TALES OF WONDER

Jane Yolen

TALES OF WONDER

SCHOCKEN BOOKS
NEW YORK

First published by Schocken Books 1983
10 9 8 7 6 5 4 2 1   83 84 85 86
Copyright © 1983 by Jane Yolen
All rights reserved

Library of Congress Cataloging in Publication Data

Yolen, Jane.
Tales of wonder.

1. Fantastic fiction, American. I. Title.
PS375.O43T3   1983   813'.54   82-62359

Designed by Lynn Braswell
Manufactured in the United States of America
ISBN 0-8052-3843-3

Grateful acknowledgment is made to the following for permission to reprint copyrighted material.

"The Pot Child" from *The Magazine of Fantasy and Science Fiction*. Copyright © 1978 by Jane Yolen. Reprinted by permission of Curtis Brown, Ltd.

"Sun/Flight" from *The Magazine of Fantasy and Science Fiction*. Copyright © 1982 by Jane Yolen. Reprinted by permission of Curtis Brown, Ltd.

"The Moon Ribbon" from *The Moon Ribbon and Other Tales* (Thomas Y. Crowell). Copyright © 1976 by Jane Yolen. Reprinted by permission of Harper & Row, Publishers, Inc.

"The Sleep of Trees" from *The Magazine of Fantasy and Science Fiction*. Coypright © 1980 by Jane Yolen. Reprinted by permission of Curtis Brown, Ltd.

"Boris Chernevsky's Hands" from *Hecate's Cauldron* (DAW Books). Copyright © 1982 by Jane Yolen. Reprinted by permission of Curtis Brown, Ltd.

"In the Hall of Grief" from *Elsewhere, Vol. II* (Ace Books). Copyright © 1982 by Jane Yolen. Reprinted by permission of Curtis Brown, Ltd.

"Sule Skerry" from *The Magazine of Fantasy and Science Fiction*. Copyright © 1982 by Jane Yolen. Reprinted by permission of Curtis Brown, Ltd.

"The White Seal Maid" from *Parabola, Myth and the Quest for Meaning*. Also appeared in *The Hundredth Dove and Other Tales* (Thomas Y. Crowell). Copyright

All these tales—and more—
are for David
and my favorite tellers: Connie
and Barbara, Laura, and Carol

Contents

vii

Introduction
The Bright Ring of Words

I AM A STORYTELLER who tells onto the printed page and often find myself recalling Montaigne's poignant phrase "We are, I know not how, double in ourselves." For the maker of literary fairy stories is both a part of and apart from the great tradition of Story. Most successful when invisible, the author of such tales should be anonymous. Yet my stories are written not by Anon, that centuries-old master of many forms, but by a particular twentieth-century eclectic mythologizer (horrid word) living in America, in New England, surrounded by children, an Apple computer, cable TV, a nearby McDonald's—in fact all the accoutrements of modern life.

There is a charming verse by Robert Louis Stevenson that begins:

> Bright is the ring of words
>   When the right man rings them,
> Fair the fall of songs
>   When the singer sings them.

> Still they are carolled and said,
>   On wings they are carried
> After the singer is dead
>   And the maker buried.

And that same sentiment was reiterated to me by a young correspondent who wrote: "Your tales will live forever. I hope you live to 99 or 100, but who cares." Who cares, indeed. Outside of my own family and friends, it is not the "I" who matters but the tales told on the page. If they can then leap from the page onto the lips of a dedicated oral teller and live on, kept alive by the folk process of mouth-to-mouth resuscitation, that is glory indeed.

For any storyteller there are two starting places for a tale. One is physical, touchable, knowable, and immediate. The other lies deep in the hidden recesses of the heart. Often years stretch between the two starting places, and the author feels like a weary traveler trudging through an unknown landscape with a tatter of map clutched in a desiccated hand. Suddenly the map matches a place, the squiggles of line translate into a river or a mountain, a moment in map time becomes a meeting. A story begins.

The Japanese have a word for it: *saku-taku-no-ki.*

Saku—the special sound a mother hen makes tapping on the egg with her beak.
Taku—the sound the chick makes tapping from within.
No-ki—the moment when the tappings come together.

Saku-taku-no-ki is the instant when the chick pecking on the inside of the egg and its mother pecking on the outside reach the same spot. The egg cracks open. New life emerges. In just that way a story begins, with the physical tapping on the outside and the answering emotion tapping from within.

After the story emerges—sometimes long afterward—one can chart its course. For example, "Names" began when I met a woman whose mother had survived Dachau. This woman was on such a severe diet that she had lost forty pounds in two

months and looked, according to her husband, like a concen-
tration-camp victim. Though the irony seemed lost on her, it
was not lost on me. Yet the story is not *about* the woman,
whom I scarcely knew. It is about me, for it was written at a
time when I was struggling with my teenage daughter who
was feeling bowed under by the weight of my "name" as a
writer. Still, I hope the story is now about neither the dieting
woman or me but about Rachel Zuckerman, the girl in the tale.
Similarly, "The Lady and the Merman" had its ostensible beginning at a poetry reading where a young man read a very bad
poem about the ocean washing away words he had written in
the sand. At that time I was immersed in research about the
legends and lore of the Mer, the underwater seafolk. But the
tale is about my relationship with my own father, though the
woman, Borne, solves her problem in a way I would not.

Saku-taku-no-ki.

The tale, then, is both a map of the human psyche who
began it and a map of the characters within. But a story needs
more than an author. It needs a reader as well before it is
complete. Often I receive mail from readers who have found in
one story or another of mine their own "tale of the heart." That
is when I know I have succeeded.

In fact, I most often describe the tales I write as "tales of
the heart." They are not old stories retold, straight from the
folk, a direct link with the oral tradition, copyrighted in my
name. Nor are they modern variants on an old tale, transcribed
and branded mine in the manner of a Charles Perrault or a
Madame Le Prince de Beaumont. Rather they are stories of my
own devising—biography mixed with dream, real life crossed
with visions—lent tone and style by a conscious and uncon-
scious remembering of folk rhythms which I have come to by
prodigious readings of old stories and singings of ballads and
come-all-ye's and cante-fables. If Jungian archetypes inform
them as well, so be it. If modern science fiction has lent occa-
sional substance, I am guilty of that, too. There is an eclecti-
cism to modern telling. Stories lean on stories, art on art. I can
only trace my own sources so far before I realize that, in the

end, it is the story that matters, not the parts: the tapestry of tale and not the individual threads. And just as kings and dragons and the Mer-folk swimming through the murmurations of the sea do not necessarily signal the old, so one cannot sum up all of modernity with a computer chip.

In a world of cable television and video arcades, I write about magical things because, like Emily Dickinson, "I dwell in possibility." I tell tales of transformations and transfigurations knowing that I use folk metaphor as a kind of literary shorthand—at times. But there is something more. I would *like* to believe that there is that of faerie in each of us, a little trickle or stream that, if we could but tap it, would lead us back to the great wellspring of magic we share with every human being, every creature—and the world.

JANE YOLEN

Phoenix Farm
Hatfield, Massachusetts

TALES OF WONDER

The Pot Child

THERE WAS ONCE an ill-humored potter who lived all alone and made his way by shaping clay into cups and bowls and urns. His pots were colored with the tones of the earth, and on their sides he painted all creatures excepting man.

"For there was never a human I liked well enough to share my house and my life with," said the bitter old man.

But one day, when the potter was known throughout the land for his sharp tongue as well as his pots, and so old that even death might have come as a friend, he sat down and on the side of a large bisque urn he drew a child.

The child was without flaw in the outline, and so the potter colored in its form with earth glazes: rutile for the body and cobalt blue for the eyes. And to the potter's practiced eye, the figure on the pot was perfect.

So he put the pot into the kiln, closed up the door with bricks, and set the flame.

Slowly the fires burned. And within the kiln the glazes matured and turned their proper tones.

It was a full day and a night before the firing was done. And a full day and a night before the kiln had cooled. And it was a full day and a night before the old potter dared unbrick the kiln door. For the pot child was his masterpiece, of this he was sure.

At last, though, he could put it off no longer. He took down the kiln door, reached in, and removed the urn.

Slowly he felt along the pot's side. It was smooth and still warm. He set the pot on the ground and walked around it, nodding his head as he went.

The child on the pot was so lifelike, it seemed to follow him with its lapis eyes. Its skin was a pearly yellow-white, and each hair on its head like beaten gold.

So the old potter squatted down before the urn, examining the figure closely, checking it for cracks and flaws, but there were none. He drew in his breath at the child's beauty and thought to himself, "*There* is one I might like well enough." And when he expelled his breath again, he blew directly on the image's lips.

At that, the pot child sighed and stepped off the urn.

This so startled the old man that he fell back into the dust.

After a while, though, the potter saw that the pot child was waiting for him to speak. So he stood up and in a brusque tone said, "Well, then, come here. Let me look at you."

The child ran over to him and, ignoring his tone, put its arms around his waist and whispered, "Father," in a high sweet voice.

This so startled the old man that he was speechless for the first time in his life. And as he could not find the words to tell the child to go, it stayed. Yet after a day, when he had found the words, the potter knew he could not utter them, for the child's perfect face and figure had enchanted him.

When the potter worked or ate or slept, the child was by his side, speaking when spoken to but otherwise still. It was a pot child, after all, and not a real child. It did not join him in his work but was content to watch. When other people came to the old man's shop, the child stepped back onto the urn and did not move. Only the potter knew it was alive.

One day several famous people came to the potter's shop. He showed them all around, grudgingly, touching one pot and then another. He answered their questions in a voice that was crusty and hard. But they knew his reputation and did not answer back.

At last they came to the urn.

The old man stood before it and sighed. It was such an uncharacteristic sound that the people looked at him strangely. But the potter did not notice. He simply stood for a moment more, then said, "This is the Pot Child. It is my masterpiece. I shall never make another one so fine."

He moved away, and one woman said after him, "It *is* good." But turning to her companions, she added in a low voice, "But it is *too* perfect for me."

A man with her agreed. "It lacks something," he whispered back.

The woman thought a moment. "It has no heart," she said. "That is what is wrong."

"It has no soul," he amended.

They nodded at each other and turned away from the urn. The woman picked out several small bowls, and, paying for them, she and the others went away.

No sooner were the people out of sight than the pot child stepped down from the urn.

"Father," the pot child asked, "what is a heart?"

"A vastly overrated part of the body," said the old man gruffly. He turned to work the clay on his wheel.

"Then," thought the pot child, "I am better off without one." It watched as the clay grew first tall and then wide between the potter's knowing palms. It hesitated asking another question, but at last could bear it no longer.

"And what is a soul, Father?" said the pot child. "Why did you not draw one on me when you made me on the urn?"

The potter looked up in surprise. "Draw one? No one can draw a soul."

The child's disappointment was so profound, the potter added, "A man's body is like a pot, which does not disclose what is inside. Only when the pot is poured, do we see its contents. Only when a man acts, do we know what kind of soul he has."

The pot child seemed happy with that explanation, and the potter went back to his work. But over the next few weeks the child continually got in his way. When the potter worked the clay, the pot child tried to bring him water to keep the clay moist. But it spilled the water, and the potter pushed the child away.

When the potter carried the unfired pots to the kiln, the pot child tried to carry some, too. But it dropped the pots, and many were shattered. The potter started to cry out in anger, bit his tongue, and was still.

When the potter went to fire the kiln, the pot child tried to light the flame. Instead, it blew out the fire.

At last the potter cried, "You heartless thing. Leave me to do my work. It is all I have. How am I to keep body and soul together when I am so plagued by you?"

At these words, the pot child sat down in the dirt, covered its face, and wept. Its tiny body heaved so with its sobs that the potter feared it would break in two. His crusty old heart softened, and he went over to the pot child and said, "There, child. I did not mean to shout so. What is it that ails you?"

The pot child looked up. "Oh, my father, I know I have no heart. But that is a vastly overrated part of the body. Still, I was trying to show how I was growing a soul."

The old man looked startled for a minute, but then, recalling their conversation of many weeks before, he said, "My poor pot child, no one can *grow* a soul. It is there from birth." He touched the child lightly on the head.

The potter had meant to console the child, but at that the child cried even harder than before. Drops sprang from its eyes and ran down its cheeks like blue glaze. "Then I shall never have a soul," the pot child cried. "For I was not born but made."

Seeing how the child suffered, the old man took a deep breath. And when he let it out again, he said, "Child, as I made you, now I will make you a promise. When I die, you shall have *my* soul, for then I shall no longer need it."

"Oh, then I will be truly happy," said the pot child, slipping its little hand gratefully into the old man's. It did not see the look of pain that crossed the old man's face. But when it looked up at him and smiled, the old man could not help but smile back.

That very night, under the watchful eyes of the pot child, the potter wrote out his will. It was a simple paper, but it took a long time to compose, for words did not come easily to the old man. Yet as he wrote, he felt surprisingly lightened. And the pot child smiled at him all the while. At last, after many scratchings out, it was done. The potter read the paper aloud to the pot child.

"It is good," said the pot child. "You do not suppose I will have long to wait for my soul?"

The old man laughed. "Not long, child."

And then the old man slept, tired after the late night's labor. But he had been so busy writing, he had forgotten to bank his fire, and in the darkest part of the night, the flames went out.

In the morning the shop was ice cold, and so was the old man. He did not waken, and without him the pot child could not move from its shelf.

Later in the day, when the first customers arrived, they found the old man. And beneath his cold fingers lay a piece of paper that said:

> When I am dead, place my body in my kiln and light the flames. And when I am nothing but ashes, let those ashes be placed inside the Pot Child. For I would be one, body and soul, with the earth I have worked.

So it was done as the potter wished. And when the kiln was opened up, the people of the town placed the ashes in the ice-cold urn.

At the touch of the hot ashes, the pot cracked: once across the breast of the child, and two small fissures under its eyes.

"What a shame," said the people to one another on seeing that. "We should have waited until the ashes cooled."

Yet the pot was still so beautiful, and the old potter so well known, that the urn was placed at once in a museum. Many people came to gaze on it.

One of those was the woman who had seen the pot that day so long ago at the shop.

"Why, look," she said to her companions. "It is the pot the old man called his masterpiece. It *is* good. But I like it even better now with those small cracks."

"Yes," said one of her companions, "it was too perfect before."

"Now the pot child has real character," said the woman. "It has . . . heart."

"Yes," added the same companion, "it has soul."

And they spoke so loudly that all the people around them heard. The story of their conversation was printed and repeated throughout the land, and everyone who went by the pot stopped and murmured, as if part of a ritual, "Look at that pot child. It has such heart. It has such soul."

Sun/Flight

THEY CALL ME the nameless one. My mother was the sea, and the sun itself fathered me. I was born fully clothed, and on my boyish cheeks was the beginnings of a beard. Whoever I was, wherever I came from, had been washed from me by the waves in which I was found.

And so I have made many pasts for myself. A honey-colored mother cradling me. A father with his beard short and shaped like a Minoan spade. Sisters and brothers have I gifted myself. And a home that smelled of fresh-strewn reeds and olives ripening on the trees. Sometimes I make myself a king's son, godborn, a javelin in my hand and a smear of honeycake on my lips. Other times I am a craftsman's child, with a length of golden string threaded around my thumbs. Or the son of a *dmos,* a serf, my back bent over the furrows where little birds search for seeds like farmers counting the crop. With no remembered pasts, I can pick a different one each day to suit my mood, to cater to my need.

But most of the time I think myself the child of the birds,

for when the fishermen pulled me up from the sea, drowned of my past, I clutched a single feather in my hand. The feather was golden—sun-colored—and when it dried it was tufted with yellow rays. I carried it with me always, my talisman, my token back across the Styx. No one knew what bird had carried this feather in its wing or tail. The shaft is strong and white, and the barbs soft. The little fingers of down are no color at all; they change with the changing light.

So I am no-name, son of no-bird, pulled from the waters of the sea north and east of Delos, too far for swimming, my only sail the feather in my hand.

The chief of the fishermen who rescued me was a morose man called Talos who would have spoken more had he no tongue at all. But he was a good man, for all that he was silent. He gave me advice but once, and had I listened then, I would not be here now, in a cold, dark cavern listening to voices from my remembered past and fearing the rising of the sun.

When Talos plucked me from the water, he wrung me out with hands that were horned from work. He made no comment at all about my own hands, whose softness the water-wrinkles could not disguise. He brought me home to his childless wife. She spread honey balm on my burns, for my back and right side were seared as if I had been drawn from the flames instead of from the sea. The puckered scars along my side are still testimony to that fire. Talos was convinced I had come from the wreckage of a burning ship, though no sails or spars were ever found. But the only fire I could recall was red and round as the sun.

Of fire and water was I made, Talos' wife said. Her tongue ran before her thoughts always. She spoke twice, once for herself and once for her speechless husband. "Of sun and sea, my only child," she would say, fondly stroking my wine-dark hair, touching the feather I kept pinned to my *chiton*. "Bird–child. A gift of the sky, a gift from the sea."

So I stayed with them. Indeed, where else could I—still a boy—go? And they were content. Except for the scar seaming my side, I was thought handsome. And my fingers were clever with memories of their own. They could make things of which I had no conscious knowledge: miniature buildings of strange design, with passages that turned back upon themselves; a mechanical bull–man that could move about and roar when wound with a hand-carved key.

"Fingers from the gods," Talos' wife said. "Such fingers. Your father must have been Hephaestus, though you have Apollo's face." And she added god after god to my siring, a litany that comforted her until Talos' warning grunt stemmed the rising tide of her words.

At last my good looks and my clever fingers brought me to the attention of the local lord. I, the nameless one, the child of sun and sea and sky. That lord was called Circinus. He had many slaves, and many servants, but only one daughter, Perdix.

She was an ox-eyed beauty, with a long neck. Her slim, boyish body and her straight, narrow nose reminded me somehow of my time before the waves, though I could not quite say how. Her name was sighed from every man's lips, but no one dared speak it aloud.

Lord Circinus asked for my services and, reluctantly, Talos and his wife let me go. He merely nodded a slow acceptance. She wept all over my shoulder before I left, a second drowning. But I, eager to show Lord Circinus my skills, paid them scant attention.

It was then that Talos unlocked his few words for me.

"Do not fly too high, my son," he said. And, like his wife, repeated himself: "Do not fly too high."

He meant Perdix, of course, for he had seen my eyes on her. But I was just newly conscious of my body's desires. I could not—did not—listen.

That was how I came into Lord Circinus' household, bringing nothing but the clothes I wore, the feather of my past, and the strange talent that lived in my hands. In Lord Circinus' house, I was given a sleeping room and a workroom, and leave to set the pattern of my days.

Work was my joy and my excuse. I began simply, making

clay-headed dolls with wooden trunks and jointed limbs, testing out the tools that Circinus gave me. But soon I moved
away from such childish things, and constructed a dancing
floor of such intricately mazed panels of wood that I was rewarded with a pocket of gold.

I never looked boldly upon the lady Perdix. It was not
my place. But I glanced sideways, from the corners of my
eyes. And somehow she must have known. For it was not
long before she found my workroom and came to tease me
with her boy's body and quick tongue. Like my stepfather
Talos, I had no magic in my answers, only in my fingers, and
Perdix always laughed at me twice: once for my slow speech
and once for the quick flush that burned my cheeks after each
exchange.

I recall the first time she came upon me, as I worked on a
mechanical bird that could fly in short bursts toward the sun.
She entered the workroom and stood by my side watching for
a while. Then she put her right hand over mine. I could feel the
heat from her hand burn me, all the way up my arm, though
this burning left no visible scar.

"My lady," I said. So I had been instructed to address her.
She was a year younger than I. "It is said that a woman should
wait upon a man's moves."

"If that were so," she answered swiftly, "all women would
be called Penelope. But I would have woven a different ending
to *that* particular tale." She laughed. "Too much waiting, without an eye upon her, makes a maid mad."

Her wordy cleverness confounded me and I blushed. But
she lifted her hand from mine and, still laughing, left the room.

It was a week before she returned. I did not even hear her
enter, but when I turned around she was sitting on the floor
with her skirts rolled halfway up her thighs. Her tanned legs
flashed unmistakable signals at me that I dared not answer.

"Do you think it better to wait for a god or wait upon a
man?" she asked, as if a week had not come between her last
words and these.

I mumbled something about a man having but one form

and a god many, and concluded lamely that perhaps, then, waiting for a god would be more interesting.

"Oh, yes," she said, "many girls have waited for a god to come. But not I. Men can be made gods, you know."

I did not know, and confessed it.

"My cousin Danaë," she said, "said that great Zeus had come into her lap in a shower of gold. But I suspect it was a more mundane lover. After all, it has happened many times before that a man has showered gold into a girl's skirts and she opens her legs to him. That does not make *him* a god, or his coming gold." She laughed that familiar low laugh and added under her breath, "Cousin Danaë always did have a quick answer for her mistakes."

"Like you, my lady?" I asked.

She answered me with a smile and stood up slowly. As I watched, she walked toward me, stopping only inches away. I could scarcely breathe. She took the feather off the workbench where it lay among my tools and ran it down my chest. I was dressed only in a linen loincloth, my *chiton* set aside, for it was summer and very hot.

I must have sighed. I know I bit my lip. And then she dropped the feather and it fluttered slowly to the floor. She used her fingers in the feather's place, and they were infinitely more knowing than my own. They found the pattern of my scar and traced it slowly, as a blind child traces the raised fable on a vase.

I stepped through the last bit of space between us and put my arms around her, as if I were fitting the last piece of puzzle into a maze. For a moment we stood as still as any frieze. Then she pushed me backward and I tumbled down. But I held on to her, and she fell on top of me, fitting her mouth to mine.

Perdix came to my room that night, and the next I went to hers. And she made me a god. And so it continued night after night, a pattern as complicated as any I could devise, and as simple, too. I could not conceive of it ending.

But end it did.

One night she did not tap lightly at my door and slip in, a shadow in a night of shadows. I thought perhaps her moon time had come, until the next morning in the hallway near my workroom when I saw her whisper into the ear of a new slave. He had skin almost as dark as the wings of the bittern, and wild black hair. His nostrils flared like a beast's. Perdix placed her hand on his shoulder and turned him to face me. When I flushed with anger and with pain, they both laughed, he taking his cue from her, a scant beat behind.

Night could not come fast enough to hide my shame. I lay on my couch and thought I slept. A dream voice from the labyrinth that is my past cried out to me, in dark and brutish tones. I rose, not knowing I rose, and took my carving knife in hand. Wrapped only in night's cloak, the feather stuck in my hair, I crept down the corridors of the house.

I sniffed the still air. I listened for every sound. And then I heard it truly—the monster from my dream, agonizing over its meal. It screamed and moaned and panted and wept, but the tears that fell from its bullish head were as red as human blood.

I saw it, I tell you, in her room crouched over her, devouring my lady, my lost Perdix. My knife was ready, and I fell upon its back, black Minotaur of my devising. But it slid from the bed and melted away in the darkness, and my blade found her waiting heart instead.

She made no sound above a sigh.

My clever fingers, so nimble, so fast, could not hold the wound together, could not seam it closed. She seemed to be leaking away through my clumsy hands.

Then I heard a rush of wings, as if her soul had flown from the room. And I knew I had to fly after her and fetch her back before she left this world forever. So I took the feather from my hair and, dipping it into the red ocean of her life, printed great bloody wings—feathered tracings—along my shoulders and down my arms. And I flew high, high after her and fell into the bright, searing light of dawn.

When they found me in the morning, by her bedside,

crouched naked by her corpse, scarred with her blood, they took me, all unprotesting, to Lord Circinus. He had me thrown into this dark cave.

Tomorrow, before the sun comes again, I will be brought from this place and tied to a post sunk in the sand.

Oh, the cleverness of it, the cleverness! It might have been devised by my own little darling, my Perdix, for her father never had her wit. The post is at a place beyond the high-water mark and I will be bound to it at the ebb. All morning my father the sun will burn me. And my father the rising tide will melt the red feathers of blood that decorate my chest and arms and side. And I will watch myself go back into the waters from which I was first pulled, nameless but alive.

Of fire and water I came, by fire and water I return. Talos was right. I flew too high. Truly there is no second fooling of the Fates.

The Moon Ribbon

THERE WAS ONCE a plain but good-hearted girl named Sylva whose sole possession was a ribbon her mother had left her. It was a strange ribbon, the color of moonlight, for it had been woven from the gray hairs of her mother and her mother's mother and her mother's mother's mother before her.

Sylva lived with her widowed father in a great house by the forest's edge. Once the great house had belonged to her mother, but when she died, it became Sylva's father's house to do with as he willed. And what he willed was to live simply and happily with his daughter without thinking of the day to come.

But one day, when there was little enough to live on, and only the great house to recommend him, Sylva's father married again, a beautiful widow who had two beautiful daughters of her own.

It was a disastrous choice, for no sooner were they wed when it was apparent the woman was mean in spirit and meaner in tongue. She dismissed most of the servants and gave their chores over to Sylva, who followed her orders without complaint. For simply living in her mother's house with her loving father seemed enough for the girl.

After a bit, however, the old man died in order to have some peace, and the house passed on to the stepmother. Scarcely two days had passed, or maybe three, when the step-mother left off mourning the old man and turned on Sylva. She dismissed the last of the servants without their pay.

"Girl," she called out, for she never used Sylva's name, "you will sleep in the kitchen and do the charring." And from that time on it was so.

Sylva swept the floor and washed and mended the family's clothing. She sowed and hoed and tended the fields. She ground the wheat and kneaded the bread, and she waited on the others as though she were a servant. But she did not complain.

Yet late at night, when the stepmother and her own two daughters were asleep, Sylva would weep bitterly into her pillow, which was nothing more than an old broom laid in front of the hearth.

One day, when she was cleaning out an old desk, Sylva came upon a hidden drawer she had never seen before. Trembling, she opened the drawer. It was empty except for a silver ribbon with a label attached to it. *For Sylva* read the card. *The Moon Ribbon of Her Mother's Hair.* She took it out and stared at it. And all that she had lost was borne in upon her. She felt the tears start in her eyes, and, so as not to cry, she took the tag off and began to stroke the ribbon with her hand. It was rough and smooth at once, and shone like the rays of the moon.

At that moment her stepsisters came into the room.

"What is that?" asked one. "Is it nice? It is mine."

"I want it. I saw it first," cried the other.

The noise brought the stepmother to them. "Show it to me," she said.

Obediently, Sylva came over and held the ribbon out to her. But when the stepmother picked it up, it looked like no more than strands of gray hair woven together unevenly. It was prickly to the touch.

"Disgusting," said the stepmother dropping it back into Sylva's hand. "Throw it out at once."

"Burn it," cried one stepsister.

"Bury it," cried the other.

"Oh, please. It was my mother's. She left it for me. Please let me keep it," begged Sylva.

The stepmother looked again at the gray strand. "Very well," she said with a grim smile. "It suits you." And she strode out of the room, her daughters behind her.

Now that she had the silver ribbon, Sylva thought her life would be better. But instead it became worse. As if to punish her for speaking out for the ribbon, her sisters were at her to wait on them both day and night. And whereas before she had to sleep by the hearth, she now had to sleep outside with the animals. Yet she did not complain or run away, for she was tied by her memories to her mother's house.

One night, when the frost was on the grass turning each blade into a silver spear, Sylva threw herself to the ground in tears. And the silver ribbon, which she had tied loosely about her hair, slipped off and lay on the ground before her. She had never seen it in the moonlight. It glittered and shone and seemed to ripple.

Sylva bent over to touch it and her tears fell upon it. Suddenly the ribbon began to grow and change, and as it changed the air was filled with a woman's soft voice speaking these words:

> Silver ribbon, silver hair,
> Carry Sylva with great care,
> Bring my daughter home.

And there at Sylva's feet was a silver river that glittered and shone and rippled in the moonlight.

There was neither boat nor bridge, but Sylva did not care.

She thought the river would wash away her sorrows. And without a single word, she threw herself in.

But she did not sink. Instead, she floated like a swan and the river bore her on, on past houses and hills, past high places and low. And strange to say, she was not wet at all.

At last she was carried around a great bend in the river and deposited gently on a grassy slope that came right down to the water's edge. Sylva scrambled up onto the bank and looked about. There was a great meadow of grass so green and still it might have been painted on. At the meadow's rim, near a dark forest, sat a house that was like and yet not like the one in which Sylva lived.

"Surely someone will be there who can tell me where I am and why I have been brought here," she thought. So she made her way across the meadow, and only where she stepped down did the grass move. When she moved beyond, the grass sprang back and was the same as before. And though she passed larkspur and meadowsweet, clover and rye, they did not seem like real flowers, for they had no smell at all.

"Am I dreaming?" she wondered, "or am I dead?" But she did not say it out loud, for she was afraid to speak into the silence.

Sylva walked up to the house and hesitated at the door. She feared to knock and yet feared equally not to. As she was deciding, the door opened of itself and she walked in.

She found herself in a large, long, dark hall with a single crystal door at the end that emitted a strange glow the color of moonlight. As she walked down the hall, her shoes made no clatter on the polished wood floor. And when she reached the door, she tried to peer through into the room beyond, but the crystal panes merely gave back her own reflection twelve times.

Sylva reached for the doorknob and pulled sharply. The glowing crystal knob came off in her hand. She would have wept then, but anger stayed her; she beat her fist against the door and it suddenly gave way.

Inside was a small room lit only by a fireplace and a round

white globe that hung from the ceiling like a pale, wan moon. Before the fireplace stood a tall woman dressed all in white. Her silver-white hair was unbound and cascaded to her knees. Around her neck was a silver ribbon.

"Welcome, my daughter," she said.

"Are you my mother?" asked Sylva wonderingly, for what little she remembered of her mother, she remembered no one as grand as this.

"I am if you make me so," came the reply.

"And how do I do that?" asked Sylva.

"Give me your hand."

As the woman spoke, she seemed to move away, yet she moved not at all. Instead the floor between them moved and cracked apart. Soon they were separated by a great chasm which was so black it seemed to have no bottom.

"I cannot reach," said Sylva.

"You must try," the woman replied.

So Sylva clutched the crystal knob to her breast and leaped, but it was too far. As she fell, she heard a woman's voice speaking from behind her and before her and all about her, warm with praise.

"Well done, my daughter. You are halfway home."

Sylva landed gently on the meadow grass, but a moment's walk from her house. In her hand she still held the knob, shrunk now to the size of a jewel. The river shimmered once before her and was gone, and where it had been was the silver ribbon, lying limp and damp in the morning frost.

The door to the house stood open. She drew a deep breath and went in.

"What is that?" cried one of the stepsisters when she saw the crystalline jewel in Sylva's hand.

"I want it," cried the other, grabbing it from her.

"I will take that," said the stepmother, snatching it from them all. She held it up to the light and examined it. "It will fetch a good price and repay me for my care of you. Where did you get it?" she asked Sylva. Sylva tried to tell them of the ribbon and the river, the tall woman and the black crevasse.

But they laughed at her and did not believe her. Yet they could not explain away the jewel. So they left her then and went off to the city to sell it. When they returned, it was late. They thrust Sylva outside to sleep and went themselves to their comfortable beds to dream of their new riches.

Sylva sat on the cold ground and thought about what had happened. She reached up and took down the ribbon from her hair. She stroked it, and it felt smooth and soft and yet hard, too. Carefully she placed it on the ground.

In the moonlight, the ribbon glittered and shone. Sylva recalled the song she had heard, so she sang it to herself:

> Silver ribbon, silver hair,
> Carry Sylva with great care,
> Bring my daughter home.

Suddenly the ribbon began to grow and change, and there at her feet was a silver highway that glittered and glistened in the moonlight.

Without a moment's hesitation, Sylva got up and stepped out onto the road and waited for it to bring her to the magical house.

But the road did not move.

"Strange," she said to herself. "Why does it not carry me as the river did?"

Sylva stood on the road and waited a moment more, then tentatively set one foot in front of the other. As soon as she had set off on her own, the road set off, too, and they moved together past fields and forests, faster and faster, till the scenery seemed to fly by and blur into a moon-bleached rainbow of yellows, grays, and black.

The road took a great turning and then quite suddenly stopped, but Sylva did not. She scrambled up the bank where the road ended and found herself again in the meadow. At the far rim of the grass, where the forest began, was the house she had seen before.

Sylva strode purposefully through the grass, and this time

the meadow was filled with the song of birds, the meadowlark and the bunting and the sweet jug-jug-jug of the nightingale. She could smell fresh-mown hay and the pungent pine.

The door of the house stood wide open, so Sylva went right in. The long hall was no longer dark but filled with the strange moonglow. And when she reached the crystal door at the end, and gazed at her reflection twelve times in the glass, she saw her own face set with strange gray eyes and long gray hair. She put her hand up to her mouth to stop herself from crying out. But the sound came through, and the door opened of itself.

Inside was the tall woman all in white, and the globe above her was as bright as a harvest moon.

"Welcome, my sister," the woman said.

"I have no sister," said Sylva, "but the two stepsisters I left at home. And you are none of those."

"I am if you make me so."

"How do I do that?"

"Give me back my heart which you took from me yesterday."

"I did not take your heart. I took nothing but a crystal jewel."

The woman smiled. "It was my heart."

Sylva looked stricken. "But I cannot give it back. My stepmother took it from me."

"No one can take unless you give."

"I had no choice."

"There is always a choice," the woman said.

Sylva would have cried then, but a sudden thought struck her. "Then it must have been your choice to give me your heart."

The woman smiled again, nodded gently, and held out her hand.

Sylva placed her hand in the woman's and there glowed for a moment on the woman's breast a silvery jewel that melted and disappeared.

"Now will you give me your heart?"

"I have done that already," said Sylva, and as she said it, she knew it to be true.

The woman reached over and touched Sylva on her breast, and her heart sprang out onto the woman's hand and turned into two fiery red jewels. "Once given, twice gained," said the woman. She handed one of the jewels back to Sylva. "Only take care that you give each jewel with love."

Sylva felt the jewel warm and glowing in her hand, and at its touch felt such comfort as she had not had in many days. She closed her eyes and a smile came on her face. And when she opened her eyes again, she was standing on the meadow grass not two steps from her own door. It was morning, and by her feet lay the silver ribbon, limp and damp from the frost.

The door to her house stood open.

Sylva drew in her breath, picked up the ribbon, and went in.

"What has happened to your hair?" asked one stepsister.

"What has happened to your eyes?" asked the other.

For indeed Sylva's hair and eyes had turned as silver as the moon.

But the stepmother saw only the fiery red jewel in Sylva's hand. "Give it to me," she said, pointing to the gem.

At first Sylva held out her hand, but then quickly drew it back. "I *can*not," she said.

The stepmother's eyes became hard. "Girl, give it here."

"I *will* not," said Sylva.

The stepmother's eyes narrowed. "Then you shall tell me where you got it."

"That I shall, and gladly," said Sylva. She told them of the silver ribbon and the silver road, of the house with the crystal door. But strange to say, she left out the woman and her words.

The stepmother closed her eyes and thought. At last she said, "Let me see this wondrous silver ribbon, that I may believe what you say."

Sylva handed her the ribbon, but she was not fooled by her stepmother's tone.

The moment the silver ribbon lay prickly and limp in the stepmother's hand, she looked up triumphantly at Sylva. Her face broke into a wolfish grin. "Fool," she said, "the magic is herein. With this ribbon there are jewels for the taking." She marched out of the door, and the stepsisters hurried behind her.

Sylva walked after them, but slowly, stopping in the open door.

The stepmother flung the ribbon down. In the early morning sun it glowed as if with a cold flame.

"Say the words, girl," the stepmother commanded.

From the doorway Sylva whispered:

> Silver ribbon, silver hair,
> Lead the ladies with great care,
> Lead them to their home.

The silver ribbon wriggled and writhed in the sunlight, and as they watched, it turned into a silver-red stair that went down into the ground.

"Wait," called Sylva. "Do not go." But it was too late.

With a great shout, the stepmother gathered up her skirts and ran down the steps, her daughters fast behind her. And before Sylva could move, the ground had closed up after them and the meadow was as before.

On the grass lay the silver ribbon, limp and dull. Sylva went over and picked it up. As she did so, the jewel melted in her hand and she felt a burning in her breast. She put her hand up to it, and she felt her heart beating strongly beneath. Sylva smiled, put the silver ribbon in her pocket, and went back into her house.

After a time, Sylva's hair returned to its own color, except for seven silver strands, but her eyes never changed back. And when she was married and had a child of her own, Sylva plucked the silver strands from her own hair and wove them into the silver ribbon, which she kept in a wooden box. When Sylva's child was old enough to understand, the box with the ribbon was put into her safekeeping, and she has kept them for her own daughter to this very day.

The Gwynhfar

THE *GWYNHFAR*—THE WHITE ONE, the pure one, the anointed one—waited. She had waited every day since her birth, it seemed, for this appointed time. Attended by her voiceless women in her underground rooms, the *gwynhfar's* limbs had been kept oiled, her bone-white hair had been cleaned and combed. No color was allowed to stain her dead-white cheeks, no *maurish* black to line her eyes. White as the day she had been born, white as the foam on a troubled sea, white as the lilybell grown in the wood, she waited.

Most of her life had been spent on her straw bed in that half-sleep nature spent on her. She moved from small dream to small dream, moment to moment, hour to hour, day to day, without any real knowledge of what awaited her. Nor did she care. The *gwynhfar* did not have even creature sense, nor had she been taught to think. All she had been taught was waiting. It was her duty, it was her life.

She had been the firstborn of a dour landholder and his wife. Pulled silently from between her mother's thighs,

bleached as bone, her tiny eyes closed tight against the agonizing light, the *gwynhfar* cried only in the day—a high, thin,
mewling call. At night, without the sun to torment her, she
seemed content; she waited.

They say now that the old mage attended her birth, but
that is not true. He did not come for weeks, even months, till
word of the white one's birth had traveled mouth to ear,
mouth to ear, over and over the intervening miles. He did not
come at first, but his messengers came, as they did to every
report of a marvel. They had visited two-headed calves, fish-
scaled infants, and twins joined at the hip and heart. When they
heard of the white one, they came to her, too.

She waited for them as she waited for everything else.

And when the messengers saw that the stories were true
enough, they reported back to the stone hall. So the Old One
himself came, wrapped in his dignity and the sour trappings of
state.

He had to bend down to enter the cottage, for age had not
robbed him of the marvelous height that had first brought *him*
to the attention of the Oldest Ones, those who dwell in the
shadows of the Circle of Stones. He bent and bent till it
seemed he would bend quite in two, and still he broke his head
on the lintel.

"A marvel," it was said. "The blood anointed the door."
That was no marvel, but a failing of judgment and the blood a
mere trickle where the skin broke apart. But that is what was
said. What the Old One himself said was in a language far
older than he and twice as filled with power. But no one reported *it,* for who but the followers of the oldest way even
know that tongue?

As the Old One stood there, gazing at the mewling white
babe in her half-sleep before the flickering fire, he nodded and
stroked his thin beard. This, too, they say, and I have seen him
often enough musing in just that way, so it could have been so.

Then he stretched forth his hand, that parchment-colored,
five-fingered magician's wand that could make balls and cards
and silken banners disappear. He stretched forth his hand and

touched the child. She shivered and woke fully for the first time, gazing at a point somewhere beyond his hand but not as far as his face with her watery pink eyes.

"So," he said in that nasal excuse for a voice. "So." He was never profligate with words. But it was enough.

The landholder gladly gave up the child, grateful to have the monster from his hearth. Sons could help till the lands. Only the royals crave girls. They make good counters in the bargaining games played across the castle boundary lines. But this girl was not even human enough to cook and clean and wipe the bottoms of her sisters and brothers to come. The landholder would have killed the moon-misbegotten thing on its emergence from his child-bride's womb had not the midwife stayed him. He sold the child for a single gold piece and thought himself clever in the bargain.

And did the Old One clear his throat then and consecrate their trade with words? Did he speak of prophecy or pronounce upon omens? If the landholder's wife had hoped for such to ease her guilt, she got short shrift of him. He had paid with a coin and a single syllable.

"So," he had said. And so it was.

The Old One carried the *gwynhfar* back over the miles with his own hands. "*With his own hands*," run the wonder tales, as if this were an awesome thing, carrying a tiny, witless babe. But think on it. Would he have trusted her to another, having come so far, across the years and miles, to find her? Would he have given her into clumsier hands when his own could still pull uncooked eggs from his sleeves without a crack or a drop?

Behind him, they say, came his people: the priests and the seers, a grand processional. But I guess rather he came by himself and at night. She would have been a noisesome burden to carry through the bright, scalding light; squalling and squealing at the sun. The moon always quieted her. Besides, he wanted to surprise them with her, to keep her to himself till the end. For was it not written that the *gwynhfar* would arise and bind the kingdom:

Gwynhfar, white as bone,
Shall make the kingdom one.

Just as it had been written in the entrails of deer and the
bloody leavings of carrion crow that the Tall One, blessed be,
would travel the length of the kingdom to find her. Miracles
are made by hands such as his, and prophecies can be invented.

And then, too, he would want to be sure. He would want
time to think about what he carried, that small, white-haired
marvel, that unnature. For if the Old One was anything, he
was a planner. If he had been born better, he would have been
a mighty king. So, wrapped in the cloak of night, keeping the
babe from her enemy light, which drained even the small
strength she had, and scheming—always scheming—the Old
One moved through the land.

By day, of course, there would have been no mistaking
him. His height ever proclaimed him. Clothes were no disguise. A mask but pointed the finger. At night, though, he was
only a long shadow in a world of long shadows.

I never saw him then, but I know it all. I can sort through
stories as a crow pecks through grain. And though it is said he
rode a whirlwind home, it was a time of year for storms. They
were no worse than other years. It is just that legend has a
poor memory, and hope an even worse.

The Old One returned with a cough that wracked his long,
thin body and an eye scratched out by a tree limb. The black
patch he wore thereafter gave rise to new tales. They say he
had been blinded in one eye at his first sight of her, the *gwynhfar.* But I have it from the physician who attended him that
there was a great scar on his cheek and splinters still in the
flesh around the eye.

And what did the Old One say of the wound?

"Clean it," he said. And then, "So!" There is no story
there. That is why words of power have been invented for him.

The Old One had a great warren built for the child under
the ground so the light would not disturb her rest. Room upon
room was filled with things for a growing princess, but noth-

ing there to speak to a child. How could he know what would
interest a young one? It was said he had never been a babe.
This was only partly a lie. He had been raised by the Oldest
Ones himself. He had been young but he had never had a
youth. So he waited impatiently for her to grow. He wanted to
watch the unfolding of this white, alien flower, his only child.

But the *gwynhfar* was slow. Slow to sit, slow to crawl,
slow to eat. Like a great white slug, she never did learn speech
or to hold her bowels. She had to be kept wrapped in swaddling under her dresses to keep her clean, but who could see
through the silk to know? She grew bigger but not much
older, both a natural and unnatural thing. So she was never left
alone.

It meant that the Old One had to change his plan. And so
his plan became this. He had her beaten every day, but never
badly. And on a signal, he would enter her underground chambers and put an end to her punishment. Again and again he
arrived just as blood was about to be drawn. Then he would
send away her tormentors, calling down horrid punishments
upon them. It was not long before the *gwynhfar* looked only to
him. She would turn that birch-white face toward the door
waiting for him to enter, her watery eyes glistening. The over-
big head on the weak neck seemed to strain for his words,
though it was clear soon enough that she was deaf as well.

If he could have found another as white as she, he would
likely have gotten rid of her. Perhaps. But there have been
stranger loves. And only he could speak to her, a language of
simple hand signs and finger plays. As she grew into womanhood, the two would converse in a limited fashion. It was some
relief from statecraft and magecraft and the tortuous imaginings of history.

On those days and weeks when he did not come to see her,
the *gwynhfar* often fell into a half-sleep. She ate when fed,
roused to go out into the night only when pulled from her
couch. The women around her kept her exercised as if she were
some exotic, half-wild beast, but they did take good care of her.
They guessed what would happen if they did not.

What they did not guess was that they were doomed anyway. Her raising was to be the Old One's secret. Only one
woman, who escaped with a lover, told what really happened.
No one ever believed her, not even her lover, and he was soon
dead in a brawl and she with him.

But I believed. I am bound to believe what cannot be true,
to take fact from fancy, fashion fancy from fact.

The plan was changed, but not the promise.

> *Gwynhfar,* white as bone,
> Shall make the kingdom one.

The rhyme was known, sung through the halls of power
and along the muddy country lanes. Not a man or woman or
child but wished it to be so: for the kingdom to be bound up,
its wounds cleansed. Justice is like a round banquet table—it
comes full circle, and none should be higher or lower than the
next. So the mage waited, for the *gwynhfar's* first signs of
womanhood. And the white one waited for the dark prince she
had been promised, light and dark, two sides of the same coin.
She of the old tribes, he of the new. She of the old faith and he
of the new. He listened to new advisers, men of action, new
gods. She had but one adviser, knew no action, had one god.
That was the promise: old and new wedded together. How else
can a kingdom be made one?

How did the mage tell her this, finger upon finger? Did
she understand? I only know she waited for the day with the
patience of the dreamer, with the solidity of a stone. For that
was what she was, a white pebble in a rushing stream, which
does not move but changes the direction of the water that
passes over it.

I know the beginning of the tale, but not yet the end. Perhaps this time the wisdom of the Old Ones will miscarry.
Naught may come of naught. Such miracles are often barren.
There have been rumors of white ones before. Beasts sometimes
bear them. But they are weak, they die young, they cannot conceive. A queen without issue is a dreadful thing. Unnatural.

And the mage has planned it all except for the dark prince. He is a young bear of a king and I think will not be bought so easily with hand-wrought miracles. His hunger for land and for women, his need for heirs, will not be checked by the mage's blanched and barren offering. He is, I fear, of a lustier mind.

And I? I am no one, a singer of songs, a teller of tales. But I am the one to be wary of, for I remake the past and call it truth. I leave others to the rote of history, which is dry, dull, and unbelievable. Who is to say which mouth's outpourings will lift the soul higher—that which *is* or that which *could be?* Did it really flood, or did Noah have a fine storymaker living in his house? I care not either way. It is enough for me to sing.

But stay. It is my turn on the boards. Watch. I stride to the room's center, where the song's echo will linger longest. I lift my hands toward the young king, toward the old mage, toward the *gwynhfar* swaddled in silk who waits, as she waits for everything else. I bow my head and raise my voice.

"Listen," I say, my voice low and cozening. "Listen, lords and ladies, as I sing of the coming days. I sing of the time when the kingdom will be one. And I call my song, the lay of the dark King Artos and of Guinevere the Fair."

The Sleep of Trees

Never invoke the gods unless
you really want them to appear.
It annoys them very much.
— G. K. CHESTERTON

IT HAD BEEN a long winter. Arrhiza had counted every line
and blister on the inside of the bark. Even the terrible binding
power of the heartwood rings could not contain her longings.
She desperately wanted spring to come so she could dance free,
once again, of her tree. At night she looked up and, through
the spiky winter branches, counted the shadows of early birds
crossing the moon. She listened to the mewling of buds making their slow, painful passage to the light. She felt the sap
veins pulse sluggishly around her. All the signs were there:
spring was coming, spring was near, yet still there was no
spring.

She knew that one morning, without warning, the rings
would loosen and she would burst through the bark into her
glade. It had happened every year of her life. But the painful
wait, as winter slouched toward its dismal close, was becoming
harder and harder to bear.

When Arrhiza had been younger, she had always slept the
peaceful, uncaring sleep of trees. She would tumble, half-

awake, through the bark and onto the soft, fuzzy green earth with the other young dryads, their arms and legs tangling in that first sleepy release. She had wondered then that the older trees released their burdens with such stately grace, the dryads and the meliades sending slow green praises into the air before the real Dance began. But she wondered no longer. Younglings simply slept the whole winter dreaming of what they knew best: roots and bark and the untroubling dark. But aging conferred knowledge; dreams change. Arrhiza now slept little, and her waking, as her sleep, was filled with sky.

She even found herself dreaming of birds. Knowing trees were the honored daughters of the All Mother, allowed to root themselves deep into her flesh; knowing trees were the treasured sisters of the Huntress, allowed to unburden themselves into her sacred groves, Arrhiza envied birds. She wondered what it would be like to live apart from the land, to travel at will beyond the confines of the glade. Silly creatures though birds were, going from egg to earth without a thought, singing the same messages to one another throughout their short lives, Arrhiza longed to fly with one, passengered within its breast. A bird lived but a moment, but what a moment that must be.

Suddenly realizing her heresy, Arrhiza closed down her mind lest she share thoughts with her tree. She concentrated on the blessings to the All Mother and the Huntress, turning her mind from sky to soil, from flight to the solidity of roots.

And in the middle of her prayer. Arrhiza fell out into spring, as surprised as if she were still young. She tumbled against one of the birch, her nearest neighbor, Phyla of the white face. Their legs touched, their hands brushing one another's thighs.

Arrhiza turned toward Phyla. "Spring comes late," she sighed, her breath caressing Phyla's budlike ear.

Phyla rolled away from her, pouting. "You make Spring Greeting sound like a complaint. It is the same every year." She sat up with her back to Arrhiza and stretched her arms. Her hands were outlined against the evening sky, the second and third fingers slotted together like a leaf. Then she turned slowly toward Arrhiza, her woods-green eyes unfocused. In the soft, filtered light her body gleamed whitely, and the darker patches were mottled beauty marks on her breasts and sides. She was up to her feet in a single fluid movement and into the Dance.

Arrhiza watched, still full length on the ground, as one after another the dryads and meliades rose and stepped into position, circling, touching, embracing, moving apart. The cleft of their legs flashed pale signals around the glade.

Rooted to their trees, the hamadryads could only lean out into the Dance. They swayed to the lascivious pipings of spring. Their silver-green hair, thick as vines, eddied around their bodies like water.

Arrhiza watched it all but still did not move. How long she had waited for this moment, the whole of the deep winter, and yet she did not move. What she wanted was more than this, this entering into the Dance on command. She wanted to touch, to walk, to run, even to dance when she alone desired it. But then her blood was singing, her body pulsating; her limbs stretched upward answering the call. She was drawn toward the others and, even without willing it, Arrhiza was into the Dance.

Silver and green, green and gold, the grove was a smear of color and wind as she whirled around and around with her sisters. Who was touched and who the toucher; whose arm, whose thigh was pressed in the Dance—it did not matter. The Dance was all. Drops of perspiration, sticky as sap, bedewed their backs and ran in slow rivulets to the ground. The Dance *was* the glade, *was* the grove. There was no stopping, no starting, for a circle has no beginning or end.

Then suddenly a hunter's horn knifed across the meadow. It was both discordant and sweet, sharp and caressing at once. The Dance did not stop, but it dissolved. The Huntress was coming. The Huntress was here.

And then She was in the middle of them all, straddling a moonbeam, the red hem of Her saffron hunting tunic pulled up to expose muscled thighs. Seven hounds lay growling at

Her feet. She reached up to Her hair and in one swift, savage movement, pulled at the golden cords that bound it up. Her hair cascaded like silver and gold leaves onto Her shoulders and crept in tendrils across Her small, perfect breasts. Her heart-shaped face, with its crescent smile, was both innocent and corrupt; Her eyes as dark blue as a storm-coming sky. She dismounted the moon shaft and turned around slowly, as if displaying Herself to them all, but She was the Huntress, and She was doing the hunting. She looked into their faces one at a time, and the younger ones looked back, both eager and afraid.

Arrhiza was neither eager nor afraid. Twice already she had been the chosen one, torn laughing and screaming from the glade, brought for a night to the moon's dark side. The pattern of the Huntress's mouth was burned into her throat's hollow, Her mark. And Her words were still in Arrhiza's ears. "You are mine. Forever. If you leave me, I will kill you, so fierce is my love." It had been spoken each time with a kind of passion, in between kisses, but the words, like the kisses, were as cold and distant and pitiless as the moon.

The Huntress walked around the circle once again, pausing longest before a young meliade, Pyrena of the apple blossoms. Under that gaze Pyrena seemed both to wither and to bloom. But the Huntress shook Her head and Her mouth formed the slightest moue of disdain. Her tongue flicked out and was caught momentarily between flawless teeth. Then She clicked to the hounds, who sprang up. Mounting the moonbeam again, She squeezed it with Her thighs and was gone, riding to another grove.

The moment She disappeared, the glade was filled with breathy gossip.

"Did you see—" began Dryope. Trembling with projected pleasure, she turned to Pyrena. "The Huntress looked at you. Truly looked. Next time it *will* be you. I *know* it will."

Pyrena wound her fingers through her hair, letting fall a cascade of blossoms that perfumed the air. She shrugged, but smiled a secret, satisfied smile.

Arrhiza turned abruptly and left the circle. She went back

to her tree. Sluggishly the softened heartwood rings admitted
her, and she leaned into them, closed her eyes, and tried to
sleep though she knew that in spring no true sleep would
come.

She half dreamed of clouds and birds, forcing them into
her mind, but really she was hearing a buzzing. Sky, she mur-
murmed to herself; remember sky.

> "Oh trees, fair and flourishing, on the high hills
> They stand, lofty. The
> Deathless sacred grove . . ."

Jeansen practiced his Homeric supplication, intoning carefully through his nose. The words as they buzzed through his
nasal passages tickled. He sneezed several times rapidly, a light
punctuation to the verses. Then he continued:

> Deathless sacred grove
> Men call them, and with iron never cut."

He could say the words perfectly now, his sounds
rounded and full. The newly learned Greek rolled off his
tongue. He had always been a fast study. Greek was his fifth
language, if he counted Esperanto. He could even, on occasion, feel the meanings that hid behind the ancient poetry, but
as often the meanings slid away, slippery little fish and he the
incompetent angler.

He had come to Greece because he wanted to be known as
the American Olivier, the greatest classical actor the States had
ever produced. He told interviewers he planned to learn
Greek—classical Greek, not the Greek of the streets—to show
them *Oedipus* from the amphitheaters where it had first been
played. He would stand in the groves of Artemis, he had said,
and call the goddess to him in her own tongue. One columnist
even suggested that with his looks and voice and reputation she
would be crazy not to come. If she did, Jeansen thought to
himself, smiling, I wouldn't treat her with any great distance.

The goddesses like to play at being shopgirls; the shopgirls, goddesses. And they all, he knew only too well, liked grand gestures.

And so he had traveled to Greece, not the storied isles of Homer but the fume-clogged port of Piraeus, where a teacher with a mouthful of broken teeth and a breath only a harpy could love had taught him. But mouth and breath aside, he was a fine teacher and Jeansen a fine learner. Now he was ready. *Artemis* first, a special for PBS, and then the big movie. *Oedipus* starring *the* Jeansen Forbes.

Only right now all he could feel was the buzz of air, diaphragm against lungs, lungs to larynx, larynx to vocal chords, a mechanical vibration. Buzz, buzz, buzz.

He shook his head as if to clear it, and the well-cut blond hair fell perfectly back in place. He reached a hand up to check it, then looked around the grove slowly, admiringly. The grass was long, uncut, but trampled down. The trees—he had not noticed it at first—were a strange mixture: birch and poplar, apple and oak. He was not a botanist, but it seemed highly unlikely that such a mix would have simply sprung up. Perhaps they had been planted years and years ago. *Note to himself: check on that.*

This particular grove was far up on Mount Cynthus, away from any roads and paths. He had stumbled on it by accident. Happy accident. But it was perfect, open enough for re-enacting some of the supplicatory dances and songs but the trees thick enough to add mystery. The guidebook said that Cynthus had once been sacred to the Huntress, virgin Artemis, Diana of the moon. He liked that touch of authenticity. Perhaps her ancient worshipers had first seeded the glade. Even if he could not find the documentation, he could suggest it in such a way as to make it sound true enough.

Jeansen walked over to one birch, a young tree, slim and gracefully bending. He ran his hands down its white trunk. He rubbed a leaf between his fingers and considered the camera focusing on the action. He slowed the movement to a sensuous stroking. *Close-up of hand and leaf, full frame.*

Next to the birch was an apple, so full of blossoms there was a small fall of petals puddling the ground. He pushed them about tentatively with his boot. Even without wind, more petals drifted from the tree to the ground. *Long tracking shot as narrator kicks through the pile of white flowers; lap dissolve to a single blossom.*

Standing back from the birch and the apple tree, tall and unbending, was a mature oak. It looked as if it were trying to keep the others from getting close. Its reluctance to enter the circle of trees made Jeansen move over to it. Then he smiled at his own fancies. He was often, he knew, too fanciful, yet such invention was also one of his great strengths as an actor. He took off his knapsack and set it down at the foot of the oak like an offering. Then he turned and leaned against the tree, scratching between his shoulder blades with the rough bark. *Long shot of man in grove; move in slowly for tight close-up. Voice-over.*

> "But when the fate of death is drawing near,
> First wither on the earth the beauteous trees,
> The bark around them wastes, the branches fall,
> And the nymph's soul, at the same moment, leaves
> The sun's fair light."

He let two tears funnel down his cheeks. Crying was easy. He could call upon tears whenever he wanted to, even before a word was spoken in a scene. They meant nothing anymore. *Extremely tight shot on tear, then slow dissolve to . . .*

A hand touched his face, reaching around him from behind. Startled, Jeansen grabbed at the arm, held, and turned.

"Why do you water your face?"

He stared. It was a girl, scarcely in her teens, with the clearest complexion he had ever seen and flawless features, except for a crescent scar at her throat which somehow made the rest more perfect. His experienced eyes traveled quickly down her body. She was naked under a light green chiffon shift. He wondered where they had gotten her, what she wanted. A part in the special?

"Why do you water your face?" she asked again. Then this time she added, "You are a man." It was almost a question. She moved around before him and knelt unselfconsciously.

Jeansen suddenly realized she was speaking ancient Greek. He had thought her English with that skin. But the hair was black with blue-green highlights. Perhaps she *was* Greek.

He held her face in his hands and tilted it up so that she met him eye to eye. The green of her eyes was unbelievable. He thought they might be lenses, but saw no telltale double impression.

Jeansen chose his words with care, but first he smiled, the famous slow smile printed on posters and magazine covers. "You," he said, pronouncing the Greek with gentle precision, his voice carefully low and tremulous, "you are a goddess."

She leaped up and drew back, holding her hands before her. "No, no," she cried, her voice and body registering such fear that Jeansen rejected it at once. This was to be a classic play, not a horror flick.

But even if she couldn't act, she was damned beautiful. He closed his eyes for a moment, imprinting her face on his memory. And he thought for a moment of her pose, the hands held up. There had been something strange about them. She had too many—or too few—fingers. He opened his eyes to check them, and she was gone.

"Damned bit players," he muttered at last, angry to have wasted so much time on her. He took the light tent from his pack and set it up. Then he went to gather sticks for a fire. It could get pretty cold in the mountains in early spring, or so he had been warned.

From the shelter of the tree, Arrhiza watched the man. He moved gracefully, turning, gesturing, stooping. His voice was low and full of music, and he spoke the prayers with great force. Why had she been warned that men were coarse, unfeeling creatures? He was far more beautiful than any of the worshipers who came cautiously at dawn in their black-beetle dresses, creeping down the paths like great *nicophori* from the hidden chambers of earth, to lift their year-scarred faces to the sky. They brought only jars of milk, honey, and oil, but he came bringing a kind of springy joy. And had he not wept when speaking of the death of trees, the streams from his eyes as crystal as any that ran near the grove? Clearly this man was neither coarse nor unfeeling.

A small breeze stirred the top branches, and Arrhiza glanced up for a moment, but even the sky could not hold her interest today. She looked back at the stranger, who was pulling oddments from his pack. He pounded small nails into the earth, wounding it with every blow, yet did not fear its cries.

Arrhiza was shocked. What could he be doing? Then she realized he was erecting a dwelling of some kind. It was unthinkable—yet this stranger had thought it. No votary would dare stay in a sacred grove past sunfall, dare carve up the soil on which the trees of the Huntress grew. To even think of being near when the Dance began was a desecration. And to see the Huntress, should She visit this glade at moonrise, was to invite death. Arrhiza shivered. She was well schooled in the history of Acteon, torn by his own dogs for the crime of spying upon Her.

Yet this man was unafraid. As he worked, he raised his voice—speaking, laughing, weeping, singing. He touched the trees with bold, unshaking hands. It was the trees, not the man, who trembled at his touch. Arrhiza shivered again, remembering the feel of him against the bark, the muscles hard under the fabric of his shirt. Not even the Huntress had such a back.

Then perhaps, she considered, this fearless votary was not a man at all. Perhaps he was a god come down to tease her, test her, take her by guile or by force. Suddenly, she longed to be wooed.

"You are a goddess," he had said. And it had frightened her. Yet only a god would dare such a statement. Only a god, such as Eros, might take time to woo. She would wait and let the night reveal him. If he remained untouched by the Huntress and unafraid, she would know.

Jeansen stood in front of the tent and watched the sun go down. It seemed to drown itself in blood, the sky bathed in an elemental red that was only slowly leeched out. Evening, however, was an uninteresting intermission. He stirred the coals on his campfire and climbed into the tent. *Lap dissolve . . .*

Lying in the dark, an hour later, still sleepless, he thought about the night. He often went camping by himself in the California mountains, away from the telephone and his fans. *Intercut other campsites.* He knew enough to carry a weapon against marauding mountain lions or curious bears. But the silence of this Greek night was more disturbing than all the snufflings and howlings in the American dark. He had never heard anything so complete before—no crickets, no wind, no creaking of trees.

He turned restlessly and was surprised to see that the tent side facing the grove was backlit by some kind of diffused lighting. Perhaps it was the moon. It had become a screen, and shadow women seemed to dance across it in patterned friezes. It had to be a trick of his imagination, trees casting silhouettes. Yet, without wind, how did they move?

As he watched, the figures came more and more into focus, clearly women. This was no trick of imagination, but of human proposing. If it was one of the columnists or some of his erstwhile friends . . . Try to frighten him, would they? He would give them a good scare instead.

He slipped into his khaki shorts and found the pistol in his pack. Moving stealthily, he stuck his head out of the tent. And froze.

Instead of the expected projector, he saw real women dancing, silently beating out a strange exotic rhythm. They touched, stepped, circled. There was no music that he could hear, yet not one of them misstepped. And each was as lovely as the girl he had met in the grove.

Jeansen wondered briefly if they were local girls hired for an evening's work. But they were each so incredibly beautiful, it seemed unlikely they could all be from any one area. Then suddenly realizing it didn't matter, that he could simply watch and enjoy it, Jeansen chuckled to himself. It was the only sound in the clearing. He settled back on his haunches and smiled.

The moon rose slowly as if reluctant to gain the sky. Arrhiza watched it silver the landscape. Tied to its rising, she was pulled into the Dance.

Yet as she danced a part of her rested still within the tree, watching. And she wondered. Always before, without willing it, she was wholly a part of the Dance. Whirling, stepping along with the other dryads. Their arms, her arms; their legs, her legs. But now she felt as cleft as a tree struck by a bolt. The watching part of her trembled in anticipation.

Would the man emerge from his hasty dwelling? Would he prove himself a god? She watched and yet she dared not watch, each turn begun and ended with the thought, the fear.

And then his head appeared between the two curtains of his house; his bare shoulders, his bronzed and muscled chest. His face registered first a kind of surprise, then a kind of wonder, and at last delight. There was no fear. He laughed, and his laugh was more powerful than the moon. It drew her to him and she danced slowly before her god.

Setting: moonlit glade; 30–35 girls dancing. No Busby Berkeley kicklines, please. Try for a frenzied yet sensuous native dance. Robbins? Sharp? Ailey? Absolutely no dirndls. Light makeup. No spots. Diffused light. Music: an insistent pounding, feet on grass. Maybe a wild piping. Wide shot of entire dance, then lap dissolve to single dancer. She begins to slow down, dizzy with anticipation, dread. Her god has chosen her . . .

Jeansen stood up as one girl turned slowly around in front of him and held out her arms. He leaned forward and caught her up, drew her to him.

A god is different, thought Arrhiza, as she fell into his arms. They tumbled onto the fragrant grass.

He was soft where the Huntress was hard, hard where She

was soft. His smell was sharp, of earth and mold; Hers was musk and air.

"Don't leave," he whispered, though Arrhiza had made no movement to go. "I swear I'll kill myself if you leave." He pulled her gently into the canvas dwelling.

She went willingly, though she knew that a god would say no such thing. Yet knowing he was but a man, she stayed and opened herself under him, drew him in, felt him shudder above her, then heavily fall. There was thunder outside the dwelling and the sound of dogs growling. Arrhiza heard it all and, hearing, did not care. The Dance outside had ended abruptly. She breathed gently in his ear, "It is done."

He grunted his acceptance and rolled over onto his side, staring at nothing, but a hero's smile playing across his face. Arrhiza put her hand over his mouth to silence him, and he brought up his hand to hers. He counted the fingers with his own and sighed. It was then that the lightning struck, breaking her tree, her home, her heart, her life.

She was easy, Jeansen thought. Beautiful and silent and easy, the best sort of woman. He smiled into the dark. He was still smiling when the tree fell across the tent, bringing the canvas down around them and crushing three of his ribs. A spiky branch pierced his neck, ripping the larynx. He pulled it out frantically and tried to scream, tried to breathe. A ragged hissing of air through the hole was all that came out. He reached for the girl and fainted.

Three old women in black dresses found him in the morning. They pushed the tree off the tent, off Jeansen, and half carried, half dragged him down the mountainside. They found no girl.

He would live, the doctor said through gold-and-plaster teeth, smiling proudly.

Live. Jeansen turned the word over in his mind, bitterer than any tears. In Greek or in English, the word meant little to him now. *Live.* His handsome face unmarred by the fallen tree seemed to crack apart with the effort to keep from crying. He shaped the word with his lips but no sound passed them. Those beautiful, melodious words would never come again. His voice had leaked out of his neck with his blood.

Camera moves in silently for a tight close-up. Only sounds are routine hospital noises; and mounting over them to an overpowering cacophony is a steady, harsh, rasping breathing, as credits roll.

Boris Chernevsky's Hands

BORIS CHERNEVSKY, son of the famous Flying Chernevskys and nephew to the galaxy's second greatest juggler, woke up unevenly. That is to say, his left foot and right hand lagged behind in the morning rituals.

Feet over the side of the bed, wiggling the recalcitrant left toes and moving the sluggish right shoulder, Boris thought about his previous night's performance.

"Inept" had been Uncle Misha's kindest criticism. In fact, most of what he had yelled was untranslatable, and Boris was glad that his own Russian was as fumbling as his fingers. It had not been a happy evening. He ran his slow hands through this thick blond hair and sighed, wondering—and not for the first time—if he had been adopted as an infant or exchanged *in utero* for a scholar's clone. How else to explain his general awkwardness?

He stood slowly, balancing gingerly because his left foot was now asleep, and practiced a few passes with imaginary *na* clubs. He had made his way to eight in the air and was starting an over-the-shoulder pass, when the clubs slipped and clattered to the floor. Even in his imagination he was a klutz.

His uncle Misha said it was eye-and-ear coordination, that the sound of the clubs and the rhythm of their passing were what made the fine juggler. And his father said the same about flying: that one had to hear the trapeze and calculate its swing by both eye and ear. But Boris was not convinced.

"It's in the hands," he said disgustedly, looking down at his five-fingered disasters. They were big-knuckled and grained like wood. He flexed them and could feel the right moving just a fraction slower than the left. "It's all in the hands. What I wouldn't give for a better pair."

"And what *would* you give, Boris Chernevsky?" The accent was Russian, or rather Georgian. Boris looked up, expecting to see his uncle.

There was no one in the trailer.

Boris turned around twice and looked under his bed. Sometimes the circus little people played tricks, hiding in closets and making sounds like old clothes singing. Their minds moved in strange ways, and Boris was one of their favorite gulls. He was so easily fooled.

"Would you, for example, give your soul?" The voice was less Georgian, more Siberian now. A touch of Tartar, but low and musical.

"What's a soul?" Boris asked, thinking that adopted children or clones probably weren't allowed any anyway.

"Two centuries ago," the voice said, and sighed with what sounded like a Muscovite gurgle, "everyone had a soul and no one wanted to sell. Today everyone is willing to sell, only no one seems to have one."

By this time, Boris had walked completely around the inside of the trailer, examining the underside of chairs, lifting the samovar lid. He was convinced he was beginning to go crazy. "From dropping so many imaginary *na* clubs on my head," he told himself out loud. He sat down on one of the chairs and breathed heavily, his chin resting on his left hand. He didn't

yet completely trust his right. After all, he had only been awake
and moving for ten minutes.

Something materialized across the table from him. It was a
tall, gaunt old woman whose hair looked as if birds might be
nesting in it. Nasty birds. With razored talons and beaks per-
manently stained with blood. He thought he spotted guano in
her bushy eyebrows.

"So," the apparition said to him, "*hands* are the topic of
our discussion." Her voice, now that she was visible, was no
longer melodic but grating, on the edge of a scold.

"Aren't you a bit old for such tricks, Baba?" asked Boris,
trying to be both polite and steady at once. His grandmother,
may she rest in pieces on the meteorite that had broken up her
circus flight to a rim world, had taught him to address old
women with respect. "After all, a grandmother should be . . ."

"Home tending the fire and the children, I suppose." The
old woman spat into the corner, raising dust devils. "The centuries roll on and on, but the Russian remains the same. The
Soviets did wonders to free women as long as they were young.
Old women, we still have the fire and the grandchildren." Her
voice began to get louder and higher. *Peh,* she spat again. "Well,
I for one, have solved the grandchildren problem."

Boris hastened to reach out and soothe her. All he needed
now, on top of last evening's disastrous performance, was to
have a screaming battle with some crazy old lady when Uncle
Misha and his parents, the Famous Flying, were asleep in the
small rooms on either side of the trailer. "Shh, shh," he cautioned.

She grabbed at his reaching right hand and held it in an
incredibly strong grip. Vised between her two claws, his hand
could not move at all. "This, then," she asked rhetorically, "is
the offending member?"

He pulled back with all his strength, embarrassment lend-
ing him muscles, and managed to snag the hand back. He held
it under the table and tried to knead feeling back into the
fingers. When he looked up at her, she was smiling at him. It
was not a pretty smile.

"Yes," he admitted.

She scraped at a wen on her chin with a long, dirty finger-nail. "It *seems* an ordinary-enough hand," she said. "Large knuckles. Strong veins. I've known peasants and czars that would have envied you that hand."

"*Ordinary,*" Boris began in a hoarse whisper and stopped. Then, forcing himself to speak, he began again. "Ordinary is the trouble. A juggler has to have *extraordinary* hands. A jug-gler's hands must be spider-web strong, bird's-wing quick." He smiled at his metaphors. Perhaps he was a poet-clone.

The old woman leaned back in her chair and stared at a spot somewhat over Boris's head. Her watery blue eyes never wavered. She mumbled something under her breath, then sat forward again. "Come," she said. "I have a closetful. All you have to do is choose."

"Choose what?" asked Boris.

"*Hands!*" screeched the old woman. "Hands, you idiot. Isn't that what you want?"

"*Boris,*" came his uncle's familiar voice through the thin walls. "*Boris,* I need my sleep."

"I'll come. I'll come," whispered Boris, just to get rid of the hag. He shooed her out the door with a movement of his hands. As usual, the right was a beat behind the left, even after half a morning.

He hadn't actually meant to go anywhere with her, just maneuver her out of the trailer, but when she leaped down the steps with surprising speed and climbed into a vehicle that looked like a mug with a large china steering rudder sticking out of the middle, his feet stepped forward of their own accord.

He fell down the stairs.

"Perhaps you could use a new pair of feet, too," said the old woman.

Boris stood up and automatically brushed off his clothes, a gesture his hands knew without prompting.

The old woman touched the rudder, and the mug moved closer to Boris.

He looked on both sides and under the mug for evidence of its motor. It moved away from his as soundlessly as a hovercraft, but when he stuck his foot under it cautiously, he could feel no telltale movement of the air.

"How do you *do* that?" he asked.

"Do what?"

"The mug," he said.

"Magic." She made a strange gesture with her hands. "After all, I am Baba Yaga."

The name did not seem to impress Boris, who was now on his hands and knees peering under the vehicle.

"Baba *Yaga*," the old woman repeated as if the name itself were a charm.

"How do you do," Boris murmured, more to the ground than to her.

"You know . . . the witch . . . Russia . . . magic . . ." Her voice trailed off. When Boris made no response, she made another motion with her hands, but this time it was an Italian gesture, and not at all nice.

Boris saw the gesture and stood up. After all, the circus was his life. He knew that magic was not real, only a matter of quick hands. "Sure," he said, imitating her last gesture. His right hand clipped his left bicep. He winced.

"*Get in!*" the old woman shouted.

Boris shrugged. But his politeness was complicated by curiosity. He wanted to see the inside anyway. There had to be an engine somewhere. He hoped she would let him look at it. He was good with circuitry and microchips. In a free world, he could have chosen his occupation. Perhaps he might even have been a computer programmer. But as he was a member of the Famous Flying Chernevsky family, he had no choice. He climbed over the lip of the mug and, to his chagrin, got stuck. The old woman had to pull him the rest of the way.

"You really are a klutz," she said. "Are you sure all you want is hands?"

But Boris was not listening. He was searching the inside of the giant mug. He had just made his third trip around when it took off into the air. In less than a minute, the circus and its ring of bright trailers were only a squiggle on the horizon.

They passed quickly over the metroplexes that jigsawed across the continent and hovered over one of the twenty forest preserves. Baba Yaga pulled on the china rudder, and the mug dropped straight down. Boris fell sideways and clung desperately to the mug's rim. Only a foot above the treetops the mug slowed, wove its way through a complicated pattern of branches, and finally landed in a small clearing.

The old woman hopped nimbly from the flier. Boris followed more slowly.

A large presence loomed to one side of the forest clearing. It seemed to be moving toward them. An enormous bird, Boris thought. He had the impression of talons. Then he looked again. It was not a bird, but a hut, and it was walking.

Boris pointed at it. "Magic?" he asked, his mouth barely shaping the syllables.

"Feet," she answered.

"Feet?" He looked down at his feet, properly encased in Naugahyde. He looked at hers, in pointed lizard leather. Then he looked again at the house. It was lumbering toward him on two scaly legs that ended in claws. They looked like giant replicas of the chicken feet that always floated nails-up in his mother's chicken soup. When she wasn't practicing being a Famous Flying, she made her great-great-grandmother's recipes. He preferred her in the air. "Feet," Boris said again, this time feeling slightly sick.

"But the subject is hands," Baba Yaga said. Then she turned from him and strolled over to the hut. They met halfway across the clearing. She greeted it, and it gave a half-bob, as if curtseying, then squatted down. The old woman opened the door and went in.

Boris followed. One part of him was impressed with the special effects, the slow part of him. The fast part was already convinced it was magic.

The house inside was even more unusual than the house outside. It was one big cupboard. Doors and shelves lined every inch of wall space. And each door and cupboard carried a hand-lettered sign. The calligraphy differed from door to door, drawer to drawer, and it took a few minutes before Boris could make out the pattern. But he recognized the lettering from the days when he had helped his uncle Misha script broadsides for their act. There was irony in the fact that he had always had a good calligraphic hand.

In Roman Bold were **Newt, eye of; Adder, tongue of;** and similar biological ingredients. Then there were botanical drawers in Carolingian Italic: ***Thornapple juice, Amanita,*** and the like. Along one wall, however, in basic Foundational Bold were five large cupboards labeled simply: **HEADS, HANDS, FEET, EARS, EYES.**

The old woman walked up to that wall and threw open the door marked **HANDS.**

"There," she said.

Inside, on small wooden stands, were hundreds of pairs of hands. When the light fell on them, they waved dead-white fingers as supple and mindless as worms.

"Which pair do you want to try?" Baba Yaga asked.

Boris stared. "But . . ." he managed at last, "they're miniatures."

"One size fits all," Baba Yaga said. "That's something I learned in the twentieth century." She dragged a pair out of the closet on the tiny stand. Plucking the hands from the stand, she held them in her palm. The hands began to stretch and grow, inching their way to normal size. They remained the color of custard scum.

Boris read the script on the stand to himself. **LOVER'S HANDS.** He hesitated.

"Try them," the old woman said again, thrusting them at him. Her voice was compelling.

Boris took the left hand between his thumb and forefinger. The hand was as slippery as rubber, and wrinkled as a prune. He pulled it on his left hand, repelled at the feel. Slowly the hand molded itself to his, rearranging its skin over his bones. As Boris watched, the left hand took on the color of new cream, then quickly tanned to a fine, overall, healthy-looking beige. He flexed the fingers, and the left hand reached over and stroked his right. At the touch, he felt a stirring of desire that seemed to move sluggishly up his arm, across his shoulder, down his back, and grip his loins. Then the left hand reached over and picked up its mate. Without waiting for a signal from him, it lovingly pulled the right hand on, fitting each finger with infinite care.

As soon as both hands were the same tanned tone, the strong, tapered, polished nails with the quarter-moons winking up at him, Boris looked over at the witch.

He was surprised to see that she was no longer old but, in fact, only slightly mature, with fine bones under a translucent skin. Her blue eyes seemed to appraise him, then offer an invitation. She smiled, her mouth thinned down with desire. His hands preceded him to her side, and then she was in his arms. The hands stroked her wind-tossed hair.

"You have," she breathed into his ear, "a lover's hands."

"Hands!" He suddenly remembered, and with his teeth ripped the right hand off. Underneath were his own remembered big knuckles. He flexed them experimentally. They were wonderfully slow in responding.

The old woman in his arms cackled and repeated, "A lover's hands."

His slow right hand fought with the left, but managed at last to scratch off the outer layer. His left hand felt raw, dry, but comfortingly familiar.

The old woman was still smiling an invitation. She had crooked teeth and large pores. There was a dark mustache on her upper lip.

Boris picked up the discarded hands by the tips of the fingers and held them up before the witch's watery blue eyes. "Not *these* hands," he said.

She was already reaching into the closet for another pair.

Boris pulled the hands on quickly, glancing only briefly at the label. **SURGEON'S HANDS.** They were supple-fingered and moved nervously in the air as if searching for something to do.

Finally they hovered over Baba Yaga's forehead. Boris felt as if he had eyes in his fingertips, and suddenly saw the old woman's skin as a map stretched taut across a landscape of muscle and bone. He could sense the subtle traceries of veins and read the directions of the bloodlines. His right hand moved down the bridge of her nose, turned left at the cheek, and descended to her chin. The second finger tapped her wen, and he could hear the faint echo of his knock.

"I could remove that easily," he found himself saying.

The witch pulled the surgeon's hands from him herself. "Leave me my wen. Leave me my own face," she said angrily. "It is the stage setting for my magic. Surgeon's hands indeed."

Remembering the clowns in their makeup, the wire-walkers in their sequined leotards, the ringmaster in his tie and tails—costumes that had not changed over the centuries of circus—Boris had to agree. He looked down again at his own hands. He moved the fingers. The right were still laggards. But for the first time he heard and saw how they moved. He dropped his hands to his sides and beat a tattoo on his outer thighs. Three against two went the rhythm, the left hitting the faster beat. He increased it to seven against five, and smiled. The right would always be slower, he knew that now.

"It's not in the hands," he said.

Baba Yaga looked at him quizzically. Running a hand through her bird's-nest hair and fluffing up her eyebrows, she spoke. But it was Uncle Misha's voice that emerged between her crooked teeth: "Hands are the daughters of the eye and ear."

"How do you *do* that?" Boris asked.

"Magic," she answered, smiling. She moved her fingers mysteriously, then turned and closed the cupboard doors.

Boris smiled at her back, and moved his own fingers in imitation. Then he went out the door of the house and fell down the steps.

"Maybe you'd like a new pair of feet," the witch called after him. "I have Fred Astaire's. I have John Travolta's. I have

Mohammed Ali's." She came out of the house, caught up with Boris, and pulled him to a standing position.

"Were they jugglers?" asked Boris.

"No," Baba Yaga said, shaking her head. "No. But they had soul."

Boris didn't answer. Instead he climbed into the mug and gazed fondly at his hands as the mug took off and headed toward the horizon and home.

In the Hall of Grief

I was Thirteen Summers, the last turning of childhood, when Great-grandmother became ill. She was exiled upstairs, to the windowless room under the thatch, to practice lying in darkness. So it is with the very old, whose lives are spent in dusk just as newborns must learn to live in the dawn.

It was not Great-grandmother's illness that made me eligible to enter the Hall of Grief, but my own signs of adulthood: the small breasts just beginning to bud, the fine curlings of hair in the cave places of my body, the rush of fresh blood from the untested nest of my womb.

I was ready. Had I not spent many childhood hours playing at the Hall game? Alone or with my brothers I had built my own Halls of willow branch and alder snappings. We had decked the tables, made signs, drawn pictures. Always, always my table was best, though I was the youngest of us all. It had more than just an innocent beauty, decked in ribbons and bordered by wildflowers: red trillium for life, blue-black elderberry for death, and the twinings of green boughs for the passage between. No, my tables had a character that was both mine and the grieven one's. It had substance and imagination and daring, even from the time I was quite young. Everyone remarked on it. The other children sensed it. But the elders who came and watched us at our play—they knew for sure. I heard one say (overheard, really), "She has a gift for grief, that one. Mark her well."

But even before that, I had known. As a child I had started crafting my own grief poems. The first aped the dirges and threnodies I had been taught, but always with a little twist of my own. One in particular I remember, for my parents shared it with the elders as a sign of my gift. It began:

> I sail out on my dark ship
> Toward the unmarked shore
> With only the grievings
> Of my family to guide me.
> The ship breasts the waves . . .

The dark ship, the unmarked shore, they were but copies of the unusual metaphors of grief. But the wording of the fifth line, the *penta*—which foreshadowed the central image, that of a carved figurehead of a nude woman, something of which I should have had no knowledge, for we were a people of the Middle Lands—convinced them all. I was a prodigy. I basked in their praises for weeks and tried hard to repeat my success. But that time I could not. It was years before I realized that, truly, I grieved best when trying for no effect at all, though the critics and the public did not always know the difference. But the craftswoman knows.

And then the day came when I was old enough to enter the Hall of Grief. I rose early and spent many minutes in front of the glass, the only one in the house not covered with the gray mourning cloth. I drew dark circles under my eyes and deep shades on my lids. Of course I overdid it. What new griever does not? I had yet to learn that true grief makes its own hollows in the face, a better sculptor of the body's contours than all our pencils and paints. Artifice should only heighten.

But I was young, as I have said. And even Great-grandmother in her dusky room was not enough to teach me then.

That first day I tried something daring. Even that first day my gift for invention showed. I painted my nails the color of my eyelids and I took a penknife and scraped the paint on the thumbnail of my left hand into a cross, to signify the bisecting of life and death. Yes, I see you understand. It was the beginning of the carvings I would later do on all my nails, the carvings that would become such a passion among young grievers and given my name. I never do it myself anymore. It seemed such a little thing then: some extra paint, an extra dab of darkness onto light. An instinctual gesture that others took—mistook—for genius. That is, after all, what genius is: a label for instinct.

I plaited my long dark hair with trillium and elderberry, too. And that was much less successful. As I recall, the trillium died before the morning was over, and the berries left my braids sticky with juice. But at the moment of leave-taking, when I went upstairs to give Great-grandmother the respect I owed her, I felt the proper griever. And she turned in her bed, the one with the carvings of wreaths on the posters, the one in which all the women of our house have died. Then she looked at me with her luminous, half-dead eyes.

"You will make them remember me?" she asked.

"Great-grandmother, I will," I replied.

"May your lines of grieving be long," she said.

"May your time of dying be short," I answered. And the ritual was complete. I left, for I was far more interested in the Hall of Grief and my part in it than her actual moment of death, when the breath leaps from the mouth in a great upward sigh. That is a private moment, after all, though grieving is all done in public. Still, I know now that all our mourning, all our grieving, all the outward signs of our rituals are nothing compared to that one quick moment of release. Do I startle you with my heresy? It is an old woman's right.

I did not look back, but ran down the stairs and into the light. My mother and her mother walked with me to the Hall of Grief. And though we marched to the slow metronome of the funerary drums, my heart skipped before.

The Hall was even larger inside than I had dreamed. Great massive pillars with fluted columns and carved capitals held up the roof. I had seen the building from afar—for who had not?—but had never been close enough to distinguish the carvings. They were appropriate to the Hall, weeping women with their long hair caught up in fanciful waterfalls. You laugh. Only in the countryside could such banal motifs still be seen. It was a very minor Hall, to be sure. But to my eyes then it was magnificent, each marble weeper a monument to grief. I drank it all in, eager to be a part.

Inside the clans had already set up their tables, and Mother and Grandmother threaded their way through the chaos to our usual stand with an ease born of long experience. Under the banner proclaiming our colors—we had always been the Queen's own, even in our little backwater—was a kidney-shaped table. It was littered with the memoria of our dying ones. We had three that year, a small number, counting Great-grandmother in our attic. I can still recite the birth lines of the other two: Cassania, of Cassapina, of Cassuella, of Cassamerra was the one. Peripia, of Perrifona, of Persivalia, of Perdonia was the other. And of course, in my own direct line, I can still go back the twenty-one requisite names. We have no gap in the line, of which I am still—though it sometimes makes me laugh at myself—inordinately proud. I am the last, as you know. No one grieves for me, no sister of the family, no blood griever, and sometimes it still bothers me that this is so, my own sisters having gone before when I was too young to grieve for them.

The daughters of Cassania and Peripia were already there, having no attic grieven of their own and no new grievers to prepare for their first Hall. They had borne only boys. And my own sisters had gone in one of the winter sicknesses, leaving me the only hope of our clan. Our table was piled high with pictographs, for this was before we had learned to capture life impressions with the photobox of the strangers. Changes come too quickly now that even boys are taught to grieve.

Since Cassania's daughters were known for their fine hand, there were many ornately lettered lamentation plaques on the table. But the table, for all its wealth of memoria, was disordered, and that disturbed me greatly.

I spoke in an undertone to my mother. "May I be allowed to arrange Great-grandmother's part?"

She did not understand my distress at the disorder, taking my request as a display of eagerness. But I was still too young to do more than look. I had yet to apprentice to a griever, to one of my older aunts. I had only a meager background, the pretendings of a child among children, and brothers at that.

So I was sent away while the older women worked, sent off to look at the other tables in the Hall, to discover for myself the many stages and presentations of Grief.

The other tables were as disordered as our own for, as I have said, we were only a minor Hall, and the grievers there unsophisticated in their arrangements. One or two had a rough feeling that I have since tried to replicate in my own work. Touching that old country grief has, I think, often given me my greatest successes.

To think of it, walking in a Hall before the days of the strangers for the first time. The sound of the mourners lining up in the galleries, waiting for the doors to open. Some of them actually wailed their distress, though in the major Halls that rarely happens anymore. Except on great occasions of state: an exiled priestess, the assassination of a princess, a fallen queen.

Inside the Hall, the grievers moved silently, setting up their tables and stalls. I remember one old woman lovingly polishing a spear, the symbol of the warrior her dying great-uncle had been. And another placing a harp with a broken string beneath the lamentation: *One last song, one final touch.* I have always liked the simplicity of that line, though the broken string was a bit overdone.

And then the doors were flung open, and the mourners came in. In the first crush, I lost sight of our own table, and was flung up against the wall. But soon the crowds sorted themselves, and I could see how the lines made a kind of pattern. There were long lines by the tables that gave away garlands and crying towels, though the longest by far was in front of the harper's stall, where a live singer recalled in song all that had been great in the harper's life.

I learned two things that day, before ever apprenticing: that to please the crowd and draw a line is easy, but to keep the lines coming back again and again and again is not. Once the garlands were gone and the towels all given away, once the singer stopped for a draught of wine, the line of mourners broke apart and formed again somewhere else. And none of the mourners remembered the grieven one's name for longer than that day, though some remembered the names of the grievers. There is no immortality in that.

By noon I had toured the entire Hall, carrying with me a wilted garland and three towels embroidered with names of grieven ones whose deeds I no longer recalled. And I came back again to the place where I had begun, the stall of my own clan, piled high with memoria.

"Let me take a turn while you eat. It will be a slow time, now, while the funeral meats are set out," I told my aunts and my mother, my grandmother having gone home to get her mother's last meal. And because they thought I could do no harm then, the left me by myself at the table.

I busied myself at once, rearranging the overwrought items in a new way so that the whole picture was one of restraint. And then I sat down and composed a threnody, the first of the ones in my so-called "Gray Wanderer" period because for the first time the figure of the cloaked soul-traveler appeared. I wrote quickly, much faster than I was to work in later years, the words tumbling over themselves. I have always had a facility which, at times, betrays me.

You know the poem, of course: *The lines of her worn and gray cloak . . . ,* which scholars insist refer to the lines of mourning. I did not mean that, just that the cloak fell from her shoulders in comfortable, familiar folds. But never mind. The scholars seem to know more about such things than we grievers do. You smile. You have heard me say all this before. Do I, in my age, repeat myself endlessly? Well, what else is there to do, lying in darkness, but retrace the steps of light? Here I throw no shadows. But once my shadow—the shadow of the Gray Wanderer—covered the entire land.

I had just finished the writing of the threnody and was tracing out the words onto a tablet, and it was slow going. I had not the grace of my aunts' hands, and each letter was painstakingly drawn. You have such grace, and that is one of the reasons why I kept you past your training. No, do not blush, child, you know it is true. Do not confuse humility with self-denial. You have an old hand grafted onto a young arm. Not for you the easy, strangers' ways, the machines that multiply machine-drawn letters. Hold to it. Pass it on.

Yes, I drew the words slowly, and my hand faltered on a phrase. Oh, the phrase was fine, but the lettering was traitor to its truth. I was casting around for a scraper when I realized that someone was standing over me. I looked up. It was a youth just past that blush of boyhood, when the skin still has a lambent glow yet is covered with soft down that has not yet coarsened into beard.

"I would have liked them," he said, nodding at the memoria to my great-grandmother and great-great-aunts.

It is the ritual opening, of course, the mildest approach to an unknown grieven one. But somehow I sensed it was sincerely meant, and though I answered with the words that have been spoken already a million million times by grievers, he knew my own sincerity in them.

"They would have grown by your friendship."

I scraped the linen free of the ink and finished the threnody while he watched. Then I pulled it free of its stretcher. The linen curled up at the edges just a bit, which was what I had hoped. It meant that a reader had to flatten it by hand and that way actually participate in the reading.

He took the time to read it, not once but several times. And then he read it aloud. His voice had already changed, and it was low and musical. He was in training for Queen's Consort, you see. And in his mouth the words took on an even more palpable sense of grief. A singer can make a song, you know.

Soon we were surrounded by the other table-watchers. He knew how to project his voice, and they had caught phrases that had beckoned them, drawn them in.

And that was how my mother and my great-aunts found us when they returned, with a long line of mourners standing by the table and all the other stalls empty, even of the watchers. The mourners were saying with him, as he repeated the threnody yet one more time, the chorus which is now so famous:

> Weep for the night that is coming,
> Weep for the day that is past.

Yes, it is simple. Every child knows it now, in the time of the strangers. But I wrote it in a fever that day, when the strangers were not even a dream, and I wove my great-grandmother's name into the body of the poem that she would not be forgotten. Her lines were long indeed. I was glad to have done it that day, for she was dead when we returned home, and already her husk had been set out on the pyre and pylons for the birds of prey.

The next seven days we mourned upon the stage of the Hall for our grieven one's passage to the world of everlasting light. How my great-grandmother must have smiled at her lines of mourning, for they lit her way through the dark cave of death. Never had there been such lines in our minor Hall, except when General Verina died, who had been born in the town next but one to ours and whose relatives numbered in the hundreds in the countryside, and of course, I was told, the last Queen. I wrote three more Gray Wanderer threnodies and one thirty-two–verse dirge which the harper set to a modal tune. The Hall throbbed with it for days, though one can hear it only occasionally now. It takes too long in the singing, and the strangers brought with them a taste for short songs. But Great-grandmother has not been forgotten and I still have pride in that, for I made it so.

After the seven days, it was incumbent upon my mother to find me a Master Griever among our clan though, by tradition, I should have had a year between my first entrance into a Hall and my formal apprenticeship. But even the elders had come to her as soon as the Seven was over and begged her to forgo that year. They even suggested seeking out some long connection in one of the coastal towns, where gold flowed along the seashore. But we did not have the means to do such a thing.

That very day there came a knock at the door. I see you are ahead of me. Have I told this before? It was the singer, the one from the Hall. He had left after the first day, gone I had assumed to finish his young man's pilgrimage from Hall to Hall. It is part of the training, you know, singing in front of different mourners, learning *all* the ways of the land. But he had not gone on along his route. Instead he had doubled back and told the queen herself what had happened in the Hall. It had taken him three days to get an audience with her, and a day for her to make up her mind. But at last she had said to him, "Bring me this Gray Wanderer, that I may see her for myself." And that, of course, was how I was named.

So I was brought before her—the queen—from whose own body would spring the next rulers. Only she was girl-barren. Her many men plowed her, but there was no harvest. She had no girl children to grieve for her, only boys. And she did not know then that her bearing days were over and that her sister's girls would rule after her, to the great tragedy of our world. For those queens invited in the strangers, who brought with them the rule of men. But none of us knew all that then, and she asked to see me out of simple curiosity.

I dressed, as was appropriate to my age and clan, in a simple long gray gown pricked through with red and black and green embroidery. I had done it myself, the trillium twined around the boughs with a sprinkling of elderberries along the hem. And my hair was plaited and pinned up on my head, a crown as simple as the queen's was ornate. I was never any great beauty, but pride in bearing can make the difference. I held my head high.

She saw me and smiled. I was so young, she told me later, and so serious, she could not help it.

"Come, child," she said, leaning forward and holding out her hand.

I did not know any better and took it, oblivious to the mutterings around me. Then I leaned forward and whispered so that she alone could hear it. "Do not fear the dark, my lady, for I am sent to light your way."

It was not the speech I had practiced with my mother, nor yet the one I had made up along the way. But when I saw her, with the grief of all those girl-barren years sitting above her eyes, I knew why I had come. So I spoke those words, not for the applause of the court but for her alone. And because I did it that way, she knew I was speaking the truth.

She bade me sit by her feet. I was never to leave.

She asked to see my grief poems, and I took the first of the Gray Wanderer ones from the basket. They are in the museum now where only the scholars can read them, but once they had been set out for anyone to see.

She read them with growing interest and called the priest-ess to her.

"A child can lead the way," the priestess said cryptically. They always speak thus, I have found, leaving a leader many paths to choose from. Grievers and priestesses have this in common, I think, though the latter would claim true knowl-edge and infallibility, while I can only speak in symbols what I feel here, here in the heart.

The queen nodded and turned to me. "And can you make me another threnody? Now. Now, while I watch so that I can see that you made these without the promptings of your elders?"

"I have no one to grieve for, my queen," I said.

She smiled.

In those days, remember, I was young and from a small

village and a minor Hall. I thought it was a pitying smile. I know better now. It was a smile of power.

Three days later word came that my grandmother had died. I had much to grieve for then. And though I was not allowed to go home to do my grieving, the queen herself set me up at a table in a major Hall, and on that stage, surrounded by sophisticated mourners, I began my public life. I wrote thirteen threnodies in the seven days and composed a master lament. My grief was fed by homesickness, and I had those hardened mourners weeping within a day. The queen herself had to take to bed out of grief for my grandmother.

The queen called the best grievers in the land to teach me in relays after the Seven was up. And within the year I knew as much as they of the history of mourning, the structure of threnodies, and the composition of the dirge. I learned the queen's birth lines to twice the twenty-one names, and the lines of her sisters as well. And once I had a prince as a lover, though I never bore a babe.

But there is a question in your eyes, child. Do not be afraid to ask. Wait, let me ask it for you. Did I regret the years of service to my queen when I learned she had had my grandmother slain? Child, you have lived too long under the influence of the strangers. One does not question a queen. My grandmother's lines were long, and full of royal mourners; her dying was short and without pain. Would that we could all start our journey that way.

It was proclaimed, then, that a Master Griever of the queen's own choosing, not a birthright griever, could mourn her and hers. It was the first change in a time full of change. Thus it was that I served the queen and her sisters' children after, both the girls and now these weak, puling boy kings. It does not matter to the griever. We have always mourned for men and women alike, for do not we all have to take those final steps into the dark cave? But, oh, the land mourns and has become as barren as my first queen. For who can tell which man is father when all men sow the same? Yet a woman in her time of ripening is each as different as a skillfully wrought dirge.

I know not if the land dies because of the kings or because of the strangers. They would have us wound the earth with our dead, and many follow them. But what does the earth want with our husks? And why set them down into a dark cave forever? Rather we must put them out above the earth, turning the dead eyes up toward the light.

Things change too quickly, my child. But remember, you promised me that you would set my husk out on the pyre and pylons we built together, hand on hand. Outside this cave, far from the strangers and their bright, short ways.

Here, I have set down a threnody of my own. The first Gray Wanderer I have composed in many years, and the last. I want you to start my mourning today with it. I know, I know. Such was never done before, that a griever should grieve for herself. But I have no child of my womb, no girl to call the lines, and even though you are my own chosen one, it is not the same. Besides, was the Gray Wanderer ever the same? Even in my dying I must be different.

Bring me the last meal now, and the cup of sleep, for the pain is great today and my head swirls with darkness. It is time. And you will make them remember me, will you not?

Say it. Say it. Do not cry. Crying does not become a griever.

And may your lines of grieving be long.

Now, paint your eyelids, but lightly. Draw a cross on the darkened thumbnails. Pinch your cheeks. Good. And may your time of dying be short, too. Now go.

Cards of Grief

YOU HAVE COME TO SEE ME about the cards? You have left your calling until it is almost too late. My voice is so weak these days, I can scarcely sing an elegy without coughing, though there are those who would tell you that singing was never my strong point. And that is true enough. While some in the Halls of Grief could bring in lines of mourners by the power of their singing, and others by the eloquence of their mouths, such was not my way. But many, many have come to watch me draw grief pictures on paper and board. Even now, when my hand, which had once been called an old hand on a young arm, is ancient beyond its years, I still can call mourners with the power in my fingertips. Oh, I try to sing as I draw, in that strange, high, fluting voice that one critic likened to "a slightly demented turtledove." But I have always known it is the pictures, not the singing, that bring mourners to our table.

That was how she found me, you know, singing and drawing at a minor, minor Hall for one of my dying great-aunts, a sister to my mother's mother. In those days, our

mother lines were quite defined. We were a family of swine-
herds and had always been so. I found it easier to talk to pigs
than people and had never played at any Hall games, having
no brothers or sisters, only pigs. Once, though, I had made
up a threnody of sow lines. I think I could recall it still—if I
tried.

No matter. The irony is that I can remember the look of
my favorite sow's face, but the great-aunt I mourned for—her
face is lost to me forever. Though, of course, I know her lines:
Grendi, of Grendinna, of Grenesta, and so forth.

The Gray Wanderer (she was still called that by backwater
folk like us) had been on a late pilgrimage. She often went back
to country Halls. "Touching true grief," she liked to call it,
though I wonder how *true* that grief really was. We tried to
ape the cities and city folk, and we copied our dirges from the
voice boxes the new men had brought. Many of my first draw-
ings were tracings of tracings. How could I, a pigkeeper, know
otherwise?

But she saw me at a Hall so minor that both pillars and
capitals were barren of carvings, though there was an ill-
conceived painting of a weeping woman decorating one wall.
Its only value was its age. Paint flaked off it like colorful
scabs. The arms were stiff, the pose awkward. I know that
now.

"The girl, let me take her," the Gray Wanderer said.

My mother and her sisters did not want to let me go. It
was not love that bound us, but greed. I worked hard, and the
pigs would suffer from my going. Besides, I had become quite
a success as a griever in our little town. They could not see
beyond our sties to the outside world.

But the Gray Wanderer pointed out, rightfully, that they
had no means to educate me beyond this minor Hall. "Let her
come with me and learn," the Gray Wanderer said. "And I will
give you gold besides, to find another pigkeeper."

They hesitated.

"She will bring mourners to Halls all over the land to
know the names of your lines. To remember you."

I will never know which argument decided them. But they gave me into her hands.

"You will not see her again," the Gray Wanderer told them. "Except from afar. But her name will still be your name. And I promise you that she will not forget her lines."

And so it was.

No, do not rush me. I will get to the cards. But this, this must all come first. So that you will understand.

I was sixteen summers then. Not as young as the Wanderer herself had been when she had been chosen. But young enough. Yet I left home without a backward glance, my hand on her robe. I did not even paint my face with tears for the leaving. It was such a small grief. I left them counting the gold, greedier than their own swine, who sensed my going and mourned the only way they could, by refusing a meal. Later, I heard, my mother and one of her sisters had come and asked for more gold. They were given it—along with a beating.

"If you come again," the warning had been set, "she will have more names to add to the lines of grief. And they will be your own."

Well, no one likes to be called to the cave before her time. They did not set foot in the city again.

I became, in effect, the Gray Wanderer's child. I would have taken her family name, had she let me. But she had promised I would retain my own. So I did. But in all else I was hers. I learned as much as she could teach—and more. For even when she did not teach, I learned. By watching. By listening. By loving.

But she was already old, and so all of our time added together was still short. Excuse my tears. Crying, she used to say, does not become a griever. But of course, I am not a griever now. Those who come after will grieve me. But I am as near the cave as makes no difference.

So I come to the part you wish to hear. About the cards. But first I must touch upon *her* death, for it was that which inspired the cards of grief. It is many, many years ago, but as you can see, I have not left off my grieving.

I remember it as if it were yesterday. Here, let me paint it for you and tell the pictures aloud. My paints are over there, in the corner, in the round wooden box. Yes, that is it, the one with the picture of tears that look like flowers on the top. Bring it to me.

First I will sketch the cave. It was back in the mountains above the palace, one of the many rock outcroppings in the lower hills. We were three days finding it, though it was only a walk of a day. She knew where it was, but she had a palsy, a halting gait, which made walking slow. We camped at night and watched the stars together. She told me their names; strange names they were, in a language not our own. She knew tales about many of them. Does that surprise you? It should not. The Gray Wanderer remembered everything she ever heard from you starfolk. And used it, too.

Just as you say in your language, "*I see,*" when you understand something, we say, "*I hear.*" And of course the Gray Wanderer's hearing was better than anyone's.

This then is the cave. The entrance was hidden behind evergreen branches, so cleverly concealed that only she knew of it. She had discovered it when she had first come to be the Queen's own griever. Often, she told me, in that first year she had run off into the hills for quiet. She was terribly homesick. Not I. I had not ever been happy until I left my home. I would have been sick only at the thought of returning there. If I regretted anything, it was leaving my poor pigs to the mercy of my kin.

In the cave was a bed, a cot really, constructed of that same evergreen wood with weaving strung from side to side. I packed a new mattress for her each day of sweet-smelling rushes, grasses, and sharp-scented boughs. I set candles at the head and foot of the bed. There was a natural chimney in the cave, and the smoke from the candles was drawn up it and out in a thin thread. Once I fancied it was the Gray Wanderer's essence slowly unwinding from her, unwinding and threading its way out of the cave. Here, I'll draw it like that. Do you see?

She knew she was dying, of course. It was why we were

there. She set me the task of retelling all I remembered of the history of grieving, to set it for good in my memory. Since she had taught me every day I had been with her, I had many, many hours of recounting to do. But when I had told nearly all I knew, she added a new story, one I had heard only from others. It was her own tale. I still remember every word of it, as if it had been told to me just this morning.

Then she bade me bring her the Cup of Sleep, putting her hand out to me, thus. I can scarcely draw her fingers as thin and gnarled as they were. It makes me ache to see them again, but it is not that which stops me. It requires a delicacy that, alas, my own hands have forgot. But as thin and as pale and as drawn up as she was, her hair was still the vigorous dark color it had been when she was a child. I bound it up for her as she instructed, with red trillium for life, and blue-black elderberry for death. I twined green boughs around the bed for the passage between.

Then she smiled at me, and comforted me when she saw I would weep—I who never wept for anything in my life before.

I stood here, with the cup in my hands. Does the figure look strange to you? A bit cramped? Well, it should. My back and neck hurt from the tension of wanting to give the cup to her to ease her pain, and yet not wanting to because, though her pain would be over then, mine would go on and on alone. But in the end I gave it to her and left as she bid. I left, and went outside and waited two days. I sang all the grief songs I knew to keep from crying again, but I never ate. Nor did I draw.

At the end of that time, I went back into the cave. I had to cut the boughs away again, so quickly had they grown over the entrance.

She was lying there as I had left her, her face composed, her hands laced together. It surprised me to see her look so young and so peaceful.

I brought her husk out and put it on the pyre and pylons we had built together outside, though in truth she had only watched, her hand pressed against her side, while I did the work of the building. I sat another day, still as a stone, until the first birds came and settled on her, and one, a blackbird with wild white eyes, took the first bite.

Then I fled down the mountainside where I was sick several times, though I had sat pyrewatch before and had never blanched. It is funny how one can be sick with nothing in the stomach but bile and tears.

I went directly to the queen's own room and knelt and said, "The Gray Wanderer is gone."

"You will make them remember her?" she asked. She was always a cold woman, rigid. It was the proper response, but I had wanted more. I knew she had loved the Wanderer in her own way.

"Your Majesty," I said, giving her back ice for ice, "I will."

"May your lines of grieving be long," she said.

I turned and left. She knew that I had left out the last line of the ritual. I would not give her the satisfaction of my words. She would not hear "May your time of dying be short." I did not care if hers was short or long. The only one I cared about had already had too long a time of dying, too short a time of living.

I went to the rooms we had shared and wept again. Then I dried my tears with one of the many towels the Wanderer had collected in her years of grieving in Halls. I pinched my cheeks for color and sat down with a harp to compose a small dirge, a threnody, a lament. But nothing would come. Even the Gray Wanderer's own words could not contain my feelings.

I stared at my reflection in the glass. Real tears marked a passage down my cheeks. I could paint over them with tear lines in any color I wanted. But I could not just paint my face and let her go.

I spoke to her under my breath. *Forgive me, Gray,* I said. *Forgive my excess of sorrow.* She would have shuddered at the ocean of my tears. But though I was no girl of her lines, I was her true apprentice. She was dearer to me than a line mother, and I had to do more to honor her. She would have long, long lines of mourners to remember her. I would give her immortality for sure.

So all that night in the royal Hall of Grief, with mourners passing in and out, speaking their ritual parts with as much sincerity as they could manage, I began to devise the cards of grief.

I was silent while I worked, and it may be that it was my silence that first called the mourners in, for if I had any reputation at all as a young griever, it was not for silence. But if it was the silence that drew them in, it was the cards of grief that brought them back.

It took a week of days and sleepless nights before I was done with the painting of them. And then I slept for another week, hardly knowing who I was or what I was or where it was I was sleeping. My hands were so stained with paint that it was months before they were clean again. The clothes I had worn for that week I burned. I do not think I ever truly recovered my health. But I brought her a line of grievers as had never been seen before, long solemn rows of mourners; young and old, men as well as women. Even the starfarers came, borne in by curiosity I am sure, but staying to weep with the rest. And each time the cards are seen, another griever is added to her line. Oh, the Gray Wanderer is an immortal for sure.

The cards? I have not forgotten. Here, put the paints away. The painting? It is nothing, a quick sketch. Certainly you may keep it. And each time you see it, you will remember the Gray Wanderer.

You would have liked her? I see you know our rituals. So I will answer you in kind. She would have grown by your friendship. And *that* is quite true. Though she eschewed the ways of your people, she did not forget to grow in her art by understanding.

And now the cards. You see, I have not forgotten. Now is the time to show you.

That first pack was an eleven, not the more ornate thirteen plus thirteen that gamesters now use. I drew the cards on a heavy paper that I made of pressed reeds. I drew lightly so that only I could see the outline. Then I colored them in with the paints and chalks I should have used for my grief mask. That is why the colors are so basic: not the wider palette of art but the monochromatic range of the body's grief paints. The red? That color has been so remarked upon. Here is the truth of it. It was not paint at all. It was my own blood. I drew it from the soft inside of my left elbow, the turning closest to the heart. You can still see the scar. It is no more than a raised pinprick now.

To this day, the original thirteen is called the Prime Pack. Does that confuse you? You are counting on your fingers. There were eleven done at the Hall of Grief. And then, after my week of sleep, I rose and painted two more. The Prime Pack is kept on velvet in the Queen's Museum, under glass. They are arranged at each month's turning in a new order. As if the order mattered now.

That first pack spoke directly to my need. There was no arcane symbology. The Seven Grievers were one for each of the great families. The Cave That Is Fed By No Light—the darkest card—is of course the death card. For as we come from the womb cave, so we go to that other cave in the end. And, of course, my beloved Wanderer came to her end in a real cave. The picture on the card is an exact rendering of her last resting.

The Queen of Shadows is the major card, for the Wanderer was always loyal to the queen on the throne. And the Singer of Dirges is the minor card. The moving card, the card that goes with ease from high place to low, was the card I called after my master, the Gray Wanderer. Its face is her face, and the dark hair under the cloak of gray is twined with flowers. But it is the Wanderer as she was when she was young, not crabbed with age and in pain, but when her face was unlined and she had a prince for a lover.

Seven Grievers. The Cave. The Queen. The Singer. And the Gray Wanderer. Eleven cards in all. And after my sleep I added two: the Man Without Tears and the Cup.

I sometimes think it was only a sentimental gesture. Gray often told me I must not confuse true sentiment with sentimentality. I wonder what she would have thought of it. But I meant it for her, I meant it as all true grievers mean the poems and scriptings and songs they make. Those are the old, slow ways, but for all that they were old and slow, they were about life and death and the small passage between.

I did not have to explain the cards to the many lines of mourners who came to honor my master. Not the way I have to explain them today. Over and over, to those like you who have come from the far stars with voice boxes and light boxes and faulty memories, who say "I see" even when you see nothing at all. And over and over to those of my own people who now ape grief with comic songs and dances and who turn even the cards of grief into a game.

But I will do it once more. One final time. I will tell the Prime Pack. Forgive me if the telling is one whose parts you have heard before. And this time I will tell it with infinite care, for there have been times that I, even I, have told them as a rota, a list, without meaning. This time I will unwind the thread of honest grief. For the Gray Wanderer. And for myself. For the story must be told.

I lay out the cards, one by one. Listen well. Do not rely on your boxes. Use your eyes. Use your ears. Memory is the daughter of the eye and ear.

Here are the Seven Grievers.

The figure on each card is dressed as one of the great families. There is not a person in our world who cannot trace connection to them. I am myself of Lands. And all who work the soil—farmers and stockmen, harrowers and pigkeepers—are here. So it is the Number One card because it is mine. We Lands were first before all the rest, and will remain when all the rest lie forgotten. In the Prime Pack, Lands wears the brown tunic and trews of our family and rides astride a white sow because that is, in a sense, how I was found.

The Number Two card is Moon, those who know the seasons' turning and can reckon the changes—the seers and priestesses, dressed in white. Three, Arcs and Bows: the warrior–hunters. Four, Waters and all who plow there. Five, Rocks who wrest gemstones from the mountain face and craft them. Six, Stars, who carry our world's knowledge and script that knowledge into books. And Seven, the queen's own, the Royals, the smallest family of all.

Seven Grievers, seven families, all who were touched by and who touched my master.

Then the Cave card. The Queen of Shadows. The Gray Wanderer. The Singer of Dirges. I have spoken of them already. The Cup of Sleep and the Man Without Tears.

The first thirteen were known as the Cards of Dark, for all the faces on the original pack were dark since I drew them in in my grief. The thirteen cards added later by the gamesters are called the Cards of Light, and all the figures grin, their whitened faces set in a rictus, a parody of all we hold sacred.

Here, you can see the difference even in this pack. In my drawing of the Man Without Tears, he wears a landing suit and holds his hands outstretched by his sides, the light streaming through a teardrop in each palm. But his face cannot be seen, obscured as it is by the blackened bubble of his headgear. Yet in the gamesters' thirteen, he wears a different uniform, one with stars and bars on the shoulders. And though his hands are still outstretched, with the light reflecting through the palms, his face is drawn as plain as any griever's, and he smiles a painful, sad grimace.

You can see the difference also in the Queen of Shadows card. In my pack, she is dressed in red and black, and her picture was a dark portrait of the queen then on the throne. But the packs today are no-faced and every-faced, the features as bland as the mash one feeds a child. There is no meaning there. *My* queen wore a real face, but the card looked back to an even older tale. You know it, of course? The queen mourning for her dead consort who went into the cave at the center of the world. She wore a red dress and a black cloak and carried a bag of her most precious jewels to purchase his release from Death. In those days Death was thought to live in a great stone palace in the world's center surrounded by circles of unmourned folk who had to grieve for themselves.

The queen followed the twisting, winding cave for miles, learning to see in the dark land with a night sight as keen as that she had used to see with in the day. Many long night-days passed, and at last she stopped by a pool and knelt down to drink. She saw, first, the dartings of phosphorescent fish, as numerous as stars. Then she saw, staring up from the pool, her own reflection, with shining night-eyes, big and luminous. She did not recognize herself, so changed was she from her journey. But she fell in love with the image, a queen from the dark sky, she thought. And she stayed by the poolside, weeping her diamonds and pearls into it, begging the jewel-eyed star woman to come up to her.

After thirteen days of weeping, her grief for her consort was forgotten and her precious gems were all gone. She returned home empty-handed. But her eyes remained wide and dark-seeing; she had become a visionary and seeress who spoke in riddles and read signs in the stars and was never again quite sane. She was called Queen of Shadows.

You do not understand the other cards in my deck? The Singer of Dirges? It is named after the simple singer who first brought my master into her fame. He was of no great importance otherwise—a helper, a pointer of ways. And so the Singer card within the deck simply helps the other cards along, leading them from place to place within the pattern, being nothing in itself, only indicating the path to take.

And the Cup of Sleep? It is the changer. If it precedes a card, it changes the card and the pattern. If it follows a card, it does no harm. And the only card it cannot change is the Cave.

There, now you know the deck as well as I. Are you a player with the cards? Do you use them to tell you what will be, waiting on the message before you make a choice? Neither? Good. Only a fool uses them thus. They are grief cards, to help you understand your own grieving, as they helped me with mine.

We are each a card, you know. I am like the Singer card, a pointer of ways. I point back to the old ways of the Wanderer, and forward to what will come.

And you, starfarer, bring change. You and your people are like cups of sleep. Without changing yourselves, you deal out death to our ways. The Wanderer knew this, but she could do nothing to stop it. And neither can I. I can but tell you what you do, force you to look backward and forward. That was the real reason I said that you could come and capture me in your boxes. But you, yourself, starfarer, who are a woman and might have been a griever or a queen, listen to me well. Forget your boxes, and hear my words in your heart and bones. Do you mean to be a death card? Do you know what it is you do?

So much telling. My mouth is dry. Hand me that cup, the one on the table. Yes, it is a lovely thing. The engravings are quite old. From the third kingdom, I believe. I need to moisten my tongue. That is good.

What do the writings mean? I will read them to you. "Here is the Cup. Take it willingly. May your time of dying be short."

Do not look so startled. I know what I do. And now you know, too. Remember, there is no penalty in our world for giving a peaceful death. Tell your people that. Mine already know.

But you can do something for me. Grieve for me. Grieve for all of us in this quiet, dying land. You owe us that immortality at least.

Now go, for I feel sleep coming on me. The time of dying will, indeed, be short. I hope my lines of mourning will be very, very long, for I want to see my beloved Gray Wanderer again in the cave beyond all stars.

Old Herald

OLD HERALD CLOSED HIS EYES and reveled in the dancing stars. The last few days had become darker and darker. He did not begrudge his dying, only the loss of light. He wanted to see the world brightly as he went out of it. He wanted to glimpse again the riot of color that he had captured so lovingly and well during his life. His hands could barely hold the color sticks; his veins were all but dried up of paint. But his eyes could still praise color and light. He did not want to fail now. Not now. Surely, he thought, the greatest of all the Life Painters—those who quite literally bled onto the canvas— should not end in darkness but in a great rainbow burst of eternal light.

"Critics!" he cried out, refusing to disguise the agony in his voice. His crabbed hands scuttled into the air.

The two hurried to his side. Prime, a short, stocky woman with a noticeable mustache and a brilliant smile, put her arm around him and whispered into his ear, "I am here. I am always here."

Secondary, a gray-haired boy-man with faded good looks, hovered by Old Herald's feet. His hands fluttered nervously, crossing and recrossing as if they were pale butterflies seeking a place to land.

"Bring me the sticks," Old Herald ordered. "I feel a painting. I want to paint one last canvas before I die."

"But . . . but you can't . . . can't . . ." Secondary began in his hesitant way. It was that stuttering, an affliction of judgment rather than tongue, that made him a Secondary. He would never rise to Prime in the pantheon of artists. It was only because he had been around for so long, serving his apprenticeship under boy-loving Life Painters, that he had ever risen so high.

"Of course, Visionary," said Prime. She plumped the pillows around the old man's head and pushed him gently but sternly back against them. "And the colors?"

Old Herald had drifted off to sleep, but awoke with a start at her questions. "Reds. Bloods. Crimsons. The Phoenix rises."

"I serve," said Prime, placing her hand over her heart.

The old artist did not seem to hear, falling back into the half-sleep of age.

Prime nodded to her companion critic and went out of the room. His hands touching one another helplessly, Secondary followed. When they were out of the old man's hearing, he pulled on Prime's sleeve.

"He can't see," Secondary said. "We both know that."

Prime turned on him, her eyes severe behind the thick glasses. "Our duty is to serve him and criticize his work. If *he* wants to paint a final picture, then we get him the paint. And the canvas. We serve art. We do not dictate to it."

She turned from him and her white robe billowed around her, making her look even broader than she was. Her feet, surprisingly small and well shaped, tapped out a steady rhythm on the mosaic floor. Secondary followed.

He caught up with her in the Color Room. While she rinsed the paint sticks first in water, then in the antiseptic solution, he tried to argue with her.

"How can he paint if he cannot see?" Secondary began.

"We are not artists," she answered. "We are critics. How can we know what he sees or does not see until it is on the canvas?" She took the paint sticks and set them in the auto-clave, untangling the tubing and making sure that there were no weak, spongy sections where paint or blood might leak out. Her knowing fingers found no soft spots.

Secondary tried again. "But . . . but it is our . . . our duty to know."

"That has always been your mistake," Prime said, closing the top of the autoclave and setting the dial at maximum heat. With the older artists it was especially important that germ-free tools be used. After a lifetime of painting, they were easy prey to infection. "You equate *knowing* with *understanding:* you think that knowing how to mix colors and insert the color tubes with the minimum of pain gives you an insight into the artist's mind. But all you have is access to his veins."

The autoclave hummed its single note at them, and Prime nodded back at it, satisfied. She went to the palette, a large, many-drawered counter rimmed with tubes of paint in plastic holders. Taking out a spray can from one of the drawers, she sprayed antiseptic on the marble countertop. Then she took the array of reds from their side of the palette and squeezed them with practiced care onto the marble, creating a rainbow of reds. With a palette knife from a second autoclave she spread the colors, mixed them, swirling one red into another, pulling ribands of lighter shades through the darker, twining tints into a loose braid. Finally she blended several of the darker crimsons to create the mix Old Herald had dubbed "the Phoenix" and which he was famous for. Her memory for color was as good as his. She was, in her own way, an artist, though she would have denied it. She knew she was the best Prime Critic in the world, just as Old Herald was the best Life Painter. They had worked together for over fifty years. Prime had sometimes wondered, heretically, if Herald could have been as good an artist without her. The Trinity of Artist and Critics was an article of faith to her. But the artist was first. Still . . .

what if Herald had only had this Secondary, who was good with the tubings but whose eye for color was, at best, only a Landseer to her Turner. She called silently on the old gods and crossed her hands briefly in front of her, wrists up—the old ritual—to ward off the full brunt of the gods' anger.

The autoclave signaled the end of its work with a loud bell. Secondary went over and claimed the instruments, his hands encased in the formfitting plastigloves.

Prime nodded and put on a pair of gloves herself. Then she took the paint sticks from him and carefully scraped the color mix into the tubes. In the artificial light of the Color Room, the red paint in the coils of tubing looked like human veins. She held the color sticks straight up. It would not do for them to receive any paint before Old Herald was ready. Not that they could, with the color clamp on so tight at the end. She tested the clamps. They were secure.

Prime and Secondary marched back into the old painter's room. It was such a contrast to the rest of the house: spare where the artist's manse was sumptuous. It was a deliberate attempt to reproduce the garret where the god Modigliani, one of the true precursors of the suffering artist-gods, had worked. Prime had apprenticed in a much different atmosphere to an artist whose painting room was yellow outside, with a red-tiled floor and whitewashed walls like the studio of Van Gogh. Prime remembered sourly how she had left when the artist had tried to emulate the crazed god, insisting on unantiseptic coffee grounds being mixed into the paints. Not surprisingly, the artist had died of sepsis and in agony, his critics being unable to dissuade him from his folly. He had not, Prime thought uncharitably, been a particularly good painter either.

Old Herald was still asleep when they entered the room, but their footsteps on the uneven wooden floor wakened him. His eyes flew open, the faded blue of the irises contrasting sharply with the rainbowed veins running a zigzag course across the whites.

"Who is it?" he shouted at them.

"Your critics, Visionary," said Prime.

"Your second eyes, Maestro," said her companion, the ritual words coming unbidden to his lips.

"Damned if I want *your* eyes," muttered the old man. Then he shouted, "I want my own eyes back. The light, the light is fading. I will not have it." He sat up in bed, his eyes rheumy with pink tears. "I will not have it." His voice broke, but he would not cry.

Prime put the coils of tubing down beside the bed in the bowl of solution on the floor. She set the sticks upright in their holders. "Do you still wish to paint?"

"Paint? Paint?" the old man mumbled, then looked up again, a sly expression on his face. "What would I like to paint?" he asked.

Prime soothed his forehead with her gloved hand. "You said something about 'Reds. Bloods. Crimsons. The Phoenix' . . ."

"Rises!" shouted the old man triumphantly. "I was just testing you. But you always know, don't you. Too bad you're so damned homely, Prime, or I'd have married you long ago."

Secondary gave a quick smile behind Prime's back.

Prime nodded. "I know. I know," she said. She did not remind the old man that they had been married forty years before, when she was young and her small, dark body had attracted him. She had never begrudged him his subsequent mistresses, most of them models. Nor had she ever mentioned their marriage to any of his Secondaries. It was enough that she remembered. She wondered, briefly, if Old Herald, the god, remembered; indeed, if any gods remembered.

"I don't know," Old Herald suddenly whimpered. "It hurts, the brushes, the paint. It is painful to put color on canvas. I don't know. . . ."

Secondary knelt by his bed. "I would never hurt you knowingly, Visionary. My hands are gentle. You always said you liked my hands. I can rub painkiller on the tubes. That way you would feel nothing as they slipped in."

"Idiot!" murmured Prime.

"*Idiot!*" shouted Old Herald. "It is the pain that makes the artist. How can a man be a god without pain? Art—truly great art—is lifeblood spilled upon the canvas. Here, here are my wrists. Shove away. And do not spare me the pain."

He turned his hand upward toward them, and they could see the mark of the artist, the suffering god, stamped on his wrists. Set in the center of the large vein, where it crossed the wristline, was the brush hole, the circle of hard plastic with the valve that only opened inward. Because Old Herald had been an artist for so many years, the valve was yellowed with age. His branching veins stood high above the skin of his arms, like the traceries of a bas-relief sculpture. The thin, still-muscular arms disappeared into the flowing sleeves of his blue-black robe.

Prime unrolled the plastic apron, shaking it out, then tied the strings around his neck. Helping him sit up, she placed a backrest behind him that braced against the wall. Finally she got out a canvas that had been newly stretched that morning. She placed it before him.

"A new one?" he asked. He could see that much.

"I stretch a new one every day for you," she said, her voice soft, on the edge of tears. "Just in case." She started to turn away.

"I *should* have married you," he said. Then he winked.

Secondary moved toward the bed, and Prime stepped back. She picked up the coils of tubing and fed them slowly to her brother critic.

Secondary concentrated on the old man's hands. Sometimes they shook with the palsy of old age, but this time they lay like two withered leaves in his lap. Secondary picked up one, turned it so that the wrist was facing him, and, matching the tube's end to the valve, began the careful threading process. Slowly, carefully, he pushed the tube through the radial artery, never forcing. A forced vein was a severed vein: that was the first rule a critic learned. They practiced on lemurs first. The tube tracked its way up Old Herald's arm. Secondary could feel it slip into the brachial artery and snake its way across the old painter's chest, then turn and make a path down into his heart.

Old Herald did not speak again, though his labored breathing was comment enough. The threading was always painful to some extent. Young artists usually bore it stoically, though deep breathing and self-hypnosis damped the worst of it. The mediocre artists were the ones who insisted on pain-killers. But sometimes an old artist, even a great one, called for relief, and no one thought the worse of him.

The slight *pop* told Secondary when the tube had reached Old Herald's heart, but he already knew from long experience when it would happen, just seconds after the easy push through the larger subclavian artery. The second tube, into the artist's right wrist, went as smoothly. Secondary was, as always, very good with his hands.

Prime set the paint sticks into Old Herald's palms and turned the clamps.

There was an instant of spurting which coated the brush tips.

"It flows," Old Herald said, nodding his head. Then he turned by instinct alone to the canvas.

The mixture of paint and blood oozed out of the stick and onto the canvas. Old Herald moved his arms in great swoops and swings, the faultless penmanship of the true artist. The reds coruscated onto the canvas and trailed down the face of it as if weeping crimson tears. Then his right hand faltered and stopped. The left hand stuttered and was still. His eyes were closed.

"He is asleep," whispered Secondary.

"Perhaps," answered Prime.

Something in their voices woke the old man. "Is it done?" he asked, his eyes opening.

"There is nothing . . ." Secondary began, but trailed off into silence when he was pushed aside by Prime.

She placed her massive body between the old man and the canvas. "It is done," she said to him, pushing him gently back against the pillows, removing the backrest at the same time. "It is your best work."

"My best," he mumbled back to her. "You have never said

that before. My *best*. And a critic never lies to her artist. Never."

"Never," Prime agreed, pulling the covers up over his feet and legs. She untied the apron strings and stripped the plastic from him.

Old Herald smiled up at her. "One must always rage against the dying of the light. Some ancient poet-god said that. He was right. We must end our lives in a burst of color. Remember that. Tell them all—all who come after—that I said that. I did. Old Herald." He paused, then asked again as a child might, "It was my best?"

"Your heart's blood is there, there on the canvas. Would a critic lie?" Prime answered. "It is done."

"Done," Old Herald sighed. Then, with his eyes still open, he ceased breathing.

Prime disengaged the paint sticks and tugged at the tubes. Slowly they slipped out of the hole, slippery with old blood. She let the pieces clatter onto the germ-laden floor. She wept openly as she pulled the covers up over his thin body.

"You lied to him," hissed Secondary. "You did not tell him the truth about the painting. It is nothing but a few sweeps of color. Any child could do better."

Prime closed Old Herald's right eye and spoke fiercely. "All these years he has made us—forced us—to see what he wanted us to see. It was his greatest gift. Surely there was no reason at the end to let him know he had failed us."

"I thought . . . thought a critic was chosen to speak . . . speak truth to art," said Secondary. "It's in our oath."

"But mercy is in the oath, too. How would it have served Old Herald's art now?" asked Prime. "Besides—it is his final statement—rage against the dying of the light. A proper title for the picture, wouldn't you say? Rage and blood and tears. What more could an artist—a god—do?"

Secondary said nothing, but cautiously closed Old Herald's color-clotted left eye.

Wordlessly, the two critics crossed the artist's desiccated hands across his genitals, signaling the public parts over the private. They turned the hands wrist up to show the paint-clogged veins. The plug of color, a dull red, showed at the brush hole. They tied a white cloth over his head and under his chin to keep his jaw from dropping open, and Secondary picked up the tubes and brushes from the floor.

Prime looked around the room one last time. By law she could never return to it. She looked longest at the man she had loved, the artist she had served. Then she opened the outer door into the gallery where lines of mourners were already threading their way down the passage, and left Old Herald to his worshipers and to eternal light.

Sule Skerry

MAIRI ROWED THE CORACLE with quick, angry strokes, watching the rocky shoreline and the little town of Caith perched on its edge recede. She wished she could make her anger disappear as easily. She was sixteen, after all, and no longer a child. The soldiers whistled at her, even in her school uniform, when she walked to and from the Academy. And wasn't Harry Stones, who was five years older than she and a lieutenant in the RAF, a tail gunner, mad about her? Given a little time, he might have asked her dad for her hand, though she was too young yet, a schoolgirl. Whenever he came to visit, he brought her something. Once even a box of chocolates, though they were very dear.

But to be sent away from London for safekeeping like a baby, to her gran's house, to this desolate, isolated Scottish sea town because of a few German raids—it was demeaning. She could have helped, could have at least cooked and taken care of the flat for her father now that the help had all gone off to war jobs. She had wanted to be there in case a bomb *did* fall, so she could race out and help evacuate all the poor unfortunates, maybe even win a medal, and wouldn't Jenny Eivensley look green then. But he had sent her off, her dad, and Harry had agreed, even though it meant they couldn't see each other very often. It was not in the least fair.

She pulled again on the oars. The little skin boat tended to wallow and needed extra bullying. It wasn't built like a proper British rowboat. It was roundish, shaped more like a turtle shell than a ship. Mairi hated it, hated all of the things in Caith. She knew she should have been in London helping rather than fooling about in a coracle. She pulled on the oars and the boat shot ahead.

The thing about rowing, she reminded herself, was that you watched where you had been, not where you were heading. She could see the town, with its crown of mewing seabirds, disappear from sight. Her destination did not matter. It was all ocean anyway—cold, uninviting, opaque; a dark green mirror that reflected nothing. And now there was ocean behind as well as ahead, for the shore had thinned out to an invisible line.

Suddenly, without warning, the coracle fetched up against a rock, one of a series of water-smoothed amphibious mounds that loomed up out of the sea. Only at the bump did Mairi turn and look. Out of the corner of her eye she saw a quick scurry of something large and gray and furry on the far side of the rocks. She heard a splash.

"Oh," she said out loud. "A seal!"

The prospect of having come upon a seal rookery was enough to make her leap incautiously from the coracle onto the rock, almost losing the skin boat in her eagerness, her anger forgotten. She leaned over and pulled the little boat out of the water, scraping its hull along the gray granite. Then she upended the coracle and left it; it looked for all the world like a great dozing tortoise drying in the hazy sun.

Mairi shrugged out of her mackintosh and draped it on the rock next to the boat. Then, snugging the watch cap down over her curls and pulling the bulky fisherman's sweater over her slim hips, she began her ascent.

The rocks were covered with a strange purple-gray lichen that was both soft and slippery. Mairi fell once, bruising her right knee without ripping her trousers. She cursed softly, trying out swearwords that she had never been allowed to use at home or in Gran's great house back on shore. Then she started up again, on her hands and knees, more carefully now, and at last gained the high point on the rock after a furious minute of climbing that went backward and sideways almost as often as it went up. The top of the gray rock was free of the lichen, and she was able to stand up, feeling safe, and look around.

She could not see Caith, with its little, watchful wind-scored houses lined up like a homefront army to face the oncoming tides in the firth, Gran's grand old house standing to one side, the sergeant-major. She could not even see the hills behind, where cliffs hunched like the bleached fossils of some enormous prehistoric ocean beast washed ashore. All that she could see was the unbroken sea, blue and black and green and gray, with patterns of color that shifted as quickly as the pieces in a child's kaleidoscope. Gray-white foam skipped across wave tops, then tumbled down and fractured into bubbles that popped erratically, leaving nothing but a grayish scum that soon became shiny water again. She thought she saw one or two dark seal heads in the troughs of the waves, but they never came close enough for her to be sure. And overhead the sky was lowering, a color so dirty that it would have made even the bravest sailor long for shore. There was a storm coming, and Mairi guessed she should leave.

She shivered, and suddenly knew where she was. These rocks were the infamous Sule Skerry rocks that Gran's cook had told her about.

"Some may call it a rookery," Cook had said one morning when Mairi had visited with her in the dark kitchen. Cook's cooking was awful—dry, bland, and unvaried. But at least she knew stories and always imparted them with an intensity that made even the strangest of them seem real. "Aye, some may call it a rookery. But us from Caith, we know. It be the home of the selchies, who are men on land and seals in the sea. And

the Great Selchie himself lives on that rock. Tall he is. And
covered with a sealskin when he tumbles in the waves. But he
is a man for all that. And no maiden who goes to Sule Skerry
returns the same."

She had hummed a bit of an old song then, with a haunting melody that Mairi, for all her music training at school,
could not repeat. But the words of the song, some of them,
had stuck with her:

> An earthly nourrice sits and sings,
> And aye she sings, "Ba, lily wean!
> Little ken I my bairn's father,
> Far less the land that he staps in."

> Then ane arose at her bed-fit,
> An' a grumly guest I'm sure was he:
> "Here am I, thy bairn's father,
> Although I be not comelie.

> I am a man upon the land,
> I am a selchie in the sea,
> And when I'm far frae ev'ry strand
> My dwelling is in Sule Skerry."

A warning tale, Mairi thought. A bogeyman story to keep
foolish girls safe at home. She smiled. She was a Londoner,
after all, not a silly Scots girl who'd never been out of her own
town.

And then she heard a strange sound, almost like an echo of
the music of Cook's song, from the backside of the rocks. At
first she thought it was the sound of wind against water, the
sound she heard continuously at Gran's home where every room
rustled with the music of the sea. But this was different somehow, a sweet, low throbbing, part moan and part chant. Without knowing the why of it, only feeling a longing brought on by
the wordless song, and excusing it as seeking to solve a mystery,
she went looking for the source of the song. The rock face was
smooth on this side, dry, without the slippery, somber lichen;
and the water was calmer so it did not splash up spray. Mairi
continued down the side, the tune reeling her in effortlessly.

Near the waterline was a cave opening into the west face of the rock, a man-sized opening as black and uninviting as a collier's pit. But she took a deep, quick breath, and went in.

Much to her surprise, the inside of the cave glowed with an incandescent blue-green light that seemed to come from the cave walls themselves. Darker pockets of light illuminated the concave sections of the wall. Pieces of seaweed caught in these niches gave the appearance of household gods.

Mairi could scarcely breathe. Any loud sound seemed sacrilegious. Her breath itself was a violation.

And then she heard the moan-song again, so loud that it seemed to fill the entire cave. It swelled upward like a wave, then broke off in a bubbling sigh.

Mairi walked in slowly, not daring to touch the cave walls in case she should mar the perfection of the color, yet fearing that she might fall, for the floor of the cave was slippery with scattered puddles of water. Slowly, one foot in front of the other, she explored the cave. In the blue-green light, her sweater and skin seemed to take on an underwater tinge, as if she had been transformed into a mermaid.

And then the cave ended, tapering off to a rounded apse with a kind of stone altar the height of a bed. There was something dark lying on the rock slab. Fearfully, Mairi inched toward it, and when she got close, the dark thing heaved up slightly and spoke to her in a strange, guttural tongue. At first Mairi thought it was a seal, a wounded seal, but then she saw it was a man huddled under a sealskin coat. He suddenly lay back, feverish and shuddering, and she saw the beads of dried blood that circled his head like a crown.

Without thinking, Mairi moved closer and put her hand on his forehead, expecting it to burn with temperature, but he was cold and damp and slippery to the touch. Then he opened his eyes, and they were the same blue-green color as the walls, as the underside of a wave. She wondered for a moment if he were blind, for there seemed to be no pupils in those eyes. Then he closed the lids and smiled at her, whispering in that same unknown tongue.

"Never mind, never mind, I'll get help," whispered Mairi. He might be a fisherman from the town or an RAF man shot down on a mission. She looked at his closed-down face. Here, at last, was her way to aid the war effort. "Lie still. First I'll see to your wounds. They taught us first aid at school."

She examined his forehead under the slate-gray hair, and saw that the terrible wound that had been there was now closed and appeared to be healing, though bloody and seamed with scabs. But when she started to slip the sealskin coat down to examine him for other wounds, she was shocked to discover he had no clothes on under it. No clothes at all.

She hesitated then. Except for the statues in the museum, Mairi had never seen a man naked. Not even in the first-aid books. But what if he were *hurt unto death*? The fearsome poetry of the old phrase decided her. She inched back the sealskin covering as gently as she could.

He did not move except for the rise and fall of his chest. His body was covered with fine hairs, gray as the hair on his head. He had broad, powerful shoulders and slim, tapering hips. The skin on his hands was strangely wrinkled, as if he had been under water too long. She realized with a start that he was quite, quite beautiful—but alien. As her grandmother often said, "Men are queer creatures, so different from us, child. And someday you will know it."

Then his eyes opened again and she could not look away from them. He smiled, opened his mouth, and began to speak, to chant really. Mairi bent down over him and he opened his arms to her, the gray webbing between his fingers pulsing strongly. And without willing it, she covered his mouth with hers. All the sea was in that kiss, cold and vast and perilous. It drew her in till she thought she would faint with it, with his tongue darting around hers as quick as a minnow. And then his arms encircled her and he was as strong as the tide. She felt only the briefest of pain, and a kind of drowning, and she let the land go.

When Mairi awoke, she was sitting on the stone floor

of the cavern, and cold, bone-chillingly cold. She shivered and pushed her hand across her cheeks. They were wet, though whether with tears or from the damp air she could not say.

Above her, on the stone bed, the wounded man breathed raggedly. Occasionally he let out a moan. Mairi stood and looked down at him. His flesh was pale, wan, almost translucent. She put her hand on his shoulder but he did not move. She wondered if she had fallen and hit her head; if she had dreamed what had happened.

"Help. I must get help for him," she thought. She covered him again with the coat and made her way back to the cave mouth. Her entire body ached, and she decided she must have fallen and blacked out.

The threatening storm had not yet struck, but the dark slant of rain against the horizon was closer still. Mairi scrambled along the rocks to where the coracle waited. She put on her mac, then heaved the boat over and into the water and slipped in, getting only her boots wet.

It was more difficult rowing back, rowing against the tide. Waves broke over the bow of the little boat, and by the time she was within sight of the town, she was soaked to the skin. The stones of Sule Skerry were little more than gray wave tops then, and with one pull on the oars, they disappeared from sight. The port enfolded her, drew her in. She felt safe and lonely at once.

When Mairi reached the shore, there was a knot of fishermen tending their boats. A few were still at work on the bright orange nets, folding them carefully in that quick, intricate pattern that only they seemed to know.

One man, in a blue watch cap, held up a large piece of tattered white cloth, an awning of silk. It seemed to draw the other men to him. He gestured with the silk and it billowed out as if capturing the coming storm.

Suddenly Mairi was horribly afraid. She broke into the circle of men. "Oh, please, please," she cried out, hearing the growing wail of wind in her voice. "There's a man on the rocks. He's hurt."

"The rocks?" The man with the silk stuffed it into his pocket, but a large fold of it hung down his trouser leg. "Which rocks?"

"Out there. Beyond the sight line. Where the seals stay."

"Whose child is she?" asked a man who still carried an orange net. He spoke as if she were too young to understand him or as if she were a foreigner.

"Old Mrs. Goodleigh's grandchild. The one with the English father," came an answer.

"Mavis' daughter, the one who became a nurse in London."

"Too good for Caith, then?"

Mairi was swirled about in their conversation.

"Please," she tried again.

"Suppose'n she means the Rocks?"

"Yes," begged Mairi. "The rocks out there. Sule Skerry."

"Hush, child. Must na say the name in sight of the sea," said the blue-cap man.

"Toss it a coin, Jock," said the white-silk man.

The man called Jock reached into his pocket and flung a coin out to the ocean. It skipped across the waves twice, then sank.

"That should quiet en. Now then, the Rocks you say?"

Mairi turned to the questioner. He had a face like a map, wrinkles marking the boundaries of nose and cheek. "Yes, sir," she said breathily.

"Aye, he might have fetched up there," said the white-silk man, drawing it out of his pocket again for the others to see.

Did they know him, then? Mairi wondered.

"Should we leave him to the storm?" asked Jock.

"He might be one of ours," the map-faced man said.

They all nodded at that.

"He's sheltered," Mairi said suddenly. "In a cave. A grotto, like. It's all cast over with a blue and green light."

"Teched, she is. There's no grotto there," said blue-cap.

"No blue and green light either," said the map-faced man,

turning from her and speaking earnestly with his companions. "Even if he's one of them, he might tell us summat we need. Our boys could use the knowledge. From that bit of parachute silk, it's hard to say which side he's on." He reached out and touched the white cloth with a gnarled finger.

"Aye, we'd best look for him."

"He won't be hard to find," Mairi began. "He's sick. Hurt. I touched him."

"What was he wearing then?" asked blue-cap.

The wind had picked up and Mairi couldn't hear the question. "What?" she shouted.

"Wearing. *What was the fellow wearing?*"

Suddenly remembering that the man had been naked under the coat, she was silent.

"She doesn't know. Probably too scared to go close. Come on," said Jock.

The men pushed past her and dragged along two of the large six-man boats that fished the haaf banks. The waves were slapping angrily at the shore, gobbling up pieces of the sand and churning out pebbles at each retreat. Twelve men scrambled into the boats and headed out to sea, their oars flashing together.

Three men were left on shore, including the one holding the remnant of white silk. They stood staring out over the cold waters, their eyes squinted almost shut against the strange bright light that was running before the storm.

Mairi stood near them, but apart.

No one spoke.

It was a long half-hour before the first of the boats leaped back toward them, across a wave, seconds ahead of the rain.

The second boat beached just as the storm broke, the men jumping out onto the sand and drawing the boat up behind them. A dark form was huddled against the stern.

Mairi tried to push through to get a close glimpse of the man, but blue-cap spoke softly to her.

"Nay, nay, girl, don't look. He's not what you would call a

pretty sight. He pulled a gun on Jock and Jock took a rock to him."

But Mairi had seen enough. The man was dressed in a flier's suit, and a leather jacket with zippers. His blond hair was matted with blood.

"That's not the one I saw," she murmured. "Not the one I . . ."

"Found him lying on the Rocks, just as the girl said. Down by the west side of the Rocks," said Jock. "We threw his coins to the sea and bought our way home. Though I don't know that German coins buy much around here. Bloody Huns."

"What's a German flier doing this far west, I'd like to know," said map-face.

"Maybe he was trying for America," Jock answered, laughing sourly.

"Ask him. When he's fit to talk," said blue-cap.

The man with the white silk wrapped it around the German's neck. The parachute shroud lines hung down the man's back. Head down, the German was marched between Jock and blue-cap up the strand and onto the main street. The other men trailed behind.

With the rain soaking through her cap and running down her cheeks, Mairi took a step toward them. Then she turned away. She kicked slowly along the water's edge till she found the stone steps that led up to her gran's house. The sea pounded a steady reminder on her left, a *basso continuo* to the song that ran around in her head. The last three verses came to her slowly.

> Now he has ta'en a purse of goud
> And he has put it upon her knee,
> Sayin', "Gie to me my little young son
> And tak ye up thy nourrice-fee."

She shivered and put her hands in her pockets to keep them warm. In one of the mac's deep pockets, her fingers felt something cold and rough to the touch. Reluctantly she drew it out. It was a coin, green and gold, slightly crusted, as if it had lain on the ocean bottom for some time. She had never seen it before and could only guess how it had gotten into her coat pocket. She closed her hand around the coin, so tightly a second coin was imprinted on her palm.

> An' it shall pass on a summer's day
> When the sun shines het on every stane,
> That I will tak my little young son
> An' teach him for to swim his lane.
>
> An' thu sall marry a proud gunner,
> An' a right proud gunner I'm sure he'll be.
> An' the very first shot that ere he shoots
> He'll kill baith my young son and me.

Had it truly happened, or was it just some dream brought on by a fall? She felt again those cold, compelling hands on her, the movement of the webbings pulsing on her breasts; smelled again the briny odor of his breath. And if she *did* have that bairn, that child? Why, Harry Stones would *have* to marry her, then. Her father could not deny them that.

And laughing and crying at the same time, Mairi began to run up the stone steps. The sound of the sea followed her all the way home, part melody and part unending moan.

The White Seal Maid

ON THE NORTH SEA SHORE there was a fisherman named Merdock who lived all alone. He had neither wife nor child, nor wanted one. At least that was what he told the other men with whom he fished the haaf banks.

But truth was, Merdock was a lonely man, at ease only with the wind and waves. And each evening, when he left his companions, calling out "Fair wind!"—the sailor's leave—he knew they were going back to a warm hearth and a full bed while he went home to none. Secretly he longed for the same comfort.

One day it came to Merdock as if in a dream that he should leave off fishing that day and go down to the sea-ledge and hunt the seal. He had never done such a thing before, thinking it close to murder, for the seal had human eyes and cried with a baby's voice.

Yet though he had never done such a thing, there was such a longing within him that Merdock could not say no to it. And that longing was like a high, sweet singing, a calling. He could not rid his mind of it. So he went.

Down by a gray rock he sat, a long sharpened stick by his side. He kept his eyes fixed out on the sea, where the white birds sat on the waves like foam.

He waited through sunrise and sunset and through the long, cold night, the singing in his head. Then, when the wind went down a bit, he saw a white seal far out in the sea, coming toward him, the moon riding on its shoulder.

Merdock could scarcely breathe as he watched the seal, so shining and white was its head. It swam swiftly to the sea-ledge, and then with one quick push it was on land.

Merdock rose then in silence, the stick in his hand. He would have thrown it, too. But the white seal gave a sudden shudder and its skin sloughed off. It was a maiden cast in moonlight, with the tide about her feet.

She stepped high out of her skin, and her hair fell sleek and white about her shoulders and hid her breasts.

Merdock fell to his knees behind the rock and would have hidden his eyes, but her cold white beauty was too much for him. He could only stare. And if he made a noise then, she took no notice but turned her face to the sea and opened her arms up to the moon. Then she began to sway and call.

At first Merdock could not hear the words. Then he realized it was the very song he had heard in his head all that day:

> Come to the edge,
> Come down to the ledge
> Where the water laps the shore.
>
> Come to the strand,
> Seals to the sand,
> The watery time is o'er.

When the song was done, she began it again. It was as if the whole beach, the whole cove, the whole world were nothing but that one song.

And as she sang, the water began to fill up with seals. Black seals and gray seals and seals of every kind. They swam to the shore at her call and sloughed off their skins. They were as young as the white seal maid, but none so beautiful in Merdock's eyes. They swayed and turned at her singing, and joined their voices to hers. Faster and faster the seal maidens danced, in circles of twos and threes and fours. Only the white seal maid danced alone, in the center, surrounded by the castoff skins of her twirling sisters.

The moon remained high almost all the night, but at last it went down. At its setting, the seal maids stopped their singing, put on their skins again, one by one, went back into the sea again, one by one, and swam away. But the white seal maid did not go. She waited on the shore until the last of them was out of sight.

Then she turned to the watching man, as if she had always known he was there, hidden behind the gray rock. There was something strange, a kind of pleading, in her eyes.

Merdock read that pleading and thought he understood it. He ran over to where she stood, grabbed up her sealskin, and held it high overhead.

"Now you be mine," he said.

And she had to go with him, that was the way of it. For she was a selchie, one of the seal folk. And the old tales said it: The selchie maid without her skin was no more than a lass.

They were wed within the week, Merdock and the white seal maid, because he wanted it. So she nodded her head at the priest's bidding, though she said not a word.

And Merdock had no complaint of her, his "Sel" as he called her. No complaint except this: she would not go down to the sea. She would not go down by the shore where he had found her or down to the sand to see him in his boat, though often enough she would stare from the cottage door out past the cove's end where the inlet poured out into the great wide sea.

"Will you not walk down by the water's edge with me, Sel?" Merdock would ask each morning. "Or will you not come down to greet me when I return?"

She never answered him, either "Yea" or "Nay." Indeed, if he had not heard her singing that night on the ledge, he would have thought her mute. But she was a good wife, for all that, and did what he required. If she did not smile, she did not weep. She seemed, to Merdock, strangely content.

So Merdock hung the white sealskin up over the door where Sel could see it. He kept it there in case she should want to leave him, to don the skin and go. He could have hidden it or burned it, but he did not. He hoped the sight of it, so near and easy, would keep her with him; would tell her, as he could not, how much he loved her. For he found he did love her, his seal wife. It was that simple. He loved her and did not want her to go, but he would not keep her past her willing it, so he hung the skin up over the door.

And then their sons were born. One a year, born at the ebbing of the tide. And Sel sang to them, one by one, long, longing wordless songs that carried the sound of the sea. But to Merdock she said nothing.

Seven sons they were, strong and silent, one born each year. They were born to the sea, born to swim, born to let the tide lap them head and shoulder. And though they had the dark eyes of the seal, and though they had the seal's longing for the sea, they were men and had men's names: James, John, Michael, George, William, Rob, and Tom. They helped their father fish the cove and bring home his catch from the sea.

It was seven years and seven years and seven years again that the seal wife lived with him. The oldest of their sons was just coming to his twenty-first birthday, the youngest barely a man. It was on a gray day, the wind scarcely rising, that the boys all refused to go with Merdock when he called. They gave no reason but "Nay."

"Wife," Merdock called, his voice heavy and gray as the sky. "Wife, whose sons are these? How have you raised them that they say 'Nay' to their father when he calls?" It was ever his custom to talk to Sel as if she returned him words.

To his surprise, Sel turned to him and said, "Go. My sons be staying with me this day." It was the voice of the singer on the beach, musical and low. And the shock was so great that he went at once and did not look back.

He set his boat on the sea, the great boat that usually took several men to row it. He set it out himself and got it out into the cove, put the nets over, and never once heard when his sons called out to him as he went, "Father, fair wind!"

But after a bit the shock wore thin and he began to think about it. He became angry then, at his sons and at his wife, who had long plagued him with her silence. He pulled in the nets and pulled on the oars and started toward home. "I, too, can say 'Nay' to this sea," he said out loud as he rode the swells in.

The beach was cold and empty. Even the gulls were mute.

"I do not like this," Merdock said. "It smells of a storm."

He beached the boat and walked home. The sky gathered in around him. At the cottage he hesitated but a moment, then pulled savagely on the door. He waited for the warmth to greet him. But the house was as empty and cold as the beach.

Merdock went into the house and stared at the hearth, black and silent. Then, fear riding in his heart, he turned slowly and looked over the door.

The sealskin was gone.

"Sel!" he cried then as he ran from the house, and he named his sons in a great anguished cry as he ran. Down to the sea-ledge he went, calling their names like a prayer: "James, John, Michael, George, William, Rob, Tom!"

But they were gone.

The rocks were gray, as gray as the sky. At the water's edge was a pile of clothes that lay like discarded skins. Merdock stared out far across the cove and saw a seal herd swimming. Yet not a herd. A white seal and seven strong pups.

"Sel!" he cried again. "James, John, Michael, George, William, Rob, Tom!"

For a moment, the white seal turned her head, then she looked again to the open sea and barked out seven times. The wind carried the faint sounds back to the shore. Merdock heard, as if in a dream, the seven seal names she called. They seemed harsh and jangling to his ear.

Then the whole herd dove. When they came up again they

were but eight dots strung along the horizon, lingering for a moment, then disappearing into the blue edge of sea.

Merdock recited the seven seal names to himself. And in that recitation was a song, a litany to the god of the seals. The names were no longer harsh, but right. And he remembered clearly again the moonlit night when the seals had danced upon the sand. Maidens all. Not a man or boy with them. And the white seal turning and choosing him, giving herself to him that he might give the seal people life.

His anger and sadness left him then. He turned once more to look at the sea and pictured his seven strong sons on their way.

He shouted their seal names to the wind. Then he added, under his breath, as if trying out a new tongue, "Fair wind, my sons. Fair wind."

The Bird of Time

ONCE THERE WAS A MILLER who was named Honest Hans because he never lied or gave false weight. He had an only son called Pieter, whom many considered a fool.

Pieter often sat long hours looking steadily at the sky or a bird or a flower, saying nothing and smiling softly to himself. At such times he would not answer a question, even if someone asked him the time of day or the price of a sack of flour.

Yes, many considered Pieter a fool. But his father did not.

"Pieter is a dreamer," he said. "He knows beyond things. He understands the songs of the birds. And if he prefers the company of dumb plants and animals to that of people, perhaps it is a wise choice. It is not for me to say."

But the people of the village felt it was for them to say. They said so many unkind things about Pieter that the miller grew sad. At last Pieter said to him, "Father, I will go and seek my fortune. Then, perhaps, both you and I will have peace from this ceaseless wagging of mischievous tongues."

And so Pieter made his way into the wide, wide world.

He had traveled only two days and three nights into the wide, wide world when he heard a weak cry. It sounded like a call for help. Immediately, and without a thought for his own safety, Pieter rushed in the direction of the sound and found a tiny brown bird caught in a trap. He opened the trap and set the bird free. But the bird was so weak from lack of water and food that it only had time for a few faint chirps before it folded its tired wings and died.

However, since Pieter could speak the language of the birds, those few chirps were enough to tell him something of great importance. He hurried off to a nearby tree, where a nest lay concealed in the topmost branches.

In the nest was a single egg, gleaming like marble, white and veined with red and gold. Pieter picked it up. He thought about what the dying bird had told him: "In the egg lives the bird of time. When the egg is broken open, the bird will emerge singing. As long as it continues to sing, time will flow onward like a river. But if you should hold the bird and say, *'Bird of time, make time go fast,'* time will speed up for everyone except yourself and those you hold until you loose the bird again. And," the dying bird had continued, "if you say, *'Bird of time, make time go slow,'* time will slow down for everyone around. And you and those you hold will run through time like the wind through leafless trees."

Then the little brown bird had shivered all over. "But never say, *'Bird of time, make time stop,'* for then there will be a great shaking and a great quaking, and time will stop for you and those you hold forevermore."

With that, the bird had cried out, "Good friend, goodbye," and died.

Pieter was awed by this. But not overawed, for he was a dreamer, and dreamers believe in miracles, both large and small. So he put the egg in his cap, his cap on his head, and journeyed farther into the wide, wide world.

He had hardly been gone another night and day when suddenly there came a second cry for help. This time it was not a little cry, but a great weeping and a wailing and a terrible sobbing that filled the entire kingdom through which he was traveling.

Once again, without a thought for his own safety, Pieter ran toward the sound. Soon he came upon a large palace. Before it was a crowd of men and women and children. They were all crying and moaning, twisting their kerchiefs or stomping on their caps.

"What is the matter?" asked Pieter. "Is there something wrong?"

"You must be worse than a fool," said an old man. "For even a fool could see that we weep and cry because the wicked giant has just now stolen the king's daughter dear and carried her off to Castle Gloam. And none of us is brave enough or smart enough or strong enough to rescue her."

"Well, then, I must," said Pieter.

"Indeed you *are* a fool," said another man. "For if we, who are the people of the mightiest king in the world, are not brave enough or smart enough or strong enough to rescue the princess, then only a fool would try."

"Fool I may be," said Pieter, "or worse. But I think you are more foolish than I if you will not try at all."

And off he went with not a word more toward Castle Gloam to rescue the king's beautiful daughter.

Pieter walked and walked seven days and seven nights to Castle Gloam, which teetered on the edge of the world (for in those days the world was flat). At last he found the castle and pushed through the enormous door.

It was nearly dark inside the castle, and cold. A single light shone dimly at the end of a long hall. It was toward that light that Pieter walked. When he came to where the light began and the hall ended, he saw the king's daughter. She was sitting on a golden throne in a golden cage and weeping as though her tears could wash away the bars.

"Do not cry," said Pieter when he was quite close to the cage. "I am here to bring you home." He spoke bravely, although he had no idea how to accomplish what he promised.

When she heard him, the king's daughter looked up, her

eyes shimmering with tears. And when she looked at him, Pieter felt her gaze go straight to his heart; he had never seen anyone so beautiful. He knelt before her and took off his cap. And the egg, which had been hidden there, nestled in his hair.

Just then he heard loud footsteps and a giant voice shouting.

And before Pieter could move, the floors shook and the walls trembled and the giant of Castle Gloam stomped into the room.

Pieter turned around to stare at the giant. And as he turned, the egg, which had been nestled in his hair, fell off his head and broke upon the floor. A little brown bird arose singing from the broken egg and alighted on Pieter's hand.

Pieter stood up. Reaching into the cage, he took the hand of the king's daughter gently in his. Then he said, *"Bird of time, make time go slow."*

Immediately the little brown bird began singing a very slow, measured song. And time, which had been flowing along like a swift river, suddenly became muddy and slow for the giant. And he moved awkwardly through the air as though it were water.

Without letting go of the princess's hand, Pieter quickly opened the cage with a golden key he found hanging nearby. The king's daughter ran out. Then hand in hand they raced out into the countryside, like the wind through leafless trees. There they danced and laughed. And Pieter threw his arms up into the air with joy, and the bird of time was loosed.

At once time began to move normally again. In a moment Pieter and the princess heard the loud, rattling footsteps of the giant as he searched through Castle Gloam for the king's daughter.

"Quickly," said Pieter, taking the princess by the hand. "We must run."

But run as fast as they could, they could not run faster than the giant. With loud, earth-shattering footsteps, he gained at every stride.

"Save yourself!" cried the king's daughter. "It is foolish to stay with me."

But Pieter merely held out his hand, and the bird of time flew down and nestled in it.

"Lie down," said Pieter to the king's daughter. And he lay down by her side in the tall meadow grass.

"Bird of time, make time go fast," commanded Pieter.

The little brown bird began to sing a light, quick song. And time sped up for everyone but Pieter and the lovely princess.

The giant fairly flew over to the two bodies lying side by side on the ground. He twirled around and about them. To his speeded-up eyes they seemed dead, so measured and slow was their breathing. The giant gnashed his teeth in rage at having lost his beautiful captive. Hastily he pounded his fists on the ground. Then he noticed the bird of time in Pieter's hand singing a light, quick song. Forgetting the princess, he tore the bird out of Pieter's hand with a swift, sharp, angry movement.

Gloating, the giant ran back to Castle Gloam with the bird. Pieter and the princess watched him go.

Now the giant had heard what Pieter had said to the bird, and he realized that there was magic about. He thought that if the bird could make time speed up or make time slow down, it could help him conquer the world. And because he was evil and exceptionally greedy, the giant thought what a great fortune he could gather and how many beautiful princesses he could steal, if time could be stopped altogether and no one but he could move at all.

He put out his hand as he had seen Pieter do, and the bird nestled into it, almost disappearing in his vast palm.

"Bird of time," he commanded, *"make time stop!"*

And the bird of time stopped singing.

The giant did not know that this was a calamitous thing to say. He had not heard the dying bird's warning that no one can make time stop altogether. And he was too wicked to worry about it on his own.

Suddenly there was a great quaking. And a great shaking.

The rocks that Castle Gloam stood upon began to crack. Fissures appeared in the walls. The roof began to tremble. Then, very slowly, Castle Gloam slid over the edge of the world and disappeared.

And inside the lost castle the giant and the silent bird of time were caught forever in a timeless scream.

Pieter and the king's daughter watched as the castle sank out of sight. As soon as the castle disappeared over the edge of the world, the world returned to normal again. Once more time flowed onward like a river.

Then Pieter and the princess looked at one another and smiled. And hand in hand they walked back for seven days and seven nights until they reached the palace of the king.

There Pieter and the princess were married amidst great singing and dancing. In due time, Pieter himself became king, and lived a long and full life with his beautiful wife always at his side.

And though Pieter had found another egg veined with red and gold nestled in his cap right after the bird and the giant had disappeared, he was never fool enough to tell. Instead he gave the egg into the keeping of his father, Honest Hans. And the old miller buried it under the mill in a wooden box, where it has remained safe and unbroken to this very day.

The Weaver of Tomorrow

ONCE, ON THE FAR SIDE OF YESTERDAY, there lived a girl who wanted to know the future. She was not satisfied with knowing that the grass would come up each spring and that the sun would go down each night. The true knowledge she desired was each tick of tomorrow, each fall and each failure, each heartache and each pain, that would be the portion of every man. And because of this wish of hers, she was known as Vera, which is to say, *True*.

At first it was easy enough. She lived simply in a simple town, where little happened to change a day but a birth or a death that was always expected. And Vera awaited each event at the appointed bedside and, in this way, was always the first to know.

But as with many wishes of the heart, hers grew from a wish to a desire, from a desire to an obsession. And soon, knowing the simple futures of the simple people in that simple town was not enough for her.

"I wish to know what tomorrow holds for everyone," said

Vera. "For every man and woman in our country. For every man and woman in our world."

"It is not good, this thing you wish," said her father.

But Vera did not listen. Instead she said, "I wish to know which king will fall and what the battle, which queen will die and what the cause. I want to know how many mothers will cry for babies lost and how many wives will weep for husbands slain."

And when she heard this, Vera's mother made the sign against the Evil One, for it was said in their simple town that the future was the Devil's dream.

But Vera only laughed and said loudly, "And for that, I want to know what the Evil One himself is doing with *his* tomorrow."

Since the Evil One himself could not have missed her speech, the people of the town visited the mayor and asked him to send Vera away.

The mayor took Vera and her mother and father, and they sought out the old man who lived in the mountain, who would answer one question a year. And they asked him what to do about Vera.

The old man who lived in the mountain, who ate the seeds that flowers dropped and the berries that God wrought, and who knew all about yesterdays and cared little about tomorrow, said, "She must be apprenticed to the Weaver."

"A weaver!" said the mayor and Vera's father and her mother all at once. They thought surely that the old man who lived in the mountain had at last gone mad.

But the old man shook his head. "Not *a* weaver, but *the* Weaver, the Weaver of Tomorrow. She weaves with a golden thread and finishes each piece with a needle so fine that each minute of the unfolding day is woven into her work. They say that once every hundred years there is need for an apprentice, and it is just that many years since one has been found."

"Where does one find this Weaver?" asked the mayor.

"Ah, that I cannot say," said the old man who lived in the mountain, "for I have answered one question already." And he went back to his cave and rolled a stone across the entrance, a stone small enough to let the animals in but large enough to keep the townspeople out.

"Never mind," said Vera. "I would be apprenticed to this Weaver. And not even the Devil himself can keep me from finding her."

And so saying, she left the simple town with nothing but the clothes upon her back. She wandered until the hills got no higher but the valleys got deeper. She searched from one cold moon until the next. And at last, without warning, she came upon a cave where an old woman in black stood waiting.

"You took the Devil's own time coming," said the old woman.

"It was not his time at all," declared Vera.

"Oh, but it was," said the old woman, as she led the girl into the cave.

And what a wondrous place the cave was. On one wall hung skeins of yarn of rainbow colors. On the other walls were tapestries of delicate design. In the center of the cave, where a single shaft of sunlight fell, was the loom of polished ebony, higher than a man and three times as broad, with a shuttle that flew like a captive blackbird through the golden threads of the warp.

For a year and a day, Vera stayed in the cave apprenticed to the Weaver. She learned which threads wove the future of kings and princes, and which of peasants and slaves. She was first to know in which kingdoms the sun would set and which kingdoms would be gone before the sun rose again. And though she was not yet allowed to weave, she watched the black loom where each minute of the day took shape, and learned how, once it had been woven, no power could change its course. Not an emperor, not a slave, not the Weaver herself. And she was taught to finish the work with a golden thread and a needle so fine that no one could tell where one day ended and the next began. And for a year she was happy.

But finally the day dawned when Vera was to start her second year with the Weaver. It began as usual. Vera rose and set the fire. Then she removed the tapestry of yesterday from the loom and brushed it outside until the golden threads mirrored the morning sun. She hung it on a silver hook that was by the entrance to the cave. Finally she returned to the loom which waited mutely for the golden warp to be strung. And each thread that Vera pulled tight sang like the string of a harp. When she was through, Vera set the pot on the fire and woke the old woman to begin the weaving.

The old woman creaked and muttered as she stretched herself up. But Vera paid her no heed. Instead, she went to the Wall of Skeins and picked at random the colors to be woven. And each thread was a life.

"Slowly, slowly," the old Weaver had cautioned when Vera first learned to choose the threads. "At the end of each thread is the end of a heartbeat; the last of each color is the last of a world." But Vera could not learn to choose slowly, carefully. Instead she plucked and picked like a gay bird in the seed.

"And so it was with me," said the old Weaver with a sigh. "And so it was at first with me."

Now a year had passed, and the old woman kept her counsel to herself as Vera's fingers danced through the threads. Now she went creaking and muttering to the loom and began to weave. And now Vera turned her back to the growing cloth that told the future and took the pot from the fire to make their meal. But as soon as that was done, she would hurry back to watch the growing work, for she never wearied of watching the minutes take shape on the ebony loom.

Only this day, as her back was turned, the old woman uttered a cry. It was like a sudden sharp pain. And the silence after it was like the release from pain altogether.

Vera was so startled she dropped the pot, and it spilled over and sizzled the fire out. She ran to the old woman who sat staring at the growing work. There, in the gold and shimmering tapestry, the Weaver had woven her own coming death.

There was the cave and there the dropped pot; and last the

bed where, with the sun shining full on her face, the old woman would breathe no more.

"It has come," the old woman said to Vera, smoothing her black skirts over her knees. "The loom is yours." She stood up fresher and younger than Vera had ever seen her, and moved with a springy joy to the bed. Then she straightened the covers and lay down, her faced turned toward the entrance of the cave. A shaft of light fell on her feet and began to move, as the sun moved, slowly toward her head.

"No," cried Vera at the smiling woman. "I want the loom. But not this way."

Gently, with folded hands, the old Weaver said, "Dear child, there is no other way."

"Then," said Vera slowly, knowing she lied, but lying nonetheless, "I do not want it."

"The time for choosing is past," said the old Weaver. "You chose and your hands have been chosen. It is woven. It is so."

"And in a hundred years?" asked Vera.

"You will be the Weaver, and some young girl will come, bright and eager, and you will know your time is near."

"No," said Vera.

"It is birth," said the old Weaver.

"No," said Vera.

"It is death," said the old Weaver.

A single golden thread snapped suddenly on the loom.

Then the sun moved onto the Weaver's face and she died.

Vera sat staring at the old woman but did not stir. And though she sat for hour upon hour, and the day grew cold, the sun did not go down. Battles raged on and on, but no one won and no one lost, for nothing more had been woven.

At last, shivering with the cold, though the sun was still high, Vera went to the loom. She saw the old woman buried and herself at work, and so she hastened to the tasks.

And when the old woman lay under an unmarked stone in a forest full of unmarked stones, with only Vera to weep for her, Vera returned to the cave.

Inside, the loom gleamed black, like a giant ebony cage

with golden bars as thin and fine as thread. And as Vera sat down to finish the weaving, her bones felt old and she welcomed the shaft of sun as it crept across her back. She welcomed each trip of the shuttle through the warp as it ticked off the hundred years to come. And at last Vera knew all she wanted to know about the future.

The Boy Who Sang for Death

IN A VILLAGE that lay like a smudge on the cheek of a quiet valley, there lived an old woman and the last of her seven sons. The oldest six had joined the army as they came of age, and her husband was long in his grave. The only one left at home was a lad named Karl.

Even if he had not been her last, his mother would have loved him best, for he had a sweet disposition and a sweeter voice. It was because of that voice, pure and clear, that caroled like spring birds, that she had called him Karel. But his father and brothers, fearing the song name would unman him, had changed it to Karl. So Karl he had remained.

Karl was a sturdy boy, a farmboy in face and hands. But his voice set him apart from the rest. Untutored and untrained, Karl's voice could call home sheep from the pasture, birds from the trees. In the village, it was even said that the sound of Karl's voice made graybeards dance, the lame to walk, and milk spring from a maiden's breast. Yet Karl used his voice for no such magic, but to please his mother and gentle his flock.

One day when Karl was out singing to the sheep and goats to bring them safely in from the field, his voice broke; like a piece of cloth caught on a nail, it tore. Fearing something wrong at home, he hurried the beasts. They scattered before him, and he came to the house to find that his mother had died.

"Between one breath and the next, she was gone," said the priest.

Gently Karl folded her hands on her breast and, although she was beyond the sound of his song, he whispered something in her ear and turned to leave.

"Where are you going?" called out the priest, his words heavy with concern.

"I am going to find Death and bring my mother back," cried Karl, his jagged voice now dulled with grief. He turned at the door and faced the priest who knelt by his mother's bed. "Surely Death will accept an exchange. What is one old tired woman to Death who has known so many?"

"And will you recognize Death, my son, when you meet him?"

"That I do not know," said Karl.

The priest nodded and rose heavily from his knees. "Then listen well, my son. Death is an aging but still handsome prince. His eyes are dark and empty, for he has seen much suffering in the world. If you find such a one, he is Death."

"I will know him," said Karl.

"And what can you give Death in exchange that he has not already had many times over?" asked the priest.

Karl touched his pockets and sighed. "I have nothing here to give," he said. "But I hope that he may listen to my songs. They tell me in the village that there is a gift of magic in my voice. Any gift I have I would surely give to get my mother back. I will sing for Death, and perhaps that great prince will take time to listen."

"Death does not take time," said the old priest, raising his hand to bless the boy, "for time is Death's own greatest possession."

"I can but try," said Karl, tears in his eyes. He knelt a moment for the blessing, stood up, and went out the door. He did not look back.

Karl walked for many days and came at last to a city that lay like a blemish on three hills. He listened quietly but well, as only a singer can, and when he heard weeping, he followed the sound and found a funeral procession bearing the coffin of a child. The procession turned into a graveyard where stones leaned upon stones like cards in a neglected deck.

"Has Death been here already?" asked Karl of a weeping woman.

"Death has been here many times," she answered. "But today she has taken my child."

"*She?*" asked Karl. "But surely Death is a man."

"Death is a woman," she answered him at once. "Her hair is long and thick and dark, like the roots of trees. Her body is huge and brown, but she is barren. The only way she can bear a child is to bear it away."

Karl felt her anger and sorrow then, for they matched his own, so he joined the line of mourners to the grave. And when the child's tiny box had been laid in the ground, he sang it down with the others. But his voice lifted above theirs, a small bird soaring with ease over larger ones. The townsfolk stopped singing in amazement and listened to him.

Karl sang not of death but of his village in the valley, of the seasons that sometime stumble one into another, and of the small pleasures of the hearth. He sang tune after tune the whole of that day, and just at nightfall he stopped. They threw dirt on the baby's coffin and brought Karl to their home.

"Your songs eased my little one's passage," said the woman. "Stay with us this night. We owe you that."

"I wish that I had been here before," said Karl. "I might have saved your baby with a song."

"I fear Death would not be cheated so easily of her chosen child," said the woman. She set the table but did not eat.

Karl left in the morning. And as he walked, he thought about Death, how it was a hollow-eyed prince to the priest but a jealous mother to the woman. If Death could change shapes with such ease, how would he know Death when they finally met? He walked and walked, his mind in a puzzle, until he came at last to a plain that lay like a great open wound between mountains.

The plain was filled with an army of fighting men. There were men with bows and men with swords and men with wooden staves. Some men fought on horseback, and some fought from their knees. Karl could not tell one band of men from another, could not match friend with friend, foe with foe, for their clothes were colored by dirt and by blood and every man looked the same. And the screams and shouts and the crying of horns were a horrible symphony in Karl's ears.

Yet there was one figure Karl *could* distinguish. A woman, quite young, dressed in a long white gown. Her dark braids were caught up in ribbons of white and looped like a crown on her head. She threaded her way through the ranks of men like a shuttle through a loom, and there seemed to be a pattern in her going. She paused now and then to put a hand to the head or the breast of one man and then another. Each man she touched stopped fighting and, with an expression of surprise, left his body and followed the girl, so that soon there was a great wavering line of gray men trailing behind her.

Then Karl knew that he had found Death.

He ran down the mountainside and around the flank of the great plain, for he wanted to come upon Death face to face. He called out as he ran, hoping to slow her progress, "Wait, oh, wait, Lady Death; please wait for me."

Lady Death heard his call above the battle noise, and she looked up from her work. A weariness sat between her eyes, but she did not stop. She continued her way from man to man, a hand to the brow or over the heart. And at her touch, each man left his life to follow the young girl named Death.

When Karl saw that she would not stop at his calling, he stepped into her path. But she walked through him as if through air and went on her way, threading the line of dead gray men behind her.

So Karl began to sing. It was all he knew to do.

He sang not of death but of growing and bearing, for they were things she knew nothing of. He sang of small birds on the apple spray and bees with their honeyed burden. He sang of the first green blades piercing the warmed earth. He sang of winter fields where moles and mice sleep quietly under the snow. Each tune swelled into the next.

And Lady Death stopped to listen.

As she stopped, the ribbon of soldiers that was woven behind her stopped, too, and from their dead eyes tears fell with each memory. The battlefield was still, frozen by the songs. And the only sound and the only movement and the only breath was Karl's voice.

When he had finished at last, a tiny brown bird flew out of a dead tree, took up the last melody, and went on.

"I have made you stop, Lady Death," cried Karl. "And you have listened to my tunes. Will you now pay for that pleasure?"

Lady Death smiled, a slow, weary smile, and Karl wondered that someone so young should have to carry such a burden. And his pity hovered between them in the quiet air.

"I will pay, Karel," she said.

He did not wonder that she knew his true name, for Lady Death would, in the end, know every human's name.

"Then I ask for my mother in exchange," said Karl.

Lady Death looked at him softly then. She took up his pity and gave it back. "That I cannot do. Who follows me once, follows forever. But is it not payment enough to know that you have stayed my hand for this hour? No man has ever done that before."

"But you promised to pay," said Karl. His voice held both anger and disappointment, a man and a child's voice in one.

Ending 1

"And what I promise," she said, looking at him from under darkened lids, "I do."

Lady Death put her hand in front of her, as if reaching into a cupboard, and a gray form that was strangely transparent took shape under her fingers. It became a harp, with smoke-colored strings the color of Lady Death's eyes.

"A useless gift," said Karl. "I cannot play."

But Lady Death reached over and set the harp in his hand, careful not to touch him with her own.

And as the harp molded itself under his fingers, Karl felt music surge through his bones. He put his thumb and forefinger on the strings and began to play.

At the first note, the battle began anew. Men fought, men bled, men suffered, men fell. But Karl passed through the armies untouched, playing a sweet tune that rose upward, in bursts, as the lark and its song spring toward the sun. He walked through the armies, through the battle, through the plain, playing his harp, and he never looked back again.

Ending 2

"And what I promise," Death said, looking at him from under darkened lids, "I do."

She turned and pointed to the field, and Karl's eyes followed her fingers.

"There in that field are six men whose heads and hearts I will not touch this day. Look carefully, Karel."

He looked. "They are my brothers," he said.

"Them, I will spare." And Lady Death turned and stared into Karl's face with her smoky eyes. "But I would have you sing for me again each night in the small hours when I rest, for I have never had such comfort before. Will you come?" She held out her hand.

Karl hesitated a moment, remembering his farm, remembering the fields, the valleys, the warm spring rains. Then he looked again at Lady Death, whose smile seemed a little less weary. He nodded and reached for her hand, and it was small and soft and cool in his. He raised her hand once to his lips, then set it, palm open, over his heart. He never felt the cold.

Then, hand in hand, Karl and Lady Death walked through the battlefield. Their passing made not even the slightest breeze on the cheeks of the wounded, nor an extra breath for the dying. Only the dead who traveled behind saw them pass under the shadows of the farthest hills. But long after they had gone, the little bird sang Karl's last song over and over and over again into the darkening air.

The Lady and the Merman

ONCE IN A HOUSE overlooking the cold northern sea a baby was born. She was so plain, her father, a sea captain, remarked on it.

"She shall be a burden," he said. "She shall be on our hands forever." Then, without another glance at the child, he sailed off on his great ship.

His wife, who had longed to please him, was so hurt by his complaint that she soon died of it. Between one voyage and the next, she was gone.

When the captain came home and found this out, he was so enraged, he never spoke of his wife again. In this way he convinced himself that her loss was nothing.

But the girl lived and grew, as if to spite her father. She looked little like her dead mother but instead had the captain's face, set 'round with mouse-brown curls. Yet as plain as her face was, her heart was not. She loved her father, but was not loved in return.

And still the captain remarked on her looks. He said at

every meeting, "God must have wanted me cursed to give me such a child. No one will have her. She shall never be wed. She shall be with me forever." So he called her Borne, for she was his burden.

Borne grew into a lady, and only once gave a sign of this hurt.

"Father," she said one day when he was newly returned from the sea, "what can I do to heal this wound between us?"

He looked away from her, for he could not bear to see his own face mocked in hers, and spoke to the cold stone floor. "There is nothing between us, Daughter," he said. "But if there were, I would say, *Salt for such wounds.*"

"Salt?" Borne asked, surprised, for she knew the sting of it.

"A sailor's balm," he said. "The salt of tears or the salt of sweat or the final salt of the sea." Then he turned from her and was gone next day to the farthest port he knew of, and in this way he cleansed his heart.

After this, Borne never spoke again of the hurt. Instead, she carried it silently like a dagger inside. For the salt of tears did not salve her, so she turned instead to work. She baked bread in her ovens for the poor, she nursed the sick, she held the hands of the sea widows. But always, late in the evening, she walked on the shore looking and longing for a sight of her father's sail. Only, less and less often did he return from the sea.

One evening, tired from the work of the day, Borne felt faint as she walked on the strand. Finding a rock half in and half out of the water, she climbed upon it to rest. She spread her skirts about her, and in the dusk they lay like great gray waves.

How long she sat there, still as the rock, she did not know. But a strange, pale moon came up. And as it rose, so too rose the little creatures of the deep. They leaped free for a moment of the pull of the tide. And last of all, up from the depths, came the merman.

He rose out of the crest of the wave, sea-foam crowning his green-black hair. His hands were raised high above him, and the webbings of his fingers were as colorless as air. In the moonlight he seemed to stand upon his tail. Then, with a flick of it, he was gone, gone back to the deeps. He thought no one had remarked his dive.

But Borne had. So silent and still, she saw it all, his beauty and his power. She saw him and loved him, though she loved the fish half of him more. It was all she could dare.

She could not tell what she felt to a soul, for she had no one who cared about her feelings. Instead she forsook her work and walked by the sea both morning and night. Yet, strange to say, she never once looked for her father's sail.

That is why her father returned one day without her knowing it. He watched her through slotted eyes as she paced the shore, for he would not look straight upon her. At last he went to her and said, "Be done with it. Whatever ails you, give it over." For even he could see *this* wound.

Borne looked up at him, her eyes shimmering with small seas. Grateful even for this attention, she answered, "Yes, Father, you are right. I must be done with it."

The captain turned and left her then, for his food was growing cold. But Borne went directly to the place where the waves were creeping onto the shore. She called out in a low voice, "Come up. Come up and be my love."

There was no answer except the shrieking laughter of the birds as they dove into the sea.

So she took a stick and wrote the same words upon the sand for the merman to see should he ever return. Only, as she watched, the creeping tide erased her words one by one by one. Soon there was nothing left of her cry on that shining strand.

So Borne sat herself down on the rock to weep. And each tear was an ocean.

But the words were not lost. Each syllable washed from the beach was carried below, down, down, down to the deeps of the cool, inviting sea. And there, below on his coral bed, the merman saw her words and came.

He was all day swimming up to her. He was half the night

seeking that particular strand. But when he came, cresting the currents, he surfaced with a mighty splash below Borne's rock.

The moon shone down on the two—she a grave shadow perched upon a stone and he all motion and light.

Borne reached down with her white hands, and he caught them in his. It was the only touch she could remember. She smiled to see the webs stretched taut between his fingers. He laughed to see hers webless, thin, and small. One great pull between them and he was up by her side. Even in the dark, she could see his eyes on her under the phosphorescence of his hair.

He sat all night by her. And Borne loved the man of him as well as the fish, then, for in the silent night it was all one.

Then, before the sun could rise, she dropped her hands on his chest. "Can you love me?" she dared to ask at last.

But the merman had no tongue to tell her above the waves. He could only speak below the water with his hands, a soft murmuration. So, wordlessly, he stared into her eyes and pointed to the sea.

Then, with the sun just rising beyond the rim of the world, he turned, dove arrow-slim into a wave, and was gone.

Gathering her skirts, now heavy with ocean spray and tears, Borne stood up. She cast but one glance at the shore and her father's house beyond. Then she dove after the merman into the sea.

The sea put bubble jewels in her hair and spread her skirts about her like a scallop shell. Tiny colored fish swam in between her fingers. The water cast her face in silver, and all the sea was reflected in her eyes.

She was beautiful for the first time. And for the last.

Wild Goose and Gander

From *The Magic Three of Solatia*

Before

WHEN A MAN comes to be twenty years old, it is time to leave his mother's house. At least, that is what is said in Solatia, a land of much greenness and harvest gold.

So it happened that Lann, a minstrel untried in his songs except among his neighbors and friends, decided to do more than leave his mother's house. He decided to leave her land as well.

"And if I find fortune or fame, it is fine," he said. "But more, I should like to travel to all the lands both near and far, and even to the back of beyond, to seek what I know not. To sing I know not what. And to call many 'friend' along the way."

So his mother, Sianna, blessed him and gave him an amulet to wear on his breast. But when he was but a little way off, he placed the stone in his pack, for sometimes a man wants to try his own magic without his mother's aid. And Lann had faith in the power of his songs, for there is a kind of magic in music as well.

Besides, if truth be known, Lann had a chain around his neck on which there hung a button. It held magic so powerful that it had never been used. For magic has consequences—this Lann knew. Yet he knew, too, that if sometime a terrible need arose, those consequences, no matter how dear, would have to be borne.

And so Lann traveled, lute on his back, out into the wide, wide world.

1. Wild Goose and Gander

In a forest at the back of the world lived a brother and sister. By day they were wild geese and soared in the sky high above the tops of the tallest trees. But at night they flew back to their forest hut and in human form dined on red berries, green salad, and wine.

They had no one but each other, and it had been so from the first. They had been left in the forest by their frightened nursemaid on the day after they were born. For in the evening they had been babies wrapped in swaddling, but in the daylight they turned into soft-feathered goslings in the folds.

The wizard who had changed them was named Bleakard. He lived in a gray-green stone castle perched high on a mountain crag that rose in the middle of a lake. Each day he summoned the brother and sister to his castle with a magic flute. They were forced to fly away from their forest hut and circle the mountaintop. As day closed, he would let them go, and they winged home with fear-filled speed.

So the brother and sister lived in the forest at the back of beyond with one another as company and no one else in the whole wide world to call a friend.

Late one afternoon, into the forest came the young minstrel Lann. He had been gone from his home a year and a day, and had spent each night under a different roof.

When he saw the forest hut covered with wild goose grasses, he smiled. He was tired, and it seemed a likely place to stop. So he laid his flute against the wall and tapped lightly on the door. When no one answered, he pushed the door open and went in.

Inside he saw two beds neatly made and a table neatly set for two. He saw two wardrobes filled with clothes and two stone basins brimming full. But no one was there to greet him.

"I shall wait for the owners to return," thought Lann, and settled himself outside on the ground by the door. He was so weary from traveling that he soon was fast asleep.

Scarcely had he dozed off than a great whirring filled the air, the sounds of wings beating. Two shadows fell upon the minstrel's sleeping form. A wild goose and gander sailed down from the skies and landed at his feet.

At once they changed to human form. The brother, a tall lad, was named Bred, with eyes so black they seemed to have no bottom. The sister was named Bridda. Her hair was soft as feathers, her face as gentle as the wind.

Bridda clung to her brother when she saw the sleeping stranger. But Bred was more courageous and put out his hand.

"Awake, friend, and welcome," he said, as the minstrel opened his eyes.

"I did not hear you come," said Lann, jumping up. "I beg your pardon . . ."

"It is no matter," Bred replied, and led the way into the house.

Because they had only two dishes and two cups, Bred had to wait until the minstrel finished his meal. And because the minstrel tuned his lute and sang one song after another to the smiling Bridda, Bred finished his dinner alone.

When the dishes were washed and carefully set aside for the morning, Bred joined his sister and the minstrel outside under the trees, and they talked and sang until almost dawn.

Just before the sun rose, the minstrel fell into a dreamless sleep. And when the sun had fully lit the path to the hut, Bred and Bridda returned to the air. They circled once, and the goose cast a sad backward glance at the sleeping man before she joined the gander in their wingtip-to-wingtip journey across the sky.

2 . The Enchantment

That evening the goose and gander returned. As before, they touched the earth in front of the sleeping man. He was sunk again in a magical sleep so that he would not see them change.

When he awoke at last, Lann said to Bred, "This is most strange. I was asleep when you left and asleep when you returned. Yet I was not tired. There is some enchantment here that I do not understand."

"It is no matter," said Bred, and he led Lann into the house.

That evening the minstrel and Bridda ate in silence, watching each other with love-filled eyes. For Bridda had never seen another human, except her brother and the wizard. And Lann, though he had seen many maidens in his year of traveling, had never met one who so combined silence and singing, wisdom and beauty, shyness and courage.

And Bred was content to eat alone after them.

Then the three friends talked until dawn.

For three nights it was thus. But on the fourth night, before they settled down to talk, the minstrel took the stone charm from his saddlebag. He remembered what his mother had said when she had given it to him: "If you are ever in a land of strangers and strangeness, place this amulet upon your breast."

The minstrel placed the charm over his heart. And after breakfast, though he was not tired at all, he pretended to fall asleep.

Just as the sun came up, Bred and Bridda began to change. First their hair turned to feathers, then feathers soft and white grew on their arms. At last their bodies were covered with down. And as they beat their great wings, they were transformed entirely into giant birds that rose up into the air and set off past the sun.

That evening when the geese returned to their forest home, they found the minstrel awake and waiting.

"Am I dreaming still, or is this enchantment?" Lann asked them when they touched the ground and turned back into humans.

"It is enchantment," said Bred softly.

Bridda wept silently. She feared that the minstrel could not love a girl who was a bird by day.

"I know about spells as I know about singing, for my mother is Sianna of the Song. Perhaps you have heard of her. There must be a way I can help you," said the minstrel.

"There is no help for us," replied Bred. "We were transformed as babies by a wicked wizard. We were left here in the forest by our nursemaid and must return to the wizard's castle each day."

Bridda added, "We do not know our mother or our father. We only know what Bleakard, the wizard, has told us: that we fed as goslings and grew as children until we are as you see us now. And each day we must go and fly around the bleak rock castle to his tune."

Lann looked thoughtful. "And the spell?"

Bred said, "We do not know the spell. And if we do not know the spell, how can we break it? We only know what we must do each day and how we must be each night."

Lann laughed. "If you can not break the spell, then you must break the spell-maker. So my mother, Sianna, who is the wisest person I know, taught me. And so I believe. I must go to the wizard who made this magic and wrest his secrets from him."

"Easier said than done," said Bridda. "The way leads through an enchanted forest and across a perilous lake."

"Better tried than not," replied Lann.

So in the morning, after a short nap, Lann started off. Inside his shirt he placed a feather that Bridda had plucked from her breast. It was still warm to the touch. He followed the only path through the wood, while the wild goose and gander circled above as if to point the way.

3 . Jared

It had been day by the hut, but was night in the woods. The way through the forest was long and cold and dark. The trees were hung with rags of fog.

As Lann walked along, his lute slung over his shoulder, the cold seemed like daggers of ice piercing his heart. And only where Bridda's feather touched him did he feel warm.

"Fear feeds on fear," thought he. So he unslung his lute, thinking to play a strengthening song. As each string was plucked and stretched, a small bit of light sparked the darkness.

"Aha," thought Lann, "so that is the way of it." And then, as if to reassure himself, but also to let any forest ears hear that he was not afraid, he repeated it out loud. "So that is the way of it."

And he began a cheery-sounding song which he made up as he walked along the midnight path. For minstrels are trained to sing a new song as easily as an old one.

> The way is dark, the path is long,
> And sometimes right begins as wrong.
> But I've found as I go along
> The world is warmed by just a song.

And as I'm getting warmed a bit,
And gathering up my scattered wit,
I see a pattern, I'll admit,
By just a song the world is lit.

For song is warmth and song is light,
And song can pierce the darkest night.
My lute's my weapon in this fight,
And what is wrong can be set right.

The way is dark, the path is long,
And sometimes right begins as wrong.
But I've found as I go along
The world is warmed by just a song.

And he ended on a single high, clear note.

As the song faded away like fireflies in a dark wood, winking and blinking and sparking and drifting at last into nothing, the forest was again dark. But now the dark seemed heavier and colder than before. Even the feather against his breast was cool.

Lann looked about him. "If this is the way of it," he thought, "I do not think I like the way." But he continued on, humming his tune and strumming occasionally on the lute to keep his fingers warm.

As he walked farther, Lann thought he heard another rhythm, a steady *one-two, one-two*. "Left foot, right foot," he said to himself. And soon he found his fingers playing that same steady beat on the strings. His own feet followed after, and he marched toward the sound.

As he marched on, Lann saw a small light ahead. Each step brought him nearer the light, and each step seemed to make the light bigger. Finally Lann could make out a large clearing, and the rhythmic pounding of the *one-two, one-two* was now so loud that it made his ears ring.

Through the ringing in his ears, Lann thought he could hear a difference between the *one* and the *two*. The *one* was loud and crackling, like a fire or the breaking of trees and branches. The *two* was a softer, almost melodic swish, of wind through flowers.

When at last he came to the clearing—which was only a lighter shade of the forest dark, for the sky overhead was heavy and gray with forbidding clouds—Lann saw what was making the noise. It was a giant of a man in leather pants and a leather jerkin, with leather bands around his wrists. He was stomping left foot, right foot, left foot, right foot, around and around the forest clearing.

As the gigantic left foot came down, lightning and fire flashed from the toes. Smoke curled up where the giant stepped. The ground beneath his left foot turned sere and brown, and nothing living grew there again. But where his right foot descended, cooling rains fell from the arch. Flowers dropped from his foot onto the path and took root there.

"Ho there," called Lann as the giant's right foot came down once again.

The gigantic man stopped stomping and turned toward the sound. His voice, so rough and grating on the ear, made furrows in the air. "Who speaks?"

Lann played a chord on his lute. "It is I, Lann. A wandering minstrel."

The giant's rough face broke into a smile. "And I am Jared," he said. "It has been many years since I have had company."

"It is a far way to find your clearing, friend," said Lann pleasantly. "Perhaps that is why you have so few visitors. I only happened here myself. Why don't you come and meet the world?"

Jared frowned. He pointed despairingly at his feet. "Wherever the one steps, I destroy. Wherever the other, I create. I can go nowhere without this double curse—flame and flowers, flowers and flame."

"Cursed," said Lann. It was a statement, but the giant heard a question and so replied.

"By Bleakard, the wizard. Once I was a king. And a rather foolish, cowardly king, I am afraid. But I loved to sing and dance and be entertained. My people rather enjoyed it, too. And they called me Jared the Good and said that flowers followed where I trod. But I trod once on a wizard's toes, I think.

I thought him but a visiting magician and boasted of my own worth. That blackguard Bleakard laughed and said, 'So you create flower gardens in your path, do you?' and brought his magic flute down upon my feet. I suppose I fainted. For when I came to, I was here in the forest as you see me now. And here I have stayed, for I do not think I could face either my people or that wizard again."

"And what will end the spell?" asked Lann.

"I do not know," replied Jared. "I have told you all I know—of the spell and of my past. The rest seems to be lost to me, I know not why."

"If you cannot break the spell," said Lann, remembering when he had said the same before, "you must break the spell-maker."

"But I dare not," said Jared. "The shame of visiting my people. The fear of visiting Bleakard . . ."

Lann put his hand out and touched the giant's hand. "I am off to visit Bleakard myself. Why not come along with me? A friend is always a welcome companion in the dark. And your people would not think less of you as you are now."

"I dare not," whispered the giant. Yet his whisper was loud enough to bend the trees with its noise. "For I have just now recalled a part of the curse. Bleakard will kill me if I come to the castle."

"Is that any worse than living the way you are now?" asked Lann softly. "Going around in circles of fire and flowers?"

"I daren't," said the giant. "Here at least I am still a king. And I do not want to die." He looked as if he might weep.

"But I dare," said Lann. "And I am not afraid to die." He added, "I think," under his breath, remembering Bridda.

The minstrel slung his lute over his back and crossed the clearing, over alternate stubbles of burned grass and patches of red and gold flowers. He started down the only path that led away from the clearing. Bridda's feather was again warm against his skin.

Lann had gone but four steps into the darkened forest

when he heard a cry from behind. It sounded like a sigh, like a gulp, like a plea, like a song. It was the giant.

"Wait—oh, wait, and I'll come too."

4 . Coredderoc

Lann turned and waited. In a minute, trailing fire and flowers, Jared had run to his side.

Carefully Lann stepped around the giant to his right side. Then side by side, Lann taking two steps to the giant's one, they made their way deeper into the forest. But whereas before the forest had been dark and lit only by the notes that sang from Lann's lute, now it was blazing-bright from the flames from the giant's foot.

"You see," said Lann, "there is good in every bad. Sometimes right begins as wrong."

Jared shook his head as if trying to clear it. "I do not find your meaning," he said.

"I mean that if you were not *cursed,* we could not see. At least not so clearly. Your foot shall light our way to Bleakard's castle."

"Why didn't I think of that?" exclaimed Jared.

"That is what a friend is for," replied Lann. "To turn a liability into an ability."

"It sounds quite fine when you say it," said Jared. "But it is one of those matters to which I will have to give a lot of thought."

And so he did.

For a while neither of the new friends spoke, but walked on in silent companionship, accented only by the hissing of the flames and the twanging of the lute strings being tuned.

When at last the lute was tuned again—for lute strings

need much attention, just as people do—Lann began a song especially for his new friend.

> A friend is the other side of a coin,
> A friend is an old song resung.
> A friend is the other side of your moon,
> A friend is an old lute restrung.
>
> And if I never knew it before,
> I guess I know it today.
> And if I haven't said it before,
> Then this is the right time to say:
>
> A friend is just you turned inside out,
> A friend is yourself turned around.
> And nothing's as good in a darkling wood
> As a friend who's newly found.

Jared laughed then for the first time, and clapped Lann so hard on the back in his enthusiasm that Lann pitched forward into the dark and nearly smashed his lute upon a tree.

"Hold, friend Jared," the minstrel called out. "I appreciate your gesture but not your gusto. Take care. The lute and I can be equally unstrung."

At that Jared laughed again and promised to be gentler. And the two walked on singing Lann's new-made song together. For the giant, as he had claimed, enjoyed a song and his voice was pleasing, if a bit too loud.

They had gone but a mile or maybe three when they heard the sound of fierce quarreling ahead. It was as if two men were screaming at one another at the top of their voices. Yet both voices were so similarly pitched that it was hard to distinguish one from the other.

"Hold, friend," said Lann. "I will sneak on ahead. For with your hissing and sparking, we will never creep up on these battlers unawares."

"Nay, you hold, friend," replied Jared. "You are but a stripling and I am a giant of a man. What we lose in surprise we will gain in awe. For when these two fighters see me and my fiery foot, they will set to such a shaking and quaking that their bones will play a knocking to accompany your strings."

But much to the giant's relief, Lann would not hear of it. And so, after a few words more, the two decided to go on together, which is the way of friends.

Around a final bend in the road they could distinguish another clearing, smaller than the last. And when they had come to the road's ending and the grass's beginning, they saw the strangest sight either had ever seen.

Instead of two men quarreling in the meadow, there was but a single man, so small he could be nothing but a dwarf. Stranger yet, the dwarf had not one but two heads. And it was these two heads that were quarreling, the one with the other. They shouted, "I am," and, "You are not, I am," back and forth at one another, snarling and gnashing teeth, sticking out tongues and spitting. It was a thoroughly disgusting exhibition.

"Ho there," called Lann and Jared together into one of the few silences.

The two heads turned toward the new voices at the same time. "Who speaks?" they said in unison.

"It is I, Lann, a wandering minstrel," said the lad, strumming a chord on his lute, which was sadly out of tune again.

"And I, Jared, who once was a mighty king," said the giant, stomping his left foot down with such violence that the flames shot high into the air. Lann looked over at him, and Jared added, "Well, maybe not *so* mighty."

"And I am Coredderoc," said the head on the right.

"He is not, I am Coredderoc," said the head on the left.

"He is lying," said the first head. "I always tell the truth."

The second head spat at the first and missed. "He is the one who always lies, I am telling the truth."

Lann put his head to one side and thought a minute. "It puts me in mind of an old paradox," he said. "My mother taught it to me."

"No," said the first head. "You have it wrong. It is only a paradox if I say 'I always lie.'"

"And you do," added the second.

"I do not," said the first.

"Well, it matters not," said Lann pleasantly. "You both look equally like Coredderoc to me."

"It matters indeed," said the two heads together. "I am cursed. By the wicked wizard Bleakard, blast his black soul." Both heads turned aside and spat on the ground at the wizard's name. It seemed the only thing they could agree upon.

"Cursed?" asked Jared loudly.

"Yes. Once I was a royal minister to a truly great king who had recently lost his wife in childbirth. Bleakard was but a visiting magician, or so I thought at first. But when first the queen died, bless her beautiful soul, and then the royal children disappeared, I feared something evil in the air. I first curried Bleakard's favor." All this the first head said. And when it took a breath to continue, the second head broke in.

"And when I had discovered who he really was, I denounced him to the king. But the king was so besotted with the mage, he dismissed me as two-faced. And Bleakard came to my chamber that very night," the second head said.

"And," the first inserted, finishing the story in a rush, "he said, 'Two-faced you are, then two-faced be.' He brought his magic flute down upon my head. I must have fainted, for when I awoke I was as you see me now. And that is all I remember."

Both heads turned and glared at one another for a moment, and then began to weep.

Jared, who had been shaking his head slowly from side to side during the dwarf's recital, suddenly spoke. "There is something familiar about your tale. And something familiar about your faces. But upon my very life, my head is a cloud and has been so since Bleakard enchanted me. I can think of nothing but my own sad fate. For look, friend, I too am cursed by that mage. So I have joined my young friend here to break the wizard as he has broken me."

"But do you dare to go to his castle?" asked the dwarf, the two heads again united in the question. "He would kill you, as he threatened me that night, with worse than death if I return."

"Could aught be worse than the way you are now?" asked Lann softly.

"Yes," said the one head.

"No," said the other.

"No," agreed the first.

"Yes," agreed the second.

And in the end, the two-headed dwarf joined the giant and the minstrel. As they left the meadow and entered the wood again, a wild goose and gander flew overhead in a direction opposite to that in which the friends were heading.

"Night is coming on," said Lann, as he remarked the birds' flight.

"How can you tell, with the sky so continually dark and the wood as black as a hole?" asked Coredderoc, both mouths working as one.

"Because the geese have flown home for their supper," said Lann. And then he told them of Bred and Bridda and Sianna of the Song. Both Coredderoc and Jared marveled at the tale and said it recalled something to them. But what it recalled, none of them was sure.

So arm in arm in arm, the three marched down the forest path. And it was only when Lann wanted to tune his lute again that the three friends dropped hands.

5. The Edge of the Cliff

Since it was indeed dark in the woods, whether day or night, the three friends decided to push on. They sang with great gusto. It was, Lann remarked, the first time he had ever heard a trio that could sing in four parts.

They sang many of the old songs: "Hey to the Inn" and "A

Lover and His Lady Fair" and even "Lord Muskrat and Black
Elinor."

They sang some new songs, too. One was their special
favorite, which Lann had made up for the occasion.

> There once were three who would be four,
> With a hey, hi, ho, and ho.
> There once were three who would be four,
> The tangled woods went to explore.
> With a hey and away went they.
>
> There once were four who would be three,
> With a hey, hi, ho, and ho.
> There once were four who would be three,
> A pestilence to wizardry,
> With a hey and away went they.
>
> There once were three who well-a-day,
> With a hey, hi, ho, and ho.
> There once were three who well-a-day
> A wicked wizard went to slay,
> With a hey and away went they.

But as they got closer and closer to the end of the woods,
the three friends with the four voices sang the last verse more
and more quietly. Till at last they left off singing it altogether.
"A pestilence to wizardry" was suddenly changed to "as peni-
tents to wizardry." None of the three friends would lay claim
to authorship of the new line. They didn't like it. It made no
sense. But they found themselves singing it with quiet fervor as
they drew closer to the wood's edge and the wizard.

Though the woods were beginning to thin out, it was difficult to notice it at first, for night had indeed fallen. Yet no stars
lit their path. What moon there was, a pale, thin splinter, was
shrouded with a gray blanket of cloud. And even Jared's flames
were dulled. It was no wonder that they were practically at the
edge of a cliff before they noticed they were out of the woods.

"The forest is behind us," said Jared with relief.

"The worst is ahead of us," said one of Coredderoc's
heads. The other nodded in bitter agreement.

"Come," said Lann, "let us look around for a moment and then take turns standing watch. For sleep will be the great encourager. Only tired men are afraid."

"Then I must be perennially tired," muttered Jared, but softly so that only he himself heard it.

The dark was so deep that they could see nothing. The gray blanket never moved off the moon. The three friends huddled together for warmth. But warmth there was none.

Suddenly Lann remembered the feather inside his shirt. He took it out to see if there was some way he could share it with his friends. It felt unaccountably heavy, so he shook it. A down comforter sprang from the feather, soft and warm.

"Where does that come from?" asked Jared.

"From love," said Lann. Then he added, "Here, friends, and welcome. I will stand the first watch."

But first became last, for neither the giant nor the dwarf woke up until morning. Lann too fell asleep, his hand holding fast to his amulet.

When a wild goose and gander flew across the sky, they circled once around the sleeping friends, honking so loudly the three awoke at once. With great apologies to one another and waves for the departing birds, the three friends rose to greet the sun.

It was like no sun they had ever seen before. Instead of shedding a bright and cheery light, the sun looked thin and worn out, like an old penny. It hung forlornly over the edge of the cliff.

When Lann looked over the cliff's edge he shivered. There was no way down.

Yet there, in the middle of a lake that began at the cliff's bottom, was a huge crag of scaly gray-green rocks, and on the top, hunched like a vulture on dead meat, was a castle.

"Bleakard's castle," said Lann.

"How do you know?" asked his friends, though they knew in their hearts he was right.

Lann pointed.

Around the top of the castle, circling and circling and

crying piteously into the wind, were the wild goose and gander. Their cries carried clearly in the fetid air.

6. The Singing

"We must get down there and cross to the castle," cried Lann, his eyes still on the circling birds.

Just as he spoke, a dreadful sound rent the air. It was a high, sinuous piping that repeated and repeated the same seven notes. It insinuated itself into the air, and the repetitions seemed to engrave the evil melody on their minds.

"My head is cracking from that sound," said Jared.

"Your head!" cried Coredderoc. "Pity me. I have two."

"It must be Bleakard's tune. That infernal piping," shouted Lann above the noise. "How can one think above it?"

"Think we must," shouted one of Coredderoc's heads.

"Without thought, man is an animal," stated the other, and was immediately shushed by his friends.

"There is only one way to battle a spell of music," said Lann. "Or at least that is what my mother taught me."

"Well, hurry, whatever the way," said the giant with a shout. "My ears will turn to stone if I listen a moment more. All I can think of is that one hideous tune."

"Only music can defeat music," Lann shouted back. "And love, hate," he added in an undertone as if to remind himself.

He took his lute from the ground where it had lain all night. Without even stopping to tune, for tuning with that constant piping was not possible, he began a song.

With their ears covered, the others could barely hear him. But if they could have listened with care, they would have heard the same seven notes of Bleakard's piping. But oh, the change! Lann's song took the seven notes and turned them inside out. He gentled them, calmed them, made them sing of love, not hate.

> My love is like a silver bird
> That flies to me when night is near.
> My love is like a silver bird,
> And oh, I wish my love were here.
>
> My love is like a silver boat
> That crests the currents of the air.
> And should I sink or should I float,
> It's oh, I wish my love were here.
>
> My love is like the fount of life
> That sprays into the summer air.
> My love is of my very life,
> And oh, I know my love is here.

At first Lann's song was as gentle as lapping waves. But like the waves, his song was also persistent. And as the song continued, Lann's voice became stronger. The lute, which had sounded flat and brittle because it was untuned and playing against the strident piping, became richer and rounder and stronger, too. Till at last Lann's song filled the cliffside entirely, drowning out the grating flute. And when the three friends with the four voices finished singing the last chorus together, there was no pipe to be heard at all.

The moment the piping ended, the wild goose and gander stopped circling the castle. They hesitated for a moment in flight, and stood in the air like two figures in a tapestry. Then, banking sharply to the right, they flew toward the cliff, their powerful wings beating in unison.

"We have won," shouted Jared, leaping into the air like a mighty fish out of the water. Where he leaped up, flowers sprang too. But when he came down on his left foot, flames shot out.

"We have just begun," said Lann. "For when one battles wizards, all things come in threes."

"Three?" asked the giant fearfully.

"Yes," replied Lann. "As my mother taught me—first the

singing, then the seeming, and last the slaying. If there is any need for a last."

"What does that all mean?" asked Jared.

"I am not entirely sure," admitted the minstrel.

Jared shook his head and tried again. "What I mean is, are we the ones who do the slaying? Or are we the ones who are to be slain?"

"I don't know," replied Lann. "All I know is that my mother is always right."

"A pox on mothers who are always right," said the giant, and he turned away. "I think I will go back to my forest home."

"Stay, friend," said Lann. "Perhaps this time she is not right."

"I fear she *is* right again," said Coredderoc with one head. "I seem to recall such an unholy trinity."

"I *know* she is right," said the other head. "Look!"

The friends looked where he was pointing, at the crags beneath the castle. The very rocks seemed to unwind themselves, and a giant gray-green serpent uncoiled and stretched, turning its ugly head in their direction.

As it uncurled, it moved its shoulders. Two giant wings began to unfurl.

"If that is a *seeming*," said the giant, "I do not like what it *seems* to be."

"What if it flies up to us here?" asked Coredderoc fearfully. "We have no weapons."

"Except my lute," said Lann.

"I fear that is not enough, friend," said Jared. "If that great scaly worm decides to fly here and have us for dinner, I fear it is not nearly enough. And as your revered mother has said, after the singing and the seeming comes the slaying. I fear, friends, we are all dead men."

Almost as if it heard the giant's voice, the great lizard pumped its mighty wings. The vast winds it created stirred the waters of the lake. And with an awful scream, which sounded like the seven notes of Bleakard's song, the dragon flung itself into the air and plunged after the wild goose and gander that were fleeing toward the cliff.

7. The Seeming

As the great dragon came closer, the goose and gander, who had been flying wing to wing, suddenly parted. They circled separately to each side of the gray-green monster. Then each by each, they struck at the dragon's sides. The blows they gave it were but light little flecks. But like the kingbirds which can drive off the larger crows and hawks with many petty pecks, the goose and gander annoyed the monstrous worm. It stopped its headlong flight toward the cliff to try to strike its tiny tormentors.

The goose and gander flew out of range over and over again. When one was in danger, the other would swoop down upon the dragon. And in that way, the silver birds delayed the dragon's descent upon the three friends on the cliff.

"Quick," said Coredderoc, "I have a plan. I was a king's minister and I remember something of war."

"Tell us what to do," replied Lann, "and it will be done."

"First strip your lute of its strings," said the dwarf's first head.

"But it will never sing again," protested the minstrel.

"If you do not, *you* will never sing again," said the first head.

"Lutes can be replaced," said the other head. "But men cannot be."

"We are going to make ourselves some mighty bows," the first explained.

Jared slapped his thigh. "Well said, friend. King I may have been, but now I take your orders. Command me."

"Your part is next, friend giant," said the first head. "Gather all the sticks and twigs you can find, and three large green boughs. Go to the right. I shall go to the left."

Within moments they had a pile of wood. The giant was able to gather huge mounds of twigs and branches with his large hands. The three boughs they used as bows and strung them quickly with the lute strings.

"And now, friend, some fire. But just in the center of the pile."

With a wild bellow, Jared leaped into the pile of sticks. He hopped up and down on his left foot, and the pile burst into flames. The minute the fire was well begun, Jared leaped out again.

Then the three friends reached into the pile of sticks and, grasping the faggots by their cold ends, placed the flaming arrows into their makeshift bows.

"To me!" shouted both of Coredderoc's heads together as he sighted with his first head along the arrow shaft.

Jared and Lann took up the cry.

"To me!"

"To me!"

At their voices, both the goose and gander spun away from the dragon and fled to the cliff.

The dragon came after them straightaway.

The friends let go of their arrows at once. And though the bows were but poorly made and the arrows but poorly aimed, the dragon was such a large target they hit it with all three flames. Immediately the arrows struck, the three friends took up fresh ones.

The goose and gander dived down upon the flaming pile, and each grasped a burning branch in its beak.

The gander raced toward the dragon's tail and scored the flame along its tender underside. But the goose, carrying a flame as large as her own body, flew straight toward the dragon's eyes.

When Lann saw where she was flying he dropped his bow. "Bridda, come back! Oh, come back!" he screamed.

But the silver bird never turned. At the last moment, when the dragon opened its mouth and it seemed certain it would swallow bird and brand and all, she dropped the flame into its mighty maw. At the same instant, she swept her wings to her side and plummeted straight down, down, down toward the lake.

Like a giant Roman candle, the dragon burst into bits of gray smoke and green flames, and each part fell loudly into the lake with a hiss. A great cloud of steam rose to the clifftop, and for long moments nothing could be seen.

When at last it was clear, the three friends peered over the cliff's edge. They could see waves lapping at the bottom of the cliff over hundreds of broken gray-green rocks. And far out in the middle of the lake, a silver goose swam in ever-widening circles. Her feathers were singed, and the air was filled with the smell of burned flesh. But of the dragon, there was no trace at all.

8 . Over the Perilous Lake

"So much for the seeming," said the giant.

"Do you think that also counts as the slaying?" asked one of Coredderoc's heads.

"I have not seen such a slaying in a long time," said the second head.

"But we did not slay anything," said Lann, strumming his fingers across the place where his lute strings had once been. "It *seemed* a dragon was upon us, but it was merely the gray-green rocks from the castle. Can't you see that?"

They all had to agree with him then. The slaying was yet to be.

"Now we must get off the cliff and to the castle," said Jared.

"Ah, but how?" asked Coredderoc's heads together.

"Not that I really want to go there, you understand," said Jared, "but I *do* have a plan. And if the rest is as simple as the first . . ."

"I hope the rest is simple, and it is not just we who are so," said Lann. "What is your plan, friend?"

"I will shake my right foot, and we will begin with many flowers."

"Flowers?" said the minstrel. "What good are flowers against a wizard?"

"Or lute strings against a dragon?" reminded Coredderoc's two heads together.

"We must make a strong chain of them," said the giant. "Strong enough to carry our weight."

"Down the cliff?" asked the dwarf's first head. "But what good will that be?"

The second head added, "We would still need to cross the lake. And I for one—"

"For two," interrupted the first head, "can't swim."

"Not down the cliff," said Jared. "My plan does the two steps in one." He waved the gander to him.

The gander in turn called to the goose who swam in the lake, washing her poor singed feathers. The goose shook the water from her wings as she rose into the air. In moments, the two silver birds were on the cliff.

The gander walked right over to the royal giant. The goose stayed back, as if embarrassed to be seen. At that, Lann went up to the beautiful bird and caressed her head and looked deeply into her round black eyes.

"Fair heart," he said to the goose as if talking to a girl, "you have been most courageous. But there is more courage yet to be asked."

The goose dipped her head toward the ground, then looked up at Lann. The gander crowded close to him, too.

"You must carry us across the lake," said the giant. And then he described the flower rope that was to be built.

Swiftly, the three friends worked while the goose and

gander cleaned their wings and made ready for the flight. Jared
would stomp his right foot on the ground, and the harder he
stomped, the larger the flowers. The larger the flowers, the
stronger the stems. And the stronger the stems, the more
sturdy and safe was the strand that they wove.

The giant's fingers were large and stubby, and he broke
more flowers than he could twist together. But the dwarf's
fingers were quick and eager. And Lann's fingers, used to
plucking a lute string, were the most facile of all. In less time
than it takes to tell of it, they had twined a flower rope the
length of three tall men.

"Now, I shall hang from one end, near the gander," said
the giant. "And you, Coredderoc, and you, Lann, shall balance
me on the other end, close to the goose."

The three friends helped the goose and gander slip the
rope around their bodies like a halter. Then, positioning themselves as Jared had instructed, the giant, the dwarf, and the
minstrel took hold of the rope. The goose and gander picked
up the ends in their beaks.

"Hold fast, friends, and never lack courage," called out
Jared, though he was the one who was most afraid.

The wild goose and gander began to pump their wings; up
and down, up and down they beat together. Slowly the goose
and then the gander rose in the air, the rope tight around their
bodies, the ends in their beaks. And more slowly still, the rope
stretched taut between the friends and pulled them into the air.
As each one left the earth—first the dwarf, then Lann, and
finally the giant—they said silent prayers for the safety of the
others. And Lann said a special farewell to his mother.

Once fully in the air, though their burden was heavy, the
goose and gander moved with ease. Their mighty wings beat
steadily, silently, swiftly.

But the arms of the three friends were pulled nearly free of
their sockets. And the three were soon weary beyond wondering.

Jared lost the grip of one hand less than halfway. Dangling
dangerously and screaming mightily, the giant was borne
through the air.

Coredderoc never said a word the entire trip across the lake. His two heads gazed soulfully at one another as if some important message were passing between the eyes of the two.

Lann, his unstrung lute across his back, crossed with his eyes closed the entire way. And whether he was singing to himself or praying, only the goose could have told, for she was the only one who might have heard.

But the rope stayed taut between them, and the goose and gander, bearing their heavy burden over the perilous lake, crossed the three friends to the castle that awaited them like a giant bird of prey.

9. The Slaying

The goose and gander lowered the rope with the three friends hanging from it to the crenelated castle wall.

The minute his feet touched the stones of the castle, Lann let go of the flower rope. He reached over to remove the halter from the goose's body.

After a moment, Jared did the same for the gander.

As for the dwarf, he knelt and kissed the stones with both his heads. Then he stroked the wall. "There is something familiar about this castle," said the first head.

"Yes, something like—yet not like," said the second head.

"It reminds me of my own castle," said Jared sadly. "But then, I suppose all castles are something alike."

Lann thought a bit. "It may be yet another seeming," he said.

"Is all wizardry seeming?" asked Jared.

"No, my friends," said a dark and sinuous voice. "The slaying is real. It is very real."

The three friends and the two birds turned slowly to-

ward that voice, as if they did not want to know who had
spoken. Or as if they knew and did not want to see. The
goose began to weep real tears, which fell silently to the
castle stones.

It was Bleakard. For so Jared and Coredderoc said together. But even if they had not, Lann would have known him.
It could have been no other.

Bleakard was dressed in a long, billowing, blood-red robe.
On his head was a crown of iron. On his fingers, dully gleaming, were iron rings. A large bone flute hung from a linked
chain around his waist. His golden mustache and beard were
streaked with gray and ran together down his face. His eyes
were like two hollows and so deeply set that Lann thought he
could see neither their color nor their size, though he knew
they were black. And when Bleakard spoke, his words sounded
like the hissing of a great snake.

Lann was afraid. But when he saw the goose weeping,
every tear pushed him to action. "Hold, friend wizard," he
said.

At that the wizard laughed. "I am no friend of yours, boy.
But speak, as if words would help you. You are mine to do
with as I will." As he spoke, Bleakard moved toward them.
And though he raised neither his voice nor his hand, there was
such menace in his every move that they all stepped backward
until their backs crowded the wall.

Lann spoke then, braver than he felt. "Before every step
there must be a chance," he said. "There was a chance for us
before the singing. And a chance before the seeming ended.
We *must* have a chance before the slaying. Magic is always fair.
That I know, for so my mother taught me."

"*Feh!* What do mothers know of magic?"

Lann looked calm. He even felt calm. He put his hand on
his amulet and said, "My mother is Sianna of the Song. And all
I know, she has taught me."

The wizard looked startled for a moment. Then the sneer
crept back on his face. "And you think she has taught you
well, young master? For if there is any who comes even near

to me in magic, it is she, Sianna of the Song. But you are not she. No son is ever the same as his sire nor the equal to his dam."

Lann knew that so many words were meant to keep him from his purpose. So therefore he knew what his mother had taught him was right. For one who is assured of his purpose does not need words to spur him on. He took a step forward and spoke again. "What is our chance, then, Bleakard? Tell us that we may at least try."

"You no longer call me friend?" the wizard asked.

"No, I now see you are no friend of mine, nor are ever likely to be."

"Well said. And truly said. I would be no friend to such weak, pitiful creatures as you. Hear me, then, Sianna's son. A single note is not a song. And you are not your mother. However, if you or one of your motley company will give up what is most precious to him, then you are all free. And I am slain. If not . . ." Bleakard lifted his right hand to his beard and stroked it slowly. "If not, you will join the gray-green rocks below. Alive, yet not alive. Slain, yet not quite dead. To come and to go at my call."

"What does he mean?" asked one of Coredderoc's heads.

"I am afraid I know," said the other.

"I mean—friends—" said Bleakard, "that you will *become* gray-green rocks, as have others who have incurred my wrath or displeasure."

The friends turned and looked down to the lake. Each felt he could see the shape of a man or woman in the rocks that lay broken and still in the water. As if in chorus, the three friends and two birds shuddered.

"Come, then," said Bleakard, "the little game begins. And what have you to offer—that which is most precious?"

"That is easy," said Lann, not daring to look at the goose as he said it. "Here is my lute. It is my most precious possession." He unslung the instrument from his back and handed it to the wizard.

"If it is easy," said the wizard, taking the lute and breaking it across his knee, "then it is not so important at all. A minstrel without a lute can still be a lover." He looked darkly and meaningfully at the goose, and swept the broken lute aside with his foot.

Lann looked down at the shards of his instrument. He felt doubly shamed. He had known that Bridda meant more to him than any lute. And so he had hoped to fool the magic, though he knew that magic does the fooling and is never fooled. He put his hand to his eyes and wept, and did not care who saw him weep.

"There, lad," said one of the dwarf's heads.

"There is yet a chance," said the other.

"Ah, what have we here?" asked the wizard with a laugh. "A two-faced friend. A counselor with no one to counsel? Well, counsel me. What have you to offer?"

The first head spoke softly, "Take my other head."

The second head snapped, "Wait, you can't give *me* away, I give *you* away."

"Both right and both wrong," sneered the wizard. He laughed louder still. "You cannot give someone else away. One person cannot own another. This game is funnier still."

Coredderoc's heads looked at one another. Then the eyes of the first head softened and the head spoke to its twin. "I am sorry. I mean it truly. You are precious to me. You *are* me."

The second replied, "It is true. We are both precious to each other."

The wizard fingered his bone flute with one hand and stroked his beard with the other. "Come now, I lose patience. You, giant, what have you to offer? Your marvelous feet?"

The giant looked down at his feet and shook his head miserably. He opened his mouth as if to speak, but fear closed it again.

The wizard smiled slowly and said, "And this is a company of friends. A fine rocky company you will make, too."

Lann looked around at his friends. He could scarcely see their faces in the gathering gloom. He realized that the sun had already gone down behind the cliff, as if to hide its face from what must surely happen to them in a moment. Darkness was fast coming on.

So Lann reached into his shirt and pulled out a silver button on a chain, the Magic Three. For the past seven years he had lived with it on his neck, and though often he had had a need to use its power, he had never tried its might. Briefly he remembered his mother's words those seven long years before. "Its consequences may be too hard to bear," she had said. Yet what could be worse than the certain living death of all his company? To lie forever by his beloved's side and be unable to reach out to her, a gray-green rock in a fog-bound pool? So he twisted it in his hand, first left, then right, then right again. And as he twisted it, he said the words "Magic Three, Magic Three, grant this boon I ask of thee."

From out the darkened sky there came the sound of thunder. And the button twisted by itself in his hand.

> A precious gift give us to give,
> That all this company might live.

Lann spoke the words in a whisper. There was another loud crash of thunder, and the magic button ran like quicksilver through his fingers and was gone.

Suddenly the two birds gave a moan and began to change. First the feathers on their heads turned to hair. Their faces changed from birds to those Lann knew so well—his beloved Bridda and her brother. Then the feathers, soft and white on their wings, dissolved, and the wings turned into arms.

Even before the change was complete, Bred had moved over to his sister. He took her wing in his and placed it in Lann's hand. Then he knelt before the wizard.

"I give you what is most precious to me," he said.

"And what can be most precious to a man who is part bird?" mocked the wizard.

"I give you what is most precious to any—man or bird," said Bred. "For these my friends, I give you my life."

10. And After

The wizard still sneered. But deep in his hollow eyes, for the first time there was fear. It was fear born of certain knowledge.

Lann felt his heart contract with pain and relief. He felt ashamed of such a feeling and glanced at the others. He read the same thoughts in their eyes.

The wizard reached down for the bone flute that hung at his side. And while the horrified friends watched, the flute grew in size until it was as large as an ax, and as sharp.

"*No!*" cried Lann. He leaped toward the wizard and Bred. But he was too late.

With a swift, vengeful movement, Bleakard brought the sharp edge of the flute down on Bred's bared neck. At the blow there was the red of blood and the black of night. And the entire castle moved as if shaken by an invisible hand.

When the darkness cleared, Lann looked around him in amazement. Of giant or dwarf, of goose or gander, of the wizard and his bone flute, there was no sign. The castle itself was changed. No longer were the rocks gray-green in color, but a soft, warm brown. And instead of being on the cold tower walk, Lann was lying on a fair bed hung with velvet curtains.

Slowly he set his feet on the floor and got up. A small arched window beckoned to him. He walked over to it and peered out. Instead of night it was noon, and the sun's light was warm and full. The lake had disappeared, and in its place was a great meadow with cows and sheep grazing and a company of herdsmen nearby.

Lann looked about him again, wondering if it had all been simply a seeming after all, a tale to while away an afternoon, a magic entertainment planned by his mother. But then, on a chest at the foot of the bed, he saw the pieces of his broken instrument. Picking the pieces up sadly, he shook his head. His life, he felt, was as broken as the lute. His friend's solitary death was, indeed, a consequence he could scarcely bear.

It was then Lann saw the open door. He went through it and found himself in a long hall hung with rich tapestries.

At the hall's end was yet another door. And when he opened it, Lann found himself in a large, pleasant room filled with well-dressed people. As he walked through the door, the people all bowed.

"Hail, Lann, Sianna's son," they said at once.

Lann looked about him wonderingly and approached the people. For surely someone there could explain the things that had happened to him and help him find his company of friends.

Yet as he approached, the people fell back, bowing and opening up a pathway. At the end of the path was a throne. On the throne sat a kindly man who seemed tall as a giant, for he sat straight and proud. He was dressed in royal robes, yet beneath his golden crown was a face that was familiar.

"Jared!" cried Lann.

"It is indeed I," said Jared.

To his right stood a small man in robes of blue. A gold medallion hung around his neck. He was a counselor who looked at Lann with an expression he recognized at once.

"Coredderoc, too?" asked Lann.

"Cored one," said the counselor. "Both in one head."

Lann could contain himself no longer. He ran over to the two and threw his arms around them. There was a gasp from the people and Lann drew back, suddenly remembering that Jared was a king.

But the noise from the crowd was not for that. They were drawing apart to let a beautiful girl step through. Her hair was as soft as feathers and her face as gentle as the wind.

"This is my daughter," said the king, "whom I had thought lost forever. Bridda."

But Lann had not waited for her name. He had already gone to her side.

It was then that Cored explained what had occurred. "It was, as you have probably guessed, mostly *seeming*. We have all been enchanted, for our own folly or the follies of others. The king, the prince, the princess, and I in our own sad states in which you found us; the lords and ladies and cooks and stable-boys as the gray-green rocks on which Bleakard's castle was built. For he was so evil, he could build only upon the wreckage of others' lives."

All the people gathered in the room nodded at this and whispered, "How right," and "So true," each to his neighbor.

The king broke in then, saying, "We would have remained forever thus if you had not come by. With love and courage you inspired us to great deeds."

"But it was Bred who saved us all," protested Lann. "It was his sacrifice."

"Yes, in the end it was Bred, my son, who gave his life for us all," the king agreed. "Gave it without knowing who we all were—except that we were friends." He looked around at the assembly of people and then stood up. "Brave men do that, that others may live. And it will always be my special burden to know that at the moment of asking—though I guessed what it was that was required of me—I could not do it. I was not as brave as my own son. That is a piece of knowledge that will guide me when I must judge others."

Lann turned to the princess. "But if you are of royal blood, then I fear what I hope for may not come to pass. For though there was never a one such as my mother, she is of the blood of peasants, and so am I."

"Lann, my friend, my son," said Jared, "you are ever as dear to me as the son I had for only a moment and lost. Marry my daughter and rule in my place. For any son of a woman as wise as Sianna of the Song is more than worthy to be a king. And Cored and I will serve as your counselors whenever such a need shall arise." And, taking the crown from his own head, he placed it on Lann's. Then Jared knelt before the minstrel-king. "Your servant and your friend till death," he said.

"May that be a good long time," said Lann.

"I sincerely hope so," replied Jared with such fervor that the two friends at last were able to smile.

So Lann and Bridda married with the blessings both of her father and of his mother, who came with her minstrel husband to the wedding. The young king and queen shared in the ruling of the kingdom. Jared was ever at their side, leavening their judgments with his caution and wit. And Cored, too, served them well, as wise as two men, always seeing two sides of any question and balancing them both in any answer.

It was said that every night a silver bird with a blood-red ring around its neck visited the castle tower. King Lann played it songs on his lute. Queen Bridda fed it red berries, green salad, and wine. They called it Brother Gander and swore that it brought them news of all the people, great and small, who lived under their rule. Or so it was said in the kingdom—but many things are rumored, and not all are true.

What is true, though, is this: from that day on, no one within the kingdom was allowed to draw bow against any bird that flies in the sky or swims in the streams. And a flock of geese still lives contentedly in the palace courtyard, petted and beloved as any friends.

The Boy Who Had Wings

IN A VILLAGE DEEP IN THESSALY, where horses grow like wheat in the fields, a boy was born with wings. They were long, arching wings, softly feathered, and golden-white in color. They moved with delicate grace. And they were like nothing ever seen before in the whole of the Thessalian plain.

The boy's parents named him Aetos, which means eagle, because of his wondrous wings.

But Aetos' father, who was a herdsman, could not abide him. "Who has ever heard of a child with wings?" he asked, and made a sign with his hands to protect himself from evil spirits each time the child came near. "Surely the gods must be displeased with me to have sent me so strange a son. What good is he to me? He is something for wise men and fools to wonder about, but not a fit son for a keeper of horses."

And as Aetos grew from an infant to a boy, his father found one excuse after another to stay away from home, taking his herd of horses higher and higher into the surrounding hills.

At last he came home only when the driving rains made him seek shelter or the drifting snows closed the mountain trails.

Now Aetos' mother loved her son, but she too felt uneasy at the sight of his wings. Were they really a sign of the gods' disfavor? Or were they a blessing? It was hard to tell, but one dared not take chances. And if the villagers knew of this strange thing, they might do Aetos some hurt. So she made him a black goat-hair cape to cover his shoulders and forbade him ever to fly or to let people know of his wings.

And Aetos never disobeyed her.

But gradually Aetos became the forgotten one of the family. He played by himself in the corner of the house.

When shoved outside by his older brothers, he would wander alone down by the river. There, from behind a large olive tree, he would watch the women washing clothes in the water and the children playing on the shore.

Once in a while he would raise his eyes to the birds that raced the clouds across the skies. And sometimes his own wings would respond to the sight. They would try to stretch and arch. Then Aetos would pull his goat-hair cape more tightly around his thin shoulders and carefully study the ground until the wings were quiet once more.

It happened one day that the winter winds blew icily across the plain. Snow fell steadily in the mountains for a night and a day. But Aetos' father, high in the hills, did not come home. The snow had trapped him and his horses behind a wall of white.

The days grew colder. The winds came fiercely from the north. And still the herdsman could not bring his horses home.

In the village, Aetos, his mother, and his two older brothers sat by the fire shivering with the cold and wondering about their father.

Finally, the oldest brother, Panos, arose. "I will try to find my father," he said. He took a leather pouch and filled it with olives and flat bread. Then he went out into the storm.

But scarcely a day later, Panos returned. He had been able

to go no farther than the foot of the mountain before the icy winds had driven him home.

So once more the herdsman's wife and his three sons sat by the fire. Finally, the second brother, Nikos, arose. "Now it is my turn to seek our father," he said. He took the leather pouch and filled it with goat cheese and hung a goatskin full of wine from his belt. Then Nikos went out into the storm.

But scarcely two days later he returned. He had been able to go no farther than the first mountain pass when the icy winds and the wall of snow had driven him home.

So once more the herdsman's wife and his three sons sat by the fire. As the embers began to cool, Aetos arose. He pulled his goat-hair cape tightly around his shoulders. "It is left for me to seek our father," he said. "For if I had not been born with wings, he would have been safe at home even now."

And though he was still too young to brave the winter mountains all alone, neither his mother, nor Panos, nor Nikos told him no.

So, filling the leather pouch with a crust of dark bread and the goatskin with fresh milk, Aetos went out into the storm.

As he walked toward the mountain, the icy winds tore at his clothes. One chilling blast ripped the goatskin of milk from his shoulder and sent it spilling across the plain.

"It does not matter," thought Aetos. "I will be lighter now."

As Aetos reached the mountain's steep foot, a second chilling wind tore the leather pouch from his belt and tossed it high up on the hills.

"One thing less to carry," he thought. And he began to climb the snow-covered mountain.

Yet a third blast of the icy wind ripped his goatskin cape from his shoulders, whipping it away like a giant black hawk.

Aetos uttered a sharp cry as the cold winter air found his shoulders and back, for suddenly, without his willing it, his wondrous wings arched against the wind, stretching high and pushing out beyond his shoulders. For a minute the wind seemed to grow gentle. It played with the feathers, stroking them, petting them. And then, before Aetos could think what to do, his golden-white wings had started to beat by themselves. High above the path they carried him, above the trees and above the mountain.

As he whirled, dipped, dived, and soared, Aetos felt happy and free for the first time in his life. He saw how small his house looked, how small the village looked, how small the mountain that imprisoned his father.

His father! In the joy of flying, Aetos had almost forgotten about his father, trapped behind the cold, white wall of snow. So he squinted his eyes in concentration and mastered the beating of his wings. Then carefully he glided down near the tops of the trees and began to search the steep sides and valleys for a sign of the herdsman and his herd.

At last he saw a few small, dark dots against the snow. Catching a current of air, he floated down to investigate. There, huddled between two mares shaggy in their winter coats, was his father, fainting with the cold.

Aetos swooped down and lifted his father into his arms. He marveled at how light his father felt, for the herdsman had gone many days with no food and only melted snow to drink. Then, with his wings beating against the cold air, the feathers beginning to stiffen and grow heavy with ice, Aetos took off into the mountain air once again, his father cradled in his arms.

In less time than it takes to tell it, Aetos and his father had crossed up and over the mountain, sailed across the Thessalian plain, and landed in front of the herdsman's house.

Panos, Nikos, and their mother ran out and carried the herdsman inside, where they warmed him by the fire. But it was some time before they paid any heed to the chilled and drooping boy who shivered by the door. It was even longer before they noticed his frozen wings. But finally they signaled him to stand by the fire and filled him with warm broth and even warmer thanks.

The herdsman recovered quickly, for he was a hardy man. But Aetos lay in bed, shivering first cold and then hot, for many days.

When he was finally well, his wings, which had become frostbitten by the icy winds, lost all their feathers one by one. At last the wings themselves dropped off. All that was left were two large scars on his shoulders where the wings had been.

At first Aetos was sad, remembering the wild, happy freedom of his ride in the sky. But afterward, when both his mother and father hugged, kissed, petted, and praised him, and he was allowed to join the other boys at their games, he all but forgot about his lost wings. For they had brought him no happiness except for that one brief moment.

As the years passed, and Aetos grew into a man, he was loved and respected by all. He lived as other men in the village did and became a herder of horses. His wings and his one great flight into freedom faded into a childhood memory. Except for the scars on his shoulders, he would have counted them as a dream. But now, no longer burdened by the wings, his soul could fly.

Yet generations later, the people of the village prayed to a guardian angel of the horse herders, an angel they called St. Aetos. You see, the people never knew how unhappy the boy had been before he lost his wings, and only thought of how glorious it must be to fly. And boys and girls prayed each night to grow great, arched, golden-white wings that would carry them up over the mountains. Or they prayed that their own children might be born with such wings to bring them safely home across the plain.

But from that day to this, no one else has ever been so blessed.

The Girl Who Loved the Wind

ONCE MANY YEARS AGO in a country far to the east, there lived a wealthy merchant. He was a widower and had an only daughter named Danina. She was dainty and beautiful, and he loved her more than he loved all of his treasures.

Because Danina was his only child, the merchant wanted to keep her from anything that might hurt or harm her in any way, and so he decided to shut her away from the world.

When Danina was still an infant, her father brought her to a great house which he had built on the shore of the sea. On three sides of the house rose three huge walls. And on the fourth side was the sea itself.

In this lovely, lonely place Danina grew up knowing everything that was in her father's heart, but nothing of the world.

In her garden grew every kind of fair fruit and flower, for so her father willed it. And on her table was every kind of fresh fish and fowl, for so her father ordered. In her room were the finest furnishings. Gaily colored books and happy music, light dancing and bright paintings filled her days. And the servants were instructed always to smile, never to say no, and to be cheerful all through the year. So her father wished it, and so it was done. And for many years, nothing sad touched Danina in any way.

Yet one spring day, as Danina stood by her window gazing at the sea, a breeze blew salt across the waves. It whipped her hair about her face. It blew in the corners of her room. And as it moved, it whistled a haunting little tune.

Danina had never heard such a thing before. It was sad, but it was beautiful. It intrigued her. It beguiled her. It caused her to sigh and clasp her hands.

"Who are you?" asked Danina.

And the wind answered:

> Who am I?
> I call myself the wind.
> I slap at ships and sparrows.
> I sough through broken windows.
> I shepherd snow and sandstorms.
> I am not always kind.

"How peculiar," said Danina. "Here you merely rustle the trees and play with the leaves and calm the birds in their nests."

"*I am not always kind,*" said the wind again.

"Everyone here is always kind. Everyone here is always happy."

"*Nothing is always,*" said the wind.

"My life is always," said Danina. "Always happy."

"*But life is not always happy,*" said the wind.

"Mine is," said Danina.

"*How sad,*" whispered the wind from a corner.

"What do you mean?" asked Danina. But the wind only whirled through the window carrying one of her silken scarves, and before she could speak again, he had blown out to sea.

Days went by, happy days. Yet sometimes in her room, Danina would try to sing the wind's song. She could not quite remember the words or recall the tune, but its strangeness haunted her.

Finally, one morning, she asked her father: "Why isn't life always happy?"

"Life *is* always happy," replied her father.

"That's what I told him," said Danina.

"Told who?" asked her father. He was suddenly frightened, frightened that someone would take his daughter away.

"The wind," said Danina.

"The wind does not talk," said her father.

"He called himself the wind," she replied.

But her father did not understand. And so when a passing fisherman found Danina's scarf far out at sea and returned it to the merchant's house, he was rewarded with a beating, for the merchant suspected that the fisherman was the one who called himself the wind.

Then one summer day, weeks later, when the sun was reflected in the petals of the flowers, Danina strolled in her garden. Suddenly the wind leaped over the high wall and pushed and pulled at the tops of the trees. He sang his strange song, and Danina clasped her hands and sighed.

"Who are you?" she whispered.

"*Who am I?*" said the wind, and he sang:

> Who am I?
> I call myself the wind.
> I've worked the sails of windmills.
> I've whirled the sand in deserts.
> I've wrecked ten thousand galleons.
> I am not always kind.

"I knew it was you," said Danina. "But no one believed me."

And the wind danced around the garden and made the flowers bow.

He caressed the birds in the trees and played gently with the feathers on their wings.

"You say you are not always kind," said Danina. "You say you have done many unkind things. But all I see is that you are gentle and good."

"But not always," reminded the wind. *"Nothing is always."*

"Is it sad, then, beyond the wall?"

"Sometimes sad and sometimes happy," said the wind.

"But different each day?" asked Danina.

"Very different."

"How strange," Danina said. "Here things are always the same. Always beautiful. Happy. Good."

"How sad," said the wind. *"How dull."* And he leaped over the wall and blew out into the world.

"Come back," shouted Danina, rushing to the wall. But her voice was lost against the stones.

Just then her father came into the garden. He saw his daughter standing by the wall and crying to the top. He ran over to her.

"Who are you calling? Who has been here?" he demanded.

"The wind," said Danina, her eyes bright with memory. "He sang me his song."

"The wind does not sing," said her father. "Only men and birds sing."

"This was no bird," said his daughter.

"Then," thought her father, "it must have been a man." And he resolved to keep Danina from the garden.

Locked out of her garden, Danina began to wander up and down the long corridors of the house, and what once had seemed like a palace to her began to feel like a prison. Everything seemed false. The happy smiles of the servants she saw as smiles of pity for her ignorance. The gay dancing seemed to hide broken hearts. The paintings disguised sad thoughts. And soon Danina found herself thinking of the wind at every moment, humming his song to the walls, his song about the world—sometimes happy, sometimes sad, but always full of change and challenge.

Her father, who was not cruel but merely foolish, could not keep her locked up completely. Once a day, for an hour, he allowed Danina to walk along the beach. But three maidservants walked before her. Three manservants walked behind. And the merchant himself watched from a covered chair.

One chilly day in the fall, when the tops of the waves rolled in white to the shore, Danina strolled on the beach. She pulled her cape around her for warmth. And the three maidservants before her and the three manservants behind shivered in the cold. Her father in his covered chair pulled his blanket to his chin and stared out to sea. He was cold and unhappy, but he was more afraid to leave Danina alone.

Suddenly the wind blew across the caps of the waves, tossing foam into the air.

Danina turned to welcome him, stretching out her arms. The cape billowed behind her like the wings of a giant bird.

"Who are you?" thundered Danina's father, jumping out of his chair.

The wind spun around Danina and sang:

> Who am I?
> I call myself the wind.
> I am not always happy.
> I am not always kind.

"Nonsense," roared Danina's father. "Everyone here is always happy and kind. I shall arrest you for trespassing." And he shouted, "*Guards!*"

But before the guards could come, Danina had spread her cape on the water. Then she stepped onto it, raised one corner, and waved goodbye to her father. The blowing wind filled the cape's corner like the sail of a ship.

And before Danina's father had time to call out, before he had time for one word of repentance, she was gone. And the last thing he saw was the billowing cape as Danina and the wind sailed far to the west into the ever-changing world.

Brothers of the Wind

The Foal

IN THE FAR REACHES OF THE DESERT, where men and horses are said to dwell as brothers, a foal was born with wings. The foal was unremarkable in color, a muted brown with no markings. However, the wings—small and crumpled, with fragile ribs and a membrane of gray skin—made it the center of all eyes.

But the sheik who owned the foal was not pleased. He stood over the newborn, pulling on his graying beard. He shook his head and furrowed his brow. Then he turned quickly, his white robes spinning about him, casting dervish shadows on the ground.

"This must be Allah's jest," he said contemptuously to the slave who tended his horses. "But I do not find it amusing. If horses were meant to be birds, they would be born with beaks and an appetite for flies."

"It is so," said the slave.

"Take the foal out into the desert," said the sheik. "Perhaps the sands will welcome this jest with better humor than I."

"At once, master," said the slave. He spoke to the sheik's back, for his master had already left the tent.

The slave clapped his hands twice. At the sound, so sharp in the desert's silence, a boy appeared. His name was Lateef, the tender one, the one full of pity and tears. He was an orphan's orphan and small for his age, with dark hair and skin the color of an old coin. His eyes burned fiercely, black suns in a bronze sky, but they were always quick to cloud over. And though Lateef was handsome and hardworking, the sheik's chief slave knew that the boy's tenderness was a great fault and that he was often the butt of jokes. Indeed, without a living mother or father to teach him other ways or to protect him from his tormentors, he was at the mercy of all. Lateef was always given the hardest and most unpleasant chores to do. He was the lowest slave in the sheik's household.

"I am here," Lateef said in his gentle voice.

"Ah, the tender one," said the keeper of horses. "Do you see this foal? This new one? It is not pleasing to our master. It is Allah's jest. For if a horse were meant to be a bird, it would make a nest of sticks and straw."

Lateef looked down at the foal as it sucked contentedly at its mother's teat. He loved being with the horses, for only with them did Lateef feel brave and strong. The little foal's sides moved in and out, and at each movement the fragile, membranous wings seemed to flutter. Lateef's hand moved to touch one wing, and his heart filled with wonder.

But the keeper of horses spoke cruelly, cutting across Lateef's thoughts. "You are to take this jest far out beyond the sight of the oasis and leave it in the sand." He turned in imitation of the sheik, his robes spinning around him.

Lateef spoke as the turn began. "Perhaps . . ." he said daringly. "Perhaps it is not Allah's jest at all. Perhaps . . . perhaps . . ." and he spoke so softly, he almost did not say it aloud. "Perhaps it is Allah's *test*."

The keeper of horses stopped in midturn, his exit ruined, his robes collapsing in confused folds and entangling his ankles. "You piece of carrion," he said in a loud, tight voice. "Do you dare to question the sheik?"

"Yes. No. But I thought . . ." Lateef began.

"You have no thoughts," said the keeper of horses. "You are a slave. A slave of slaves. You will do only as you are ordered."

"So let it be," murmured Lateef, his eyes filling. He looked meekly at the ground until the keeper of horses had left the tent. But though his eyes were on the ground, his mind was not. Questions spun inside his head. This wonder, this foal with wings—might it not truly be Allah's test? And what if he failed this test as he seemed to fail everything else? He *had* to think about it. And, even though a slave must *not* think, he could not stop himself.

"*And do it at once!*" came the command through the tent flap as the keeper of horses poked his head in for one last word. "You are not only too tender but also too slow."

Lateef took a wineskin that hung from a leather thong on the side of the tent to fill it with milk from the foal's mother. He shouldered the foal aside and softly squeezed the milk in steady streams into an earthen bowl, then carefully poured it from the bowl into the skin flask. While Lateef worked, the foal nuzzled his ear and even tried to suck on it.

When the skin flask was full, Lateef knelt and put his head under the foal's belly, settling the small creature around his shoulders. Then he stood slowly, holding on to the foal's thin legs. The foal made only one tiny sound, between a sigh and a whicker, and then lay still. Lateef kept up a continual flow of words, almost a song.

"Little brother, new and weak," he crooned, "we must go out into the sun. Do not fear the eye of God, for all that has happened, all that will happen, is already written. And if it is written that we brothers will survive, it will surely be so."

Then Lateef walked out of the tent.

The Desert

Lateef and the foal both blinked as the bright sun fell upon them. From the inside of the tent, the mare cried out, an anguished farewell. The foal gave a little shudder and was still.

But Lateef was not still. He looked around once at the village of tents that rimmed the oasis. He watched as some slave girls, younger even than he, bent over the well and drew up water. He had known them all his life, but they were still strangers to him. His mother had died at his birth; her mother had died the same way. He was indeed an orphan's orphan, a no-man's child, a slave of slaves. He would leave this home of familiar strangers with no regrets and take his burden—jest or test—out into the burning sands. He had thought about it, though thinking was not for slaves. He had thought about it and decided that he would stay with the foal. His orders were to take it out into the sands. And perhaps the keeper of horses expected them both to die there. But what if their deaths were not written? Could that be part of Allah's test? He would go out into the sands as ordered, and then turn north to Akbir. Akbir, the city of dreams. If it were written anywhere that the foal was to live, in Akbir that writing could be understood.

It was noon when Lateef set out, and the fierce eye of the sun was at its hottest. It was a time when no son of the desert would ordinarily dare the sands. But Lateef had no choice. If he did not leave at once, he would be beaten for disobedience. If he did not leave at once, his courage—what little there was— would fail him. And if he did not leave at once, some other slave would take the foal and leave it out on the desert, and then the foal with wings would surely die.

North to Akbir. Lateef felt the sand give way beneath his feet. It poured away from his sandals like water. Walking in the desert was hard, and made harder still by the heavy burden he was carrying on his back.

He turned once to look at the oasis. It was now only a

shimmering line on the horizon. He could see no movement there. He continued until even that line disappeared, until his legs were weak and his head burned beneath his *dulband*. Only then did he stop, kneel down, and place the foal gently onto the sand. He shaded it with his own shadow.

The foal looked up at the boy, its eyes brown and pleading.

"Only one small drink now," cautioned Lateef. He held the wineskin out and pressed its side. Milk streamed into the foal's mouth and down the sides of its cheeks.

"*Aiee*," Lateef said to himself, "too quickly!" He gave one more small squeeze on the wineskin, then capped it. All the while he watched the foal. It licked feebly at the remaining milk on its muzzle. Its brown flanks heaved in and out. At each outward breath, the membranous wings were pushed up, but they seemed to have no life of their own.

Lateef sat back on his heels and matched his breathing to the foal's. Then, tentatively, he reached over and touched one wing. It looked like a crumpled veil, silken soft and slightly slippery to the touch. Yet it was tougher than it looked. Lateef was reminded suddenly of the dancing women he had glimpsed going in and out of the sheik's tent. They had that same soft toughness about them.

He touched the wing again. Then, holding it by the thin rib with one hand, he stretched it out as far as it would go. The wing unfolded like a leaf, and Lateef could see the dark brown veins running through it and feel the tiny knobs of bone. The foal gave a sudden soft grunt and, at the same moment, Lateef felt the wing contract. He let it go, and it snapped shut with a soft swishing sound.

"So," he said to the foal, "you *can* move the wing. You can shut it even if you cannot open it. That is good. But now I wonder: will you ever fly? Perhaps *that* is Allah's real test."

He stood up and looked around. All was sand. There was no difference between what was behind him and what was before. Yet he was a boy of the desert. He knew how to find directions from the traveling sun. Akbir lay to the north.

"Come, winged one," he said, bending down to lift the

foal to his shoulders again. "Come, little brother. There is no way for us but north."

The foal made no noise as Lateef set out again. And except for Lateef's own breathing, the desert was silent. It drank up all sound. So, with the sand below, the sky above, and only the wind-sculpted dunes to break the unending horizon, Lateef walked on. He felt that he labored across a painted picture, so still was the land.

Then suddenly, rising up from the place where sand and sky meet, Lateef saw a great watery shape. First it was a beast, then a towered city, then an oasis surrounded by trees. The changes were slow, one image running into the next as a river is absorbed into the sea. Something in Lateef leaped with the sight, and for a moment he let himself cry out in hope. But as the tears filled his eyes, Lateef reminded himself: "It is not a beast, not an oasis, not Akbir. It is only a mirage. Sun on the brain and sand in the eye." He spoke over his shoulder to the foal. "And I wonder what it is *you* see there, little brother." Then, closing his eyes and heart to the mocking vision, he trudged on, over the wind-scoured ripples, the changing, changeless designs on the desert floor.

When night came, he walked many miles farther under the light of the indifferent stars. Finally exhausted, he set his burden down and slept. But his sleep was fitful and full of dreams. He dreamed of sand, of sun, of stars. But he never once dreamed of the little horse that had curled against his chest, confident of the coming day.

The City

Before dawn, before the sun could once more coax the shadow beasts and cloud cities to rise, Lateef set out again. He let the foal suck on the bottle and allowed himself a few sips as well. He dared not think about the coming heat or that his left foot had a cramp in it, or that his shoulders ached from the burden-some foal, or that his heart could not stop trembling with fear. He refused to let himself think about those things. Instead he thought about Akbir.

Akbir. His great-grandmother had been from Akbir. The daughter of a kitchenmaid, without a father to claim her, she had been sold into slavery. To the father of the father of Lateef's master, the sheik. Lateef understood well that being the son of so many generations of slaves made him a person worth nothing. Less than nothing. Yet he dared to hope that, in Akbir, the home of his ancestors, he might change his position. With the foal as his touchstone, might he not even become a free man? A trainer of horses? An owner of stables?

He closed his eyes against the rising fantasy. Best, he cau-tioned himself, to think of only one thing at a time. Allah's jest or Allah's test. After all, he had no real idea what he would be able to do when he reached the pebbled streets, the mosaic mosques, the towered palaces of Akbir.

Walking forward quickly, his mind on the desert and not on his dreams, Lateef continued on. Even when he passed some horsemen at last and a caravan that jangled across his path for hours, he did not permit himself to dream. And in all that time, he spoke to no one other than the foal with whom he shared the wineskin.

But Lateef was not fooled into thinking that they had managed to come so far without the help of some unac-knowledged miracle. After all, though he was an orphan, the great-grandson of a city dweller, he had been reared in the desert. His people had seventeen different words for sand, and not one of them was a compliment. He well knew that a solitary traveler could not hope to walk across the desert under the sun's unrelenting eye without more to stave off thirst than a single flask of mare's milk. And yet they had done so, the boy and the foal, and were alive as they finally stumbled onto one of the dirt-packed back streets of Akbir. Still, as if afraid of giving tongue to the word "miracle"—as if speech might unmake it—Lateef remained silent. He set the foal down and then, as it stood testing its wobbly legs against the ground, Lateef bowed down and kissed the road at the foal's feet.

The foal took a few steps down a road that led off to one side. Then it turned its head toward Lateef and whickered.

"*Aiee,* brother. That road it shall be," Lateef said. He caught up with the foal easily and gave it the last of the milk. Then he stroked its velvety nose and lifted it for one last ride upon his back.

Surprisingly there was no one in the street, nor in the roadways they crossed, nor in the souk, the marketplace, where stalls and stands carried handwork, and foodstuffs enough to feed a multitude. Puzzling at this, Lateef explored further, passing from dirt roads to pebbled streets, from pebbled streets to roadways studded with colorful patterned stones.

The foal nuzzled his ear, and at that moment Lateef heard a strange moaning. He turned and followed the sound until he came to a line of high walls. Standing in front of the walls were hundreds of people.

Women, dressed in black mourning robes, cried out and poured sand upon their heads. Men in black pants and ragged shirts wailed and tore at their own beards. Even the children, in their best clothes, rolled over and over in the roadway, sobbing. And the name that he heard on every lip was "Al-Mansur. Al-Mansur."

Lateef was amazed. He had never seen such extravagant grief. The dwellers of the desert, with whom he had lived all his life, were proud of their ability to endure tragedy and pain. Water, they said, was too precious to be wasted in tears. Their faces never showed hurt. That was why Lateef, who cried at another's pain and could not disguise his griefs, had been called "tender one" and despised by all.

As Lateef watched the wailing men and women and children, he felt tears start down his own cheeks. Embarrassed, he went over to one young mourner who was rolling in the street and stopped him gently with his foot.

"Tell me, city brother," said Lateef, "for whom do we weep?"

The boy looked up. "Oh, boy with horse shawl," he began, "we cry because our great king of kings, the caliph Al-Mansur, is dying for want of a strange horse, a horse that he has seen only in his dreams. And though the caliph is a man of mighty dreams, he has always before been able to have whatever he dreamed. Only this time he cannot. And none of our doctors—the greatest physicians in the world—can cure him. They cannot cure him, for now he dreams of his death and, as it is written, there is no remedy for death." Then the boy fell back and pulled up some of the pebbles in the street, digging in the dirt beneath them. He covered his head with this dirt and began wailing again, this time louder than before.

"These are strange people," thought Lateef, "the people who dwell in cities. Yet I am of their blood. My great-grandmother was a sister to theirs. Surely that is why I am such a tender one. Still," he mused, "it is true that there is no remedy for death. I have heard that said many times in the desert. I have looked on many dead people, even in my short life, and have never known any of them to be cured."

And thinking about the caliph's approaching death led him to think about the caliph's dream. What could a man as rich and powerful as Al-Mansur desire so much that he might die of wanting? A horse, the boy said. But surely Al-Mansur could have any horse he wanted, any horse he dreamed of, any horse in his land.

"Perhaps the horse I carry is the very horse of the caliph's dream," Lateef said to the weeping boy.

At his words, the boy stopped his noise and looked up. "That is no horse, but a rag around your shoulders. A rag on a rag. The caliph is a great man, a giant. His dreams are big, too. He would laugh at such a jest should he see it." The boy began to laugh, but quickly the laugh turned back into a wail and he lay down again in the dust.

Lateef stroked the nose of the foal with one hand. "You are no jest to me, little brother," he said. Then he stepped over the wailing boy, pushed through the line of weeping people, and entered a gate in the wall.

Inside he saw the palace guards. They had taken off their great scimitars and, after laying the swords carefully on the ground, were rolling in the dirt and crying out their grief in tones even louder than the rest.

Lateef walked past them all and mounted the steps, marveling at the patterns on the stairs and walls. Behind them were the hundreds of grieving people. He wondered what lay ahead.

The Dream

Room upon room seemed to open before Lateef, and he walked through each one as if in a dream. He—who had known only the tents of his sheik, thinking them rich beyond his greatest imaginings—could not even begin to comprehend the wonders that belonged to the caliph. The sheik's desert tents now seemed but tattered remnants of an old beggar's cloak.

He followed a thread of sound, a wailing as thin and pure as a piece of spun gold. And when he found its beginning, he entered a room more splendid than any he had wandered in before.

Pearl-encrusted oil lamps sat on ebony tables. Draperies of wine-and-gold-colored silks hung on the walls. The wind of fifty fans held by fifty slaves made the shadows from the lamplight dance about the floor and over the carved faces of the wooden window screens.

In the center of the room was a mountain of pillows where a man lay, his head back and his bearded face bleached nearly as white as his robes and *dulband*. Only the red jewel of his turban had color. The ghost of his flesh hovered around his bones, for he had once been a large man, but was now shrunken with illness and age. His eyes were closed, but his lips moved in and out as he breathed. Around him were seven weeping women dressed in veils, their noses and mouths covered but their eyes eloquent with tears. Four old men, wringing their hands and making sour mouths, listened by the bed.

As Lateef came closer, he could hear the man on the pillows speaking faintly.

"In my dream," the bearded man said, "I stood upon the brink of a river. I knew that I had to cross to the other side. But there was no boat to take me there, and the waters were too wild and cold to swim. As I stood on the bank, longing for the other side, a wind began to dance around me. It blew sand in my face. I brushed my hand across my eyes to clear them and, when I could see once more, there was a great horse standing before me. The wind came from its huge, shining wings, fanning the air. I leaped onto its back. It pumped those mighty wings once, twice. Then, with a leap, it rose into the air. I looked below, and the river was but a thin ribbon lying across a sandy vastness. I gave a great laugh, threw my hands above my head, and—laughing—fell from the horse and awoke again in my bed."

"It is the same dream, my caliph," said the oldest man there, a man with a long white beard as fine as several silken threads.

"Of course it is," said the caliph. "But if I do not find that horse, I will die." He sighed deeply, and his stomach moved up and down.

The women began to wail again, but the old men shook their heads. The oldest spoke again.

"Be reasonable, my caliph. To die for a dream?" he said.

"Is it better to die of old age? To die of a disease? I think," said the caliph, "that to die for a dream is the noblest course of all."

"Be reasonable, my caliph," the old man tried again. "There is no such horse."

"Then how did I dream it?" asked Al-Mansur. "Can a man dream what is not? What can never be? If there is no such horse, then tell me, you who are the wisest of my people, what is the meaning of my dream?" He looked up at the men.

"The river is the river of death," said one adviser.

"Or the river of life," said the second.

"Or the river of sleep, which runs between," said the third. The women cried out again.

"And the horse is your life," said the one.

"Or your death," said the second.

"Or it is the dream beyond, the great dream that all men and all women dream," said the third.

The caliph sat up straight and smiled at them. "But is it not possible that the dream might come true, that such things could exist? That someday a man will ride in the sky and look down on a river and see it as thin as a ribbon?" The caliph looked pityingly at his advisers. "Can we not dream what *will* be?"

"If men were meant to fly," said the oldest adviser, stroking his thin beard, "they would be born with feathers instead of hair. So it is written. And it is so."

The caliph puffed out his cheeks thoughtfully. "But in the days of my father's fathers," he said, "there were those who dared to dream of great wonders. And in time such wonders came into being in the land: the building of this palace, and of the road that now runs across the sand—these were but dreams once, and now they are real. Why do you tell me I should dream no more?"

"Wonders in one year are commonplaces in another," replied the old man. "And memory has a faulty tongue."

"But do not say this dream is impossible," said the caliph. "I will not have it." Yet even as he spoke the words, he sank back onto the pillows.

Before the men could tell the caliph no once more, Lateef spoke. The horse on his shoulders lent him courage. "In the desert we say nothing is impossible, my caliph. What one man cannot do, another may." He sank to his knees, ducked his head, and set the foal onto the floor. The little horse wobbled, and his tiny hooves clattered against the colorful tiles. "Perhaps, great Al-Mansur, this is the wonder of which you dreamed."

The caliph sat up again and laughed, his eyes nearly hidden in the flaps of his shriveled cheeks. The laugh put false color in his face. "I dreamed of a mighty horse, and you bring me a starveling foal. I dreamed of a flying white-winged wonder, and you bring me a brown mite almost too weak to walk."

But the oldest adviser looked more closely at the foal. He saw its tiny gray wings, frail as those of a dragonfly. And he saw a way to keep his caliph alive for a while longer. He spoke with great care. "Even a wonder may be weak in its youth," he whispered to the caliph. "Look again, Al-Mansur."

The caliph looked again, saw the wings, and clapped his hands. "Perhaps," he said, "I shall put off dying until this foal has grown. You, boy, shall live with it in its stall. You shall eat with it and exercise it. And when the wonder is big enough, you shall bring it to me once again, and I shall have my ride." He sat up and put his feet over the side of the pillows. "And now, bring me some food and tell my people to stop their grieving. Their caliph shall not die for this dream—but live."

The Year

And so it came to pass that Lateef, the slave of slaves, became Lateef the keeper of the winged foal. Yet his life was not so different as one might suppose. He slept in the straw by the side of the horse, warming its body with his own. He was up before dawn drawing water from the well, filling a sack with grain, always feeding the horse before he dared to feed himself. And each day, besides, he brushed the horse's long black mane and tail, grooming its sleek, dark sides.

But he paid the most attention of all to the wondrous wings. He would take the fragile ribs in his hands and gently flex them, stretching the membranes until they were taut. In the cool, dark stable the membranes were a milky white, the color of old pearl. But outside, with the sun shining through, they were as iridescent as insect wings. So the caliph called the horse "Dragonfly." But Lateef did not.

"Brother," he named the foal. "Wind Brother." And he sang the name into the horse's ears and blew a breath gently into the foal's nostrils as was the custom among the desert dwellers. And he made the horse a song:

> Wind rider,
> Sun strider,
> The dreamer's dream,
> Moon leaper,
> Star keeper,
> Are you what you seem?

It was not a great song, but Lateef whispered it over and over in an affectionate tone as he touched the horse, until it twitched its ears in reply. And the horse grew to love Lateef and would respond to his every command.

Often the caliph would stand by the stall, holding on to the door for support while Lateef cleaned the horse. Or he would sit in a chair nearby while the horse's wings were stretched and rubbed with oil. But whenever the caliph tried to come too close, both Lateef and the horse would tremble. Then the caliph would sigh, and a faint blush of color would stain his pale cheeks. "Ah, Dragonfly," Al-Mansur would say, "do not forget that you are my dream. And I must ride my dream or die."

One day, when Lateef and the horse had both trembled at the caliph's approach, and Al-Mansur had sighed and spoken,

Lateef could control his tongue no longer. Bowing low, afraid to raise his head, he spoke. "O Caliph, if what you say is so, then you are no more free than I."

The caliph was silent for a moment, and when he spoke his voice was very soft. "No one is entirely free, child. Even I, Caliph Al-Mansur, have never been free to indulge my own dreams. To be good and wise, a ruler must make real the dreams of his people. But now, for once, I would have this dream, this wonder, for myself alone. For in some small way, the dreaming makes me feel I am free, though I know I am not."

Lateef shook his head, for he did not understand the caliph. How could a man who had everything no farther away than a handclap not be free? He raised his head to ask the caliph, but the man was gone. He did not come again to the stable, and his absence troubled Lateef.

When a year had passed and Wind Brother's sides had filled out, his mane and tail grown long and silky, the caliph sent word around to the stables that he would come the very next day to ride the winged horse. Now in all this time Wind Brother had never been mounted, nor had a saddle ever been placed upon his back. And never had he opened and shut his wings on his own. Lateef had been content to walk around the ring with the horse, his hand on Wind Brother's neck. He had feared that if he were to sit on the horse's back, his heels might accidentally do injury to the iridescent wings or that a saddle might crush a fragile rib.

Lateef bowed low to the messenger. "Tell my caliph," he said fearfully, "and with many respects, that the horse is not yet strong enough for a rider."

The messenger looked even more afraid than Lateef. "I dare not deliver such a message myself. You must go."

So Lateef entered the caliph's room for the second time. Al-Mansur lay on the silken pillows as if he were only dreaming of life.

"The horse, your . . . your Dragonfly," stuttered Lateef, "he is not yet ready to be ridden."

"Then make him so," said the caliph, barely raising himself up to speak. He sank back quickly, exhausted from the effort.

Lateef started to protest, but the guards hurried him out of the room. As he walked down the long hall, the caliph's oldest adviser followed him.

"He *must* ride tomorrow," said the old man, his thin beard weaving fantastic patterns in the air as he spoke. "It is his only wish. He is growing weak. Perhaps it will keep him alive. A man is alive as long as he can dream."

"But *his* dream is of *my* horse."

"The horse is not yours, but the caliph's. His grain has kept the horse alive. You are but a slave," said the old man, shaking his finger at Lateef. "A slave cannot own a horse."

"A slave can still be brother to the wind," Lateef whispered, aghast at his tongue's boldness, "as long as the wind wills it so." But even as he spoke, he feared he had failed—failed the horse and failed the caliph—and in failing them both, failed himself.

Allah's Test

In the morning Lateef was up early. He rubbed the horse's sides with scented oils. He wove ribbons into its black mane. And all the while he crooned to the horse, "Oh, my brother, do not fail me as I fear I have failed you. Be humble. Take the caliph onto your back. For you are young and healthy, and he is old and sick. He is the dreamer and you are the dream."

The horse whickered softly and blew its warm breath on Lateef's neck.

Then Lateef took the horse out into the ring.

Soon the caliph came, borne in a chair that was carried by four strong men. Behind them came the caliph's advisers.

Then, in order of their importance, came the caliph's wives. Finally, led in by the armed guards, came the men and women and children of Akbir, for the word had gone out to the souks and mosques: "Come see Caliph Al-Mansur ride his dream."

Only then, when Lateef saw how many people waited and watched, did he truly become afraid. What would happen if the caliph failed in front of all these people? Would they blame the horse for not bearing the caliph's weight? Would they blame Lateef for not training the horse well? Or would they blame the caliph? Failure, after all, was for slaves, not for rulers.

The caliph was helped from his chair, but then he signaled his people away. Slowly he approached the horse. Putting his hand to the horse's nose, he let Wind Brother smell him. He moved his hand carefully along the horse's flanks, touching the wings in a curious, tentative gesture, as if he had never really seen them clearly before. He spoke softly, so that only the horse and Lateef could hear: "I am the dreamer, you are the dream. I think I am ready to ride."

Lateef waited.

The horse waited.

All the men and women and children of Akbir waited.

Suddenly, so swiftly it surprised them all, the caliph took a deep breath and leaped onto the horse's back. He sat very tall on Wind Brother, his hands twisted in the horse's mane, his legs carefully in front of the wings. Eyes closed, the caliph smiled. And his smile was a child's, sweetly content.

For a long, breath-held moment, nothing happened. Then the horse gave a mighty shudder and reared back on his hind legs. He spun around and dropped onto all fours, arching his back. The caliph, still smiling, flew into the air and landed heavily on the ground. He did not get up again.

The horse did not move, even when Lateef ran over to him and touched his nose, his neck, his side. But as Lateef swung himself astride, he felt the horse's flanks trembling.

"Be not afraid," Lateef whispered to the horse. "I am here. What they try to do to you, they must do to me first. In this I will not fail you."

The chief of the caliph's guards ran toward the boy and the horse, his great silver scimitar raised above his head. As the scimitar began to sing its death song on the trip down through the air, Lateef leaned forward, guarding the horse's neck with his own. But he did not feel any blow. All he felt was a rush of wind as the horse began to pump its mighty wings for the first time.

Lateef turned his head. Above them he could still see the image of the silver sword. Then at his knee he felt a hand. He looked down. A boy about his own age stood there, in white robes, with a white *dulband* on his head. In the turban's center was the caliph's red jewel.

"I am free and ready to ride," the boy said, a shadowy smile playing at the corners of his mouth.

"Then mount, my brother," whispered Lateef, putting his hand down and pulling the boy up behind him. "Ride your dream."

With a mighty motion, the horse's wings pumped once again, filling with air and sky. He lifted them beyond the sword, beyond the walls of the palace. They circled the minarets once, and Lateef looked down. He could see a crowd gathering around the fallen figures of a caliph, a horse, a ragged boy. Only here and there was a man or a woman or a child who dared to look up, who saw the dream-riders in the sky.

And then they were gone, the three: over a river that was a thin ribbon in the sand, over the changing patterns of the desert, to the place where there are neither slaves nor rulers and where all living beings truly dwell as brothers—the palace of the winds.

The Golden Balls

NOT ALL PRINCESSES ARE SELFISH. No. But it is an occupational hazard. Perhaps it is even in the genes, inbred along with fine, thin noses and high arches, along with slender fingers and a swanlike neck.

There was a princess once endowed with all those graces at birth. Her father—a robust sort, given to hunting and sharing bones with his dogs—had married well. That meant his wife came with property and looks, and was gracious enough to expire after producing an heir. The heir was a boy who looked a lot like his father and screamed in similar lusty tones from one wetnurse to another until he found an ample breast that pleased him.

The heir was not the firstborn, however. He came second, after a sister. But primogeniture ruled him first. First at school, first at play, first in the hearts of his countrymen.

His sister turned her attention to golden balls.

She dallied with these golden balls in all manner of places: behind the cookstove, in the palace garden, under privet hedges, and once—just once—on the edge of a well deep in the forest. *That* was a mistake.

The splash could be heard for no more than a meter, but her cries could be heard for a mile.

No doubt she might have remained hours weeping by the well, unheard, unsung in song or story, had not an ambitious, amphibious hero climbed flipper after flipper to the rim of his world.

He gave her back what she most desired. He took from her what she did not wish to give.

"And will we meet again?" he whispered at last, his voice as slippery as kitchen grease, as bubbly as beer.

"By the wellspring," she gasped, putting him off, pushing his knobby body from hers.

"In your bed," he said. It was not a frog's demand.

To escape him, to keep him, she agreed. Then raising her skirts to show her slim ankles and high arches, she made a charming moue with her mouth and fled.

He leaped after her but was left behind. By the hop, it was many miles to the palace door. He made it in time for dinner.

By then the princess had changed her dress. The dampness had left a rash on her swanlike neck. The front of the skirt had been spotted with more than tears. She smiled meaningfully at the table, blandly at her brother who was now the king. He recognized the implications of that smile.

"Answer the door," said the king before there was a knock. He knew it would come, had come, would come again. "Answer the door," he said to his sister, ignoring the entire servant class.

She went to the door and lifted the latch, but the frog had already slipped in.

Three hops, seven hops, nine hops, thirteen; he was at the table. He dragged one frogleg, but he was on time.

The princess would have fed him tidbits under the table. She would have put her foot against his. She would have touched him where no one could see. But the king leaned down and spoke to the frog. "You are well suited," he said lifting the creature to her plate.

"Eat," commanded the king.

It was a royal performance. The frog's quick tongue darted around the princess's plate. Occasionally it flicked her hand, between her fingers, under her rings.

"After dinner comes bed," said the king, laughing at his sister's white face. He guessed at hidden promises. She had never shared her golden balls with him.

"I am not tired," she said to her plate. "I have a headache," she said to her bowl. "Not tonight," she said to her cup.

The frog led the way up the stairs. It was very slow going.

Her bed was too high for a hop. She lay upon it, trembling, moist as a well.

The frog stood at the foot of the bed. He measured the draperies for flipper-holds. He eyed the bellpull for a rope ladder. He would have been all night on the floor but for the king, who picked him up between thumb and finger and flung him onto the bed.

The bedclothes showed no signs in the morning, but a child grew in her like a wart.

Marriage transformed the frog but not the princess. He became a prince, Prince Grenouille. She became colder than a shower to him. She gave the child her golden balls. And she gave herself to cooks and choirboys, to farriers and foresters, but never again to a frog.

And Prince Grenouille suffers from her love for others. He wanders from his desk down to the wellspring in the forest. He dips his hand into the water and drinks a drop or two. The air is full of moist memories, and his burdens, like an ill-fitting skin, drop from him while he is there.

Frogs lust, but they do not love. Human beings have a choice. And, oh, a princess is a very large and troublesome golden ball indeed.

Johanna

The Forest was Dark and the snow-covered path was merely an impression left on Johanna's moccasined feet.

If she had not come this way countless daylit times, Johanna would never have known where to go. But Hartwood was familiar to her, even in the unfamiliar night. She had often picnicked in the cool, shady copses and grubbed around the tall oak trees. In a hard winter like this one, a family could subsist for days on acorn stew.

Still, this was the first night she had ever been out in the forest, though she had lived by it all her life. It was tradition—no, more than that—that members of the Chevril family did not venture into the midnight forest. "Never, never go to the woods at night," her mother said, and it was not a warning so much as a command. "Your father went though he was told not to. He never returned."

And Johanna had obeyed. Her father's disappearance was still in her memory, though she remembered nothing else of him. He was not the first of the Chevrils to go that way. There

193

had been a great-uncle and two girl cousins who had likewise "never returned." At least, that was what Johanna had been told. Whether they had disappeared into the maw of the city that lurked over several mountains to the west, or into the hungry jaws of a wolf or bear, was never made clear. But Johanna, being an obedient girl, always came into the house with the setting sun.

For sixteen years she had listened to that warning. But tonight, with her mother pale and sightless, breathing brokenly in the bed they shared, Johanna had no choice. The doctor, who lived on the other side of the wood, must be fetched. He lived in the cluster of houses that rimmed the far side of Hartwood, a cluster that was known as "the village," though it was really much too small for such a name. The five houses of the Chevril family that clung together, now empty except for Johanna and her mother, were not called a village, though they squatted on as much land.

Usually the doctor himself came through the forest to visit the Chevrils. Once a year he made the trip. Even when the grandparents and uncles and cousins had been alive, the village doctor came only once a year. He was gruff with them and called them "strong as beasts" and went away, never even offering a tonic. They needed none. They were healthy.

But the long, cruel winter had sapped Johanna's mother's strength. She lay for days silent, eyes cloudy and unfocused, barely taking in the acorn gruel that Johanna spooned for her. And at last Johanna had said: "I will fetch the doctor."

Her mother had grunted "no" each day, until this evening. When Johanna mentioned the doctor again, there had been no answering voice. Without her mother's no, Johanna made up her own mind. She *would* go.

If she did not get through the woods and back with the doctor before dawn, she felt it would be too late. Deep inside she knew she should have left before, even when her mother did not want her to go. And so she ran as quickly as she dared, following the small, twisting path through Hartwood by feel.

At first Johanna's guilt and the unfamiliar night were a burden, making her feel heavier than usual. But as she continued running, the crisp night air seemed to clear her head. She felt unnaturally alert, as if she had suddenly begun to discover new senses.

The wind molded her short dark hair to her head. For the first time she felt graceful and light, almost beautiful. Her feet beat a steady tattoo on the snow as she ran, and she felt neither cold nor winded. Her steps lengthened as she went.

Suddenly a broken branch across the path tangled in her legs. She went down heavily on all fours, her breath caught in her throat. As she got to her feet, she searched the darkness ahead. Were there other branches waiting?

Even as she stared, the forest seemed to grow brighter. The light from the full moon must be finding its way into the heart of the woods. It was a comforting thought.

She ran faster now, confident of her steps. The trees seemed to rush by. There would be plenty of time.

She came at last to the place where the woods stopped, and cautiously she ranged along the last trees, careful not to be silhouetted against the sky. Then she halted.

She could hear nothing moving, could see nothing that threatened. When she was sure, she edged out onto the short meadow that ran in a downward curve to the back of the village.

Once more she stopped. This time she turned her head to the left and right. She could smell the musk of the farm animals on the wind, blowing faintly up to her. The moon beat down upon her head and, for a moment, seemed to ride on her broad, dark shoulder.

Slowly she paced down the hill toward the line of houses that stood like teeth in a jagged row. Light streamed out of the rear windows, making threatening little earthbound moons on the graying snow.

She hesitated.

A dog barked. Then a second began, only to end his call in a whine.

A voice cried out from the house farthest on the right, a woman's voice, soft and soothing. "Be quiet, Boy."

The dog was silenced.

She dared a few more slow steps toward the village, but her fear seemed to proceed her. As if catching its scent, the first dog barked lustily again.

"Boy! Down!" It was a man this time, shattering the night with authority.

She recognized it at once. It was the doctor's voice. She edged toward its sound. Shivering with relief and dread, she came to the backyard of the house on the right and waited. In her nervousness, she moved one foot restlessly, pawing the snow down to the dead grass. She wondered if her father, her great-uncle, her cousins had felt this fear under the burning eye of the moon.

The doctor, short and too stout for his age, came out of the back door, buttoning his breeches with one hand. In the other he carried a gun. He peered out into the darkness.

"Who's there?"

She stepped forward into the yard, into the puddle of light. She tried to speak her name, but she suddenly could not recall it. She tried to tell why she had come, but nothing passed her closed throat. She shook her head to clear the fear away.

The dog barked again, excited, furious.

"My God," the doctor said, "it's a deer."

She spun around and looked behind her, following his line of sight. There was nothing there.

"That's enough meat to last the rest of this cruel winter," he said. He raised the gun, and fired.

The Sow, the Mare, and the Cow

Not so Very Long Ago, a sow, a mare, and a cow were friends. They lived together on a farm in a green and pleasant land.

One day the sow said to her friends, "I am tired of man and his fences. I want to see the world."

She grunted this so loudly that all the other animals on the farm heard her and turned their backs. But her friends did not.

"I agree," said the mare.

"And I," said the cow.

So that very night, the cow and the mare leaped over the fence; the sow crawled under. Then the three companions went one hoof after another down the road to see the world.

But the world was full of men and fences all down the road.

The sow shook her head. "I am going into the woods," she said.

"I agree," said the mare.

"And I," said the cow.

So they pushed through branch after branch, and bramble after briar, till the way grew dark and tangled. At last they found a small clearing where no fence had ever been built and no man had ever dwelt. They settled there for the night.

The sow and the mare took turns standing guard, but the cow fell right to sleep.

The mare began to nod.

Then the sow.

Soon all three were asleep, and no one was left to guard the others in the small clearing in the dark wood.

Suddenly a low growling filled the forest.

The sow and the mare woke up with a start. The cow lowed in alarm and hid her eyes with her hooves.

The growling got louder.

The cow jumped up.

Back to back, the three friends spent the rest of the night awake and trembling.

In the morning the sow said, "I think we should build a barn. Then we will be safe from the growlers in the night."

"I agree," said the mare.

"And I," said the cow.

So the mare gathered twigs and boughs for walls. The sow rooted leaves and moss for the roof. And the cow showed them where everything should be placed.

Branch by branch, bramble after briar, they built a fine barn.

That night the three friends went inside their barn. The sow and mare took turns standing guard, but the cow fell right to sleep.

The mare began to nod.

Then the sow.

Soon all three were asleep, and no one was left to guard the others in the fine barn in the small clearing in the dark wood.

Suddenly a high howling filled the forest.

The sow and the mare woke up with a start. The cow lowed in alarm and tried to hide in a corner.

The howling got higher and closer.

The sow ran to guard the door. The mare ran to guard the window. The cow turned her face to the wall. The three friends spent the rest of the night awake and trembling.

In the morning, the sow said, "I think we should build a high fence around our fine barn to keep away the growlers and the howlers in the night."

"I agree," said the mare.

"And I," said the cow.

So the mare gathered logs and stumps. The sow pushed boulders and stones. And the cow showed them where everything should be placed.

Then stick by stone, and bramble after briar, they built themselves a high fence. The three friends went inside their fine barn which was inside their high fence, to spend the night.

The sow and the mare took turns standing guard, but the cow fell right to sleep.

The mare began to nod.

Then the sow.

Soon all three were asleep, and no one was left to guard the others in the fine barn inside the high fence in the small clearing in the dark wood.

Suddenly there was a scratching at the door and a scrabbling on the roof.

The sow and mare awoke with a start. The cow lowed in alarm and fell to her knees. They waited for someone or something to enter. But nothing did.

Still the three friends spent the rest of the night awake and trembling.

In the morning the three friends were tired and pale and a little uncertain. They looked at one another and at the fine barn inside the high fence in the small clearing in the dark wood.

Then the cow spoke. "I have a sudden great longing for man and his fences."

But the mare did not say, "I agree."

And the sow did not say, "And I."

They were suddenly both much too busy digging

ditches, fixing fences, mending roofs, and laying a path to their door.

So the cow put one hoof after another all the way back to the farm in the middle of the green and pleasant land. There she lived a long and happy life within man's fences.

But the sow and the mare opened the door that very night and met the growlers and the howlers, the scratchers and the scrabblers who were just the forest folk who had come to make them welcome. And they too lived long and happy lives within fences of their own making. And if you can tell which one of the three was the happier, you are a better judge of animals than I.

Cockfight

THE PIT-CLEANERS CIRCLED NOISILY, gobbling up the old fewmets with their iron mouths. They spat out fresh sawdust and moved on. It generally took several minutes between fights, and the mechanical clanking of the cleaners was matched by the roars of the pit-wise dragons and the last-minute betting calls of their masters.

Jakkin heard the noises through the wooden ceiling as he groomed his dragon in the under-pit stalls. It was the first fight for both of them, and Jakkin's fingers reflected his nervousness. He simply could not keep them still. They picked off bits of dust and flicked at specks on the dragon's already gleaming scales. They polished and smoothed and polished again. The red dragon seemed oblivious to first-fight jitters and arched up under Jakkin's hands.

Jakkin was pleased with his dragon's color. It was a dull red. Not the red of the holly berry or the red of the wild-flowering trillium, but the red of life's blood spilled upon the sand. It was a fighter's color, and he had known it from the

201

first. That was why he had sneaked the dragon from its nest, away from its hatchlings, when the young worm had emerged from its egg in the sand of the nursery.

The dragon had looked then like any lizard, for it had not yet shed its eggskin, which was wrinkled and yellow, like custard scum. But Jakkin had sensed, beneath the skin, a darker shadow and had known it would turn red. Not many would have known, but Jakkin had, though he was only fourteen.

The dragon was not his, not really, for it had belonged to his master's nursery, just as Jakkin did. But on Austar IV there was only one way to escape from bond, and that was with gold. There was no quicker way to get gold than as a bettor in the dragon pits. And there was nothing Jakkin wanted more than to be free. He had lived over half his life bonded to the nursery, from the time his parents had died when he was four. And most of that time he had worked as a stallboy, no better than a human pit-cleaner, for Sarkkhan's Dragonry. What did it matter that he lived and slept and ate with his master's dragons? He was allowed to handle only their fewmets and spread fresh sawdust for their needs. If he could not raise a fighting dragon himself and buy his way out of bond, he would end up an *old* stallboy, like Likkarn, who smoked blisterweed, dreamed his days away, and cried red tears.

So Jakkin had watched and waited and learned as much as a junior stallboy could about dragon ways and dragon lore, for he knew the only way out of bond was to steal that first egg and raise it up for fighting or breeding or, if need was great, for the stews. But Jakkin did not know eggs—could sense nothing through the elastic shell—and so he had stolen a young dragon instead. It was a greater risk, for eggs were never counted, but the new-hatched dragons were. At Sarkkhan's Dragonry old Likkarn kept the list of hatchlings. He was the only one of the bonders who could write, though Jakkin had taught himself to read a bit.

Jakkin had worried all through the first days that Likkarn would know and, knowing, tell. He kept the hatchling in a wooden crate turned upside down way out in the sands. He swept away his footsteps to and from the crate, and reckoned his way to it at night by the stars. And somehow he had not been found out. His reward had come as the young worm had grown.

First the hatchling had turned a dull brown and could trickle smoke through its nose slits. The wings on its back, crumpled and weak, had slowly stretched to a rubbery thickness. For days it had remained mud-colored. Another boy might have sold it then to the stews, keeping the small fee in his leather bond bag that swung from the metal bond chain around his neck. It would have been a laughable amount, a coin or two at the most, and the bag would have looked just as empty as before.

But Jakkin had waited, and the dragon finally molted, patchworking into a red. The nails on its foreclaws, which had been as brittle as jingle shells, were now as hard as golden oak and the same color. Its hindclaws were dull and strong as steel. Its eyes were two black shrouds. It had not roared yet, but Jakkin knew that roar would come, loud and full and fierce, when it was first blooded in the ring. The quality of the roar would start the betting rippling again through the crowd who judged a fighter by the timbre of its voice.

Jakkin could hear the cleaners clanking out of the ring through the mecho-holes. He ran his fingers through his straight brown hair and tried to swallow, then touched a dimple on his cheek that was as deep as a blood score. His hand found the bond bag and kneaded it several times for luck.

"Soon now," he promised the red dragon in a hoarse whisper, his hand still on the bag. "Soon. We will show them a first fight. They will remember us."

The red was too busy munching on blisterwort to reply.

A disembodied voice announced the next fight. "Jakkin's Red, Mekkle's Bottle O' Rum."

Jakkin winced. He knew a little about Mekkle's dragon already. He had heard about it that morning as they had come into the pit stalls. Dragon masters and trainers did not chatter while they groomed their fighters, but bettors did, gathering around the favorites and trading stories of other fights. Mekkle's Rum was a light-colored male that favored its left side and had won three of its seven fights—the last three. It would never be great, the whispers had run, but it was good enough, and a hard draw for a new dragon, possibly disastrous for a would-be dragon master. Jakkin knew his red could be good with time, given the luck of the draw. It had all the things a dragon fighter was supposed to have: it had heart, it listened well, it did all he asked of it. But just as Jakkin had never run a fighter before, the red had never been in a ring. It had never been blooded or given roar. It did not even have its true name yet. Already, he knew, the betting was way against the young red, and he could hear the murmur of new bets after the announcement. The odds would be so awful, he might never be able to get a sponsor for a second match. First fights were free, but seconds cost gold. And if he had no sponsor, that would leave only the stews for the dragon and a return to bond for himself.

Jakkin stroked the bond bag once more, then buttoned his shirt up over it to conceal it. He did not know yet what it felt like to be free, so he could stand more years as a bonder. And there might always be another chance to steal. But how could he ever give up the red to the stews? It was not any old dragon, it was his. They had already shared months of training, long nights together under the Austar moons. He knew its mind better than his own. It was a deep, glowing cavern of colors and sights and sounds. He remembered the first time he had really felt his way into it, lying on his side, winded from running, the red beside him, a small mountain in the sand. The red calmed him when he was not calm, cheered him when he thought he could not be cheered. Linked as he was with it now, how could he bear to hear its last screams in the stews and stay sane? Perhaps that was why Likkarn was always yelling at the younger bonders, why he smoked blisterweed that turned the mind foggy and made a man cry red tears. And perhaps that was why dragons in the stews were always yearlings or the untrained. Not because they were softer, more succulent, but because no one would hear them when they screamed.

Jakkin's skin felt slimed with perspiration and the dragon sniffed it on him, giving out a few straggles of smoke from its slits. Jakkin fought down his own fear. If he could not control it, his red would have no chance at all, for a dragon was only as good as its master. He took deep breaths and then moved over to the red's head. He looked into its black, unblinking eyes.

"Thou art a fine one, my Red," he whispered. "First fight for us both, but I trust thee." Jakkin always spoke *thou* to his dragon. He felt it somehow brought them closer. "Trust me?"

The dragon responded with slightly rounded smokes. Deep within its eyes Jakkin thought he detected small lights.

"Dragon's fire!" he breathed. "Thou *art* a fighter. I knew it!"

Jakkin slipped the ring from the red dragon's neck and rubbed its scales underneath. They were not yet as hard as a mature fighter's, and for a moment he worried that the older Bottle O' Rum might tear the young dragon beyond repair. He pulled the red's head down and whispered into its ear. "Guard thyself here," he said, rubbing with his fingers under the tender neck links and thinking danger at it.

The dragon shook its head playfully, and Jakkin slapped it lightly on the neck. With a surge, the red dragon moved out of the stall, over to the dragonlock, and flowed up into the ring.

"It's eager," the whisper ran around the crowd. They always liked that in young dragons. Time enough to grow cautious in the pit. Older dragons often were reluctant and had to be prodded with jumpsticks behind the wings or in the tender underparts of the tail. The bettors considered that a great fault. Jakkin heard the crowd's appreciation as he came up into the stands.

It would have been safer for Jakkin to remain below, guiding his red by mind. That way there would be no chance for Master Sarkkhan to find him here, though he doubted such a well-known breeder would enter a back-country pit-fight. And many trainers, Mekkle being one of them, stayed in the stalls drinking and smoking and guiding their dragons where the crowd could not influence them. But Jakkin needed to see the red as well as feel it, to watch the fight through his own eyes as well as the red's. They had trained too long at night, alone, in the sands. He did not know how another dragon in a real fight would respond. He had to see to understand it all. And the red was used to him being close by. He did not want to change that now. Besides, unlike many of the other bonders, he had never been to a fight, only read about them in books and heard about them from his bondmates. This might be his only chance. And, he further rationalized, up in the stands he might find out more about Mekkle's orange that would help him help the red.

Jakkin looked around the stands cautiously from the stair-well. He saw no one he knew, neither fellow bonders nor masters who had traded with Sarkkhan. He edged quietly into the stands, just one more boy at the fights. Nothing called attention to him but the empty bond bag beneath his shirt. He checked his buttons carefully to make sure they were closed. Then he leaned forward and watched as his red circled the ring.

It held its head high and measured the size of the pit, the height of the walls. It looked over the bettors as if it were counting them, and an appreciative chuckle went through the crowd. Then the red scratched in the sawdust several times, testing its depth. And still Bottle O' Rum had not appeared.

Then with an explosion, Bottle O' Rum came through the dragonlock and landed with all four feet planted well beneath the level of the sawdust, his claws fastened immovably to the boards.

"Good stance," shouted someone in the crowd, and the betting began anew.

The red gave a little flutter with its wings, a flapping that might indicate nervousness, and Jakkin thought at it: "He is a naught. A stander. But thy nails and wings are fresh. Do not be afraid. Remember thy training." At that the little red's head went high and its neck scales glittered in the artificial sun of the pit.

"Watch that neck," shouted a heckler. "There's one that'll be blooded soon."

"Too soon," shouted another from across the stands at him.

Bottle O' Rum charged the inviting neck.

It was just as Jakkin hoped, for charging from the fighting stance is a clumsy maneuver at best. The claws must be retracted simultaneously, and the younger the dragon the more brittle its claws. The orange, Rum, seven fights older than the red, was not yet fully mature. As Rum charged, one of the nails on his front right claw caught in the floorboards and splintered, causing him to falter for a second. The red shifted its position slightly. Instead of blooding the red on the vulnerable neck, Rum's charge brought him headlong onto the younger dragon's chest plates, the hardest and slipperiest part of a fighting dragon's armor. The screech of teeth on scale brought winces to the crowd. Only Jakkin was ready, for it was a maneuver he had taught his dragon out in the hidden sands.

"Now!" he cried out and thought at once.

The young red needed no urging. It bent its neck around in a fast, vicious slash, and blood spurted from behind the ears of Mekkle's Rum.

"First blood!" cried the crowd.

Now the betting would change, Jakkin thought with a certain pleasure, and touched the bond bag through the thin cloth of his shirt. Ear bites bleed profusely but are not important. It would hurt the orange dragon a little, like a pinprick or a splinter does a man. It would make the dragon mad and— more important—a bit more cautious. But first blood! It looked good.

Bottle O' Rum roared with the bite, loud and piercing. It was too high up in the throat, yet with surprising strength. Jakkin listened carefully, trying to judge. He had heard dragons roar at the nursery in mock battles or when the keepers blooded them for customers intent on hearing the timbre before buying. To him the roar sounded as if it had all its power in the top tones and none that resonated. Perhaps he was wrong, but if his red could *outlast* the orange, it might impress this crowd.

In his eagerness to help his dragon, Jakkin moved to the pit rail. He elbowed his way through some older men.

"Here, youngster, what do you think you're doing?" A man in a gray leather coverall spoke. He was obviously familiar with the pits. Anyone in leather knew his way around. And his face, what could be seen behind the gray beard, was scored with dragon-blood scars.

"Get back up in the stands. Leave ringside to the money men," said his companion, taking in Jakkin's leather-patched cloth shirt and trousers with a dismissing look. He ostentatiously jounced a full bag that hung from his wrist on a leather thong.

Jakkin ignored them, fingering his badge with the facs picture of the red on it. He leaned over the rail. "Away, away, good Red," he thought at his dragon, and smiled when the red immediately wheeled and winged up from its blooded foe. Only then did he turn and address the two scowling bettors. "Pit right, good sirs," he said with deference, pointing at the same time to his badge.

They mumbled, but moved aside for him.

The orange dragon in the pit shook its head, and the blood beaded its ears like a crown. A few drops spattered over the walls and into the stands. Each place a drop touched burned with that glow peculiar to the acidic dragon's blood. One watcher in the third row of the stands was not quick enough and was seared on the cheek. He reached up a hand to the wound but did not move from his place.

The orange Rum stood up tall again and dug back into the dust.

"Another stand," said the gray leather man to Jakkin's right.

"*Pah,* that's all it knows," said the dark man beside him. "That's how it won its three fights. Good stance, but that's it. I wonder why I bet on it at all. Let's go and get something to smoke. This fight's a bore."

Jakkin watched them leave from the corner of his eye, but he absorbed their information. If the orange was a stander—if the information was true—it would help him with the fight.

The red dragon's leap back had taken it to the north side of the pit. When it saw that Bottle O' Rum had chosen to stand, it circled closer warily.

Jakkin thought at it, "He's good in the stance. Do not force him there. Make him come to thee."

The dragon's thoughts, as always, came back clearly to Jakkin wordless but full of color and emotion. The red wanted to charge; the dragon it had blooded was waiting. The overwhelming urge was to carry the fight to the foe.

"No, my Red. Trust me. Be eager, but not foolish," cautioned Jakkin, looking for an opening.

But the crowd, as eager as the young dragon, was communicating with it, too. The yells of the men, their thoughts of charging, overpowered Jakkin's single line of calm. The red started to move.

When it saw the red bunching for a charge, Rum solidified his stance. His shoulders went rigid with the strain. Jakkin knew that if his red dived at that standing rock, it could quite easily break a small bone in its neck. And rarely did a dragon come back to the pit once its neckbones had been set. Then it was good only for the breeding nurseries—if it had a fine pit record—or the stews.

"Steady, steady," Jakkin said aloud. Then he shouted and waved a hand, "*No!*"

The red had already started its dive, but the movement of Jakkin's hand was a signal too powerful for it to ignore and, at the last possible minute, it pulled to one side. As it passed, Rum slashed at it with a gaping mouth and shredded its wingtip.

"Blood," the crowd roared and waited for the red dragon to roar back.

Jakkin felt its confusion, and his head swam with the red of dragon's blood as his dragon's thoughts came to him. He watched as it soared to the top of the building and scorched its wingtip on the artificial sun, cauterizing the wound. Then, still hovering, it opened its mouth for its first blooded roar.

There was no sound.

"A mute!" called a man from the stands. He spit angrily to one side. "Never heard one before."

A wit near him shouted back, "You won't hear this one, either."

The crowd laughed at this, and passed the quip around the stands.

But Jakkin only stared up at his red bitterly. "A mute," he thought at it. "You are as powerless as I."

His use of the distancing pronoun *you* further confused the young dragon, and it began to circle downward in a disconsolate spiral, closer and closer to the waiting Rum, its mind a maelstrom of blacks and grays.

Jakkin realized his mistake in time. "It does not matter," he cried out in his mind. "Even with no roar, thou wilt be great." He said it with more conviction that he really felt, but it was enough for the red. It broke out of its spiral and hovered, wings working evenly.

The maneuver, however, was so unexpected that the pit-wise Bottle O' Rum was bewildered. He came out of his stance with a splattering of dust and fewmets, stopped, then charged again. The red avoided him easily, landing on his back and raking the orange scales with its claws. That drew no blood, but it frightened the older dragon into a hindfoot rise. Balancing on his tail, Rum towered nearly eight feet high, his front claws scoring the air, a single shot of fire streaking from his slits.

The red backwinged away from the flames and waited.

"Steady, steady," thought Jakkin, in control again. He let his mind recall for them both the quiet sands and the cool nights when they had practiced with the wooden dragon form on charges and clawing. Then Jakkin repeated out loud, "Steady, steady."

A hard hand on his shoulder broke through his thoughts

and the sweet-strong smell of blisterweed assailed him. Jakkin turned.

"Not so steady yourself," came a familiar voice.

Jakkin stared up at the ravaged face, pocked with blood scores and stained with tear lines.

"Likkarn," breathed Jakkin, suddenly and terribly afraid.

Jakkin tried to turn back to the pit where his red waited. The hand on his shoulder was too firm, the fingers like claws through his shirt.

"And how did *you* become a dragon trainer?" the man asked.

Jakkin thought to bluff. The old stallboy was often too sunk in his smoke dreams to really listen. Bluff and run, for the wild anger that came after blister dreams never gave a smoker time to reason. "I found . . . found an egg, Likkarn," he said. And it could be true. There were a few wild dragons, bred from escapes that had gone feral.

The man said nothing, but shook his head.

Jakkin stared at him. This was a new Likkarn, harder, full of purpose. Then Jakkin noticed. Likkarn's eyes were clearer than he had ever seen them, no longer the furious pink of the weeder, but a softer rose. He had not smoked for several days at least. It was useless to bluff or run. "I took it from the nursery, Likkarn. I raised it in the sands. I trained it at night, by the moons."

"That's better. Much better. Liars are an abomination," the man said with a bitter laugh. "And you fed it what? Goods stolen from the master, I wager. You born bonders know nothing. Nothing."

Jakkin's cheeks were burning now. "I am no born bonder. And I would never steal from the master's stores. I planted in the sands last year and grew blisterweed and burnwort. I gathered the rest in the swamps. *On my own time.*" He added that fiercely.

"Bonders have no time of their own," Likkarn muttered savagely. "And supplements?"

"The master says supplements are bad for a fighter. They

make a fighter fast in the beginning, but they dilute the blood." Jakkin looked into Likkarn's eyes more boldly now. "I heard the master say that. To a buyer."

Likkarn's smile was wry and twisted. "And you eavesdrop as well." He gave Jakkin's shoulder a particularly vicious wrench.

Jakkin gasped and closed his eyes with the pain. He wanted to cry out, and thought he had, when he realized it was not his own voice he heard but a scream from the pit. He pulled away from Likkarn and stared. The scream was Bottle O' Rum's, a triumphant roar as he stood over the red, whose injured wing was piniurd beneath Rum's right front claw.

"*Jakkin . . .*" came Likkarn's voice behind him, full of warning. How often Jakkin had heard that tone right before old Likkarn had roused from a weed dream to the fury that always followed. Likkarn was old, but his fist was still solid.

Jakkin trembled, but he willed his focus onto the red, whose thoughts came tumbling back into his head now in a tangle of muted colors and whines. He touched his hand to the small lump under his shirt where the bond bag hung. He could feel his own heart beating through the leather shield. "Never mind, my Red," soothed Jakkin. "Never mind the pain. Recall the time I stood upon thy wing and we played at the Great Upset. Recall it well, thou mighty fighter. Remember. Remember."

The red stirred only slightly and made a flutter with its free wing. The crowd saw this as a gesture of submission. So did Rum and, through him, his master Mekkle. But Jakkin did not. He knew the red had listened well and understood. The game was not over yet. Pit-fighting was not all brawn; how often Master Sarkkhan had said that. The best fighters, the ones who lasted for years, were cunning gamesters, and it was this he had guessed about his red from the first.

The fluttering of the unpinioned wing caught Bottle O' Rum's eye, and the orange dragon turned toward it, relaxing his hold by a single nail.

The red fluttered its free wing again. Flutter and feint.

Flutter and feint. It needed the orange's attention totally on that wing. Then its tail could do the silent stalking it had learned in the sands with Jakkin.

Bottle O' Rum followed the fluttering as though laughing for his own coming triumph. His dragon jaws opened slightly in a deadly grin. If Mekkle had been in the stands instead of below in the stalls, the trick might not have worked. But the orange dragon, intent on the fluttering wing, leaned his head way back and fully opened his jaws, readying for the kill. He was unaware of what was going on behind him.

"Now!" shouted Jakkin in his mind and only later realized that the entire stands had roared the word with him. Only the crowd had been roaring for the wrong dragon.

The red's tail came around with a snap, as vicious and as accurate as a driver's whip. It caught the orange on its injured ear and across an eye.

Rum screamed instead of roaring and let go of the red's wing. The red was up in an instant and leaped for Bottle O' Rum's throat.

One, two and the ritual slashes were made. The orange throat was coruscated with blood, and Rum instantly dropped to the ground.

Jakkin's dragon backed at once, slightly akilter because of the wound in its wing.

"Game to Jakkin's Red," said the disembodied voice over the speaker.

The crowd was strangely silent. Then a loud whoop sounded from one voice buried in the stands, a bettor who had taken a chance on the First Fighter.

That single voice seemed to rouse Bottle O' Rum. He raised his head from the ground groggily. Only his head and half his neck cleared the dust. He strained to arch his neck over, exposing the underside to the light. The two red slashes glistened like thin, hungry mouths. Then Rum began a strange, horrible humming that changed to a high-pitched whine. His body began to shake, and the shaking became part of the sound as the dust eddied around him.

The red dragon swooped down and stood before the fallen Rum, as still as stone. Then it, too, began to shake.

The sound changed from a whine to a high roar. Jakkin had never heard anything like it before. He put his hands to the bond bag, then to his ears.

"What is it? What is happening?" he cried out, but the men on either side of him had moved away. Palms to ears, they backed toward the exits. Many in the crowd had already gone down the stairs, setting the thick wood walls between themselves and the noise.

Jakkin tried to reach the red dragon's mind, but all he felt were storms of orange winds, hot and blinding, and a shaft of burning white light. As he watched, the red rose up on its hind legs and raked the air frantically with its claws, as if getting ready for some last deadly blow.

"Fool's Pride," came Likkarn's defeated voice behind him, close enough to his ear to hear. "That damnable dragon wants death. He has been shamed, and he'll scream your red into it. Then you'll know. All you'll have left is a killer on your hands. I lost three that way. *Three.* Fool's Pride." He shouted the last at Jakkin's back, for at his first words, Jakkin had thrown himself over the railing into the pit. He landed on all fours, but was up and running at once.

He had heard of Fool's Pride, that part of the fighting dragon's bloody past that was not always bred out. Fool's Pride that led some defeated dragons to demand death. It had nearly caused dragons to become extinct. If men had not carefully watched the lines, trained the fighters to lose with grace, there would have been no dragons left on Austar IV. A good fighter should have a love of blooding, yes. But killing made dragons unmanageable, made them feral, made them wild.

Jakkin crashed into the red's side. "No, no!" he screamed up at it, beating on its body with his fists. "Do not wet thy jaws in his death." He reached as high as he could and held on to the red's neck. The scales slashed one of his palms, but he did not let go.

It was his touch more than his voice or his thoughts that

stopped the young red. It turned slowly, sluggishly, as if rousing from a dream. Jakkin fell from its neck to the ground.

The movement away shattered Bottle O' Rum's concentration. He slipped from screaming to unconsciousness in an instant.

The red nuzzled Jakkin, its eyes unfathomable, its mind still clouded. The boy stood up. Without bothering to brush the dust from his clothes, he thought at it, *"Thou mighty First."*

The red suddenly crowded his mind with victorious sunbursts, turned, then streaked back through the hole to its stall and the waiting burnwort.

Mekkle and two friends came up the stairs, glowering, leaped into the pit and dragged the fainting orange out through a mecho-hole by his tail.

Only then did Jakkin walk back to ringside, holding his cut hand palm up. It had just begun to sting.

Likkarn, still standing by the railing, was already smoking a short strand of blisterweed. He stared blankly as the red smoke circled his head.

"I owe you," Jakkin said slowly up to him, hating to admit it. "I did not know Fool's Pride when I saw it. Another minute and the red would have been good for nothing but the stews. If I ever get a second fight, I will give you some of the gold. *Your bag is not yet full.*"

Jakkin meant the last phrase simply as ritual, but Likkarn's eyes suddenly roused to weed fury. His hand went to his throat. "You owe me nothing," said the old man. He held his head high, and the age lines on his neck crisscrossed like old fight scars. *"Nothing.* You owe the master everything. I need no reminder that I am a bonder. *I fill my bag myself.*"

Jakkin bowed his head under the old man's assault. "Let me tend the red's wounds. Then do with me as you will." He turned and, without waiting for an answer, ducked through the mecho-hole and slid down the shaft.

Jakkin came to the stall where the red was already at work grooming itself, polishing its scales with a combination of fire and spit. He slipped the ring around its neck and knelt down by its side. Briskly he put his hand out to touch its wounded wing, in a hurry to finish the examination before Likkarn came down. The red drew back at his touch, sending a mauve landscape into his mind, dripping with gray tears.

"Hush, little flametongue," crooned Jakkin, slowing himself down and using the lullaby sounds he had invented to soothe the hatchling of the sands. "I won't hurt thee. I want to help."

But the red continued to retreat from him, crouching against the wall.

Puzzled, Jakkin pulled his hand back, yet still the red huddled away, and a spurt of yellow-red fire flamed from its slits. "Not here, furnace-lung," said Jakkin, annoyed. "That will set the stall on fire."

A rough hand pushed him aside. It was Likkarn, no longer in the weed dream but starting into the uncontrollable fury that capped a weed sequence. The dragon, its mind open with the pain of its wound and the finish of the fight, had picked up Likkarn's growing anger and reacted to it.

"You don't know wounds," growled Likkarn. "I'll show you what a *real* trainer knows." He grabbed the dragon's torn wing and held it firmly; then with a quick motion, and before Jakkin could stop him, he set his mouth on the jagged tear.

The dragon reared back in alarm and tried to whip its tail around, but the stalls were purposely built small to curb such motion. Its tail scraped along the wall and barely tapped the man. But Jakkin grabbed at Likkarn's arm with both hands and furiously tore him from the red's wing.

"I'll kill you, you weeder," he screamed. "Can't you wait till a dragon is in the stews before you try to eat it. I'll kill you." He slammed at Likkarn with his fist and feet, knowing as he did it that the man's weed anger would be turned on him and he might be killed by it, and not caring. Suddenly Jakkin felt himself being lifted up from behind, his legs dangling, kicking uselessly at the air. A strong arm around his waist held him fast. Another pushed Likkarn back against the wall.

"Hold off, boy. He was a good trainer—once. And he's right about the best way to deal with a wing wound. An open part, filled with dragon's blood, might burn the tongue surely. But a man's tongue heals quickly, and there is something in human saliva that closes these small tears."

Jakkin twisted around as best he could and saw the man he had most feared seeing. It was Master Sarkkhan himself, in a leather suit of the red-and-gold nursery colors. His red beard was brushed out, and he looked grim.

Sarkkhan put the boy down but held on to him with one hand. With the other, he brushed his hair back from a forehead that was pitted with blood scores as evenly spaced as a bonder's chain. "Now promise me you will let Likkarn look to the red's wing."

"I will not. He's a weeder and he's as likely to rip the red as heal it, and the red hates him—just as I do," shouted Jakkin. There he stopped and put the back of his hand over his mouth, shocked at his own bold words.

Likkarn raised his hand to the boy and aimed a blow at his head, but before the slap landed, the dragon nosed forward and pushed the man to the ground.

Master Sarkkhan let go of Jakkin's shoulder and considered the red for a moment. "I think the boy is right, Likkarn. The dragon won't have you. It's too closely linked. I wouldn't have guessed that, but there it is. Best leave this to the boy and me."

Likkarn got up clumsily and brushed off his clothes. His bond bag had fallen over the top of his overall bib in the scuffle, and Jakkin was shocked to see that it was halfway plump, jangling with coins. Likkarn caught his look and angrily stuffed the bag back inside, then jabbed at the outline of Jakkin's bag under his shirt with a reddened finger. "And how much have *you* got there, boy?" He walked off with as much dignity as he could muster to slump by the stairwell and watch.

Sarkkhan ignored them both and crouched down by the dragon, letting it get the smell of him. He caressed its jaws and under its neck with his large, scarred hands. Slowly the big man worked his way back toward the wings, crooning at the dragon in low tones, smoothing its scales, all the while staring into its eyes. Slowly the membranes, top and bottom, shuttered the red's eyes, and it relaxed. Only then did Sarkkhan let his hand close over the wounded wing. The dragon gave a small shudder but was otherwise quite still.

"Your red did a good job searing its wound on the light. Did you teach it that?"

"No," the boy admitted.

"Of course not, foolish of me. How could you? No light in the sands. Good breeding, then," said Sarkkhan with a small chuckle of appreciation. "And I should know. After all, your dragon's mother is my best—Heart O' Mine."

"You . . . you knew all along, then." Jakkin felt as confused as a blooded First.

Sarkkhan stood up and stretched. In the confines of the stall he seemed enormous, a red-gold giant. Jakkin suddenly felt smaller than his years.

"*Fewmets,* boy. Of course I knew," Sarkkhan answered. "I know *everything* that happens at my nursery."

Jakkin collapsed down next to his dragon and put his arm over its neck. When he finally spoke, it was in a very small voice. "Then why did you let me do it? Why did you let me steal the dragon? Were you trying to get me in trouble? Do you want me in jail?"

The man threw back his head and roared, and the dragons in neighboring stalls stirred uneasily at the sound. Even Likkarn started at the laugh, and a trainer six stalls down growled in disapproval. Then Sarkkhan looked down at the boy, crouched by the red dragon. "I'm sorry, boy, I forget how young you are. Never known anyone quite that young to successfully train a hatchling. But every man gets a chance to steal one egg. It's a kind of test, you might say. The only way to break out of bond. Some men are meant to be bonders, some masters. How else can you tell? Likkarn's tried it—endless times, eh, old man?" The master glanced over at Likkarn with a look akin to affection, but Likkarn only glared back. "Steal an egg and try. The only things it is wrong to steal are a bad egg or your master's provisions." Sarkkhan stopped talking for a minute and mused, idly running a hand over the red dragon's back as it chewed contentedly now on its burnwort, little gray straggles of smoke easing from its slits. "Of course, most *do* steal bad eggs or are too impatient to train what comes out, and instead they make a quick sale to the stews just for a few coins to jangle in their bags. Then it's back to bond again before a month is out. It's only the ones who steal provisions that land in jail, boy."

"Then you won't put me in jail? Or the red in the stews? I couldn't let you do that, Master Sarkkhan. Not even you. I wouldn't let you. I . . ." Jakkin began to stutter, as he often did in his master's presence.

"Send a First Fighter, a *winner* to the stews? *Fewmets,* boy, where's your brain. Been smoking blisterweed?" Sarkkhan hunkered down next to him.

Jakkin looked down at his sandals. His feet were soiled from the dust of the stall. He ordered his stomach to calm down, and he felt an answering muted rainbow of calm from the dragon. Then a peculiar thought came to him. "Did *you* have to steal an egg, Master Sarkkhan?"

The big red-headed man laughed and thrust his hand right into Jakkin's face. Jakkin drew back, but Sarkkhan was holding up two fingers and wiggling them before his eyes.

"Two! I stole two. A male and a female. And it was not mere chance. Even then, I knew the difference. *In the egg* I knew. And that's why I'm the best breeder on Austar IV." He stood up abruptly and held out his hand to the boy. "But enough. The red is fine, and you are due upstairs." He yanked Jakkin to his feet and seemed at once to lose his friendliness.

"Upstairs?" Jakkin could not think what that meant. "You said I was not to go to jail. I want to stay with the red. I want . . ."

"*Wormwort,* boy, have you been listening or not? You have to register that dragon, give her a name, record her as a First Fighter, a winner."

"*Her?*" Jakkin heard only the one word.

"Yes, a her. Do you challenge *me* on that? And I want to come with you and collect my gold. I bet a bagful on that red of yours—on Likkarn's advice. He's been watching you train—my orders. He said she was looking good, and sometimes I believe him." Sarkkhan moved toward the stairwell where Likkarn still waited. "I owe him, you know. He taught me everything."

"Likkarn? Taught you?"

They stopped by the old man who was slumped again in another blisterweed dream. Sarkkhan reached out and took the stringy red weed ash from the old man's hand. He threw it on the floor and ground it savagely into the dust. "He wasn't born a weeder, boy. And he hasn't forgotten all he once knew." Then shaking his head, Master Sarkkhan moved up the stairs, impatiently waving a hand at the boy to follow.

A stray strand of color-pearls passed through Jakkin's mind, and he turned around to look at the dragon's stall. Then he gulped and said in a rush at Sarkkhan's back, "But she's a mute, Master. She may have won this fight by wiles, but she's a mute. No one will bet on a dragon that cannot roar."

The man reached down and grabbed Jakkin's hand, yanking him through the doorway and up the stairs. They mounted two at a time. "You really are lizard waste," said Sarkkhan, punctuating his sentences with another step. "Why do you think I sent a half-blind weeder skulking around the sands at night watching you train a snatchling? Because I'd lost my mind? *Fewmets,* boy. I want to know what is happening to every damned dragon I have bred, because I have had a hunch and a hope these past ten years, breeding small-voiced dragons together. I've been *trying* to breed a mute. Think of it, a mute fighter—why, it would give nothing away, not to pit foes or to bettors. A mute fighter and its trainer . . ." and Sarkkhan stopped on the stairs, looking down at the boy. "Why, they'd rule the pits, boy."

They finished the stairs and turned down the hallway. Sarkkhan strode ahead, and Jakkin had to doubletime in order to keep up with the big man's strides.

"Master Sarkkhan," he began at the man's back.

Sarkkhan did not break stride but growled, "I am no longer your master, Jakkin. *You* are a master now. A master trainer. That dragon will speak only to you, go only on your command. Remember that, and act accordingly."

Jakkin blinked twice and touched his chest. "But . . . but my bag is empty. I have no gold to fill it. I have no sponsor for my next fight. I . . ."

Sarkkhan whirled, and his eyes were fierce. "*I* am sponsor for your next fight. I thought that much, at least, was clear. And when your bag is full, you will pay me no gold for your bond. Instead, I want pick of the first hatching when the red is bred—to a mate of my choosing. If she is a complete mute, she may breed true, and *I* mean to have it."

"Oh, Master Sarkkhan," Jakkin cried, suddenly realizing that all his dreams were realities, "you may have the pick of the first *three* hatchings." He grabbed the man's hand and tried to shake his thanks into it.

"*Fewmets!*" the man yelled, startling some of the passers-by. He shook the boy's hand loose. "How can you ever become a bettor if you offer it all up front. You have to disguise your feelings better than that. Offer me the pick of the *third* hatching. Counter me. Make me work for whatever I get."

Jakkin said softly, testing, "The pick of the third."

"First two," said Sarkkhan, softly back and his smile came slowly. Then he roared, "Or I'll have you in jail and the red in the stews."

A crowd began to gather around them, betting on the outcome of the uneven match. Sarkkhan was a popular figure at pit-fights, and the boy was leather-patched—obviously a bonder, an unknown, worm waste.

All at once Jakkin felt as if he were at pitside. He felt the red's mind flooding into his, a rainbow effect that gave him a rush of courage. It was a game, then, all a game. And he knew how to play. "The second," said Jakkin, smiling back. "After all, Heart's Blood is a First Fighter, and a winner. And," he hissed at Sarkkhan so that only the two of them could hear, "she's a mute." Then he stood straight and said loudly, so that it carried to the crowd, "You'll be lucky to have pick of the second."

Sarkkhan stood silently, as if considering both the boy and the crowd. He brushed his hair back from his forehead, then nodded. "Done," he said. "A hard bargain." Then he reached over and ruffled Jakkin's hair, and they walked off together.

The crowd, settling their bets, let them through.

"I *thought* you were a good learner," Sarkkhan said to the boy. "Second it is. Though," and he chuckled and said quietly, "you should remember this. There is never anything good in a first hatching. Second is the best by far."

"I didn't know," said Jakkin.

"Why should you?" countered Sarkkhan. "*You* are not the best breeder on Austar IV. I am. But I like the name you picked. Heart's Blood out of Heart O' Mine. It suits."

They went through the doorway together to register the red and to stuff Jakkin's bag with hard-earned dragon's gold.

Brother Kenan's Bell

BROTHER KENAN WOKE in the night. He had had the most wondrous dream. An angel with a great smile of joy had come to him and said:

> Take you a bell into the wilderness, a bell without clapper or tongue. And when that bell shall ring by itself— there build a house of God.

When morning prayers were over, Brother Kenan hurried along the stone hall to the abbot's cell and told him of the dream.

"It *is* a strange dream," the abbot said, "for what is a bell without clapper or tongue?"

"A piece of metal?" asked Kenan.

"Just so," said the abbot with a smile. "A piece of metal. And do you think that I would send any of my monks into the wilderness with just a piece of metal to guide him? I am supposed to be a father to you all. What kind of a father would I be to let you go because of a single strange dream?"

Brother Kenan went into the monastery garden where he was to work that day. There he saw Brother David and Brother John, and told them about his dream.

Brother David, whose clever hands were never still, said, "Perhaps it was something you ate. Dreams often proceed from the stomach."

So Brother Kenan said no more.

But that night he dreamed again. This time the angel was not smiling, and said:

> Take you a bell into the wilderness, a bell without clapper or tongue. And when that bell rings by itself—there build a house of God with Brother David and Brother John.

Brother Kenan did not even wait for the morning prayers to be rung. He put on his sandals and hurried off to the abbot's cell, where he roused the good father with a shake. The abbot was annoyed to be awakened before the bells, but he did not show it with his words or eyes. Only his mouth was angry and drawn into a hard line.

"It is certainly another strange dream," admitted the abbot. "But I myself have had many such dreams. Perhaps you are working too hard."

"But the angel knew Brother David's name," protested Kenan. "And he knew Brother John's name, too."

"Then he read your heart," said the abbot. "Surely an angel could do that." Then he turned over on his side and said, "Go back to bed, Brother Kenan."

After prayers Brother Kenan went to work in the monastery kitchen with Brother David and Brother John. He told them of his second dream.

Brother John, who could heal any ache with his herbs, said, "I have a simple that will help you sleep. And in *that* sleep you will not dream."

So Brother Kenan said no more.

But that night he dreamed again. This time the angel came and took him by the shoulder and shook him hard and said:

Take you a bell into the wilderness, a bell without
clapper or tongue. And when that bell rings by itself—there
build a house of God with Brother David and Brother John.
AND DO IT SOON!

Brother Kenan did not even stop to put on his sandals. He
hurried down the dark corridor to the abbot's cell. He burst in,
and was surprised to see the abbot sitting up in his bed. By his
side were David and John.

"I have had yet another dream," began Kenan.

"Come," said the abbot with a great smile, and opened his
arms. "So have we all. In the morning we must search for a
piece of iron for your quest."

In the morning, after prayers, the three monks and the
abbot looked all around the monastery for metal for the bell.
But except for small nails and smaller needles, the pots and
pans to cook the monastery meals, some rakes and hoes in the
garden, and a knocker on the door, no metal could be found.

The abbot gave a large sigh. "I suppose I must give you
our only bell," he said at last. "Come up with me to the bell
tower."

So the four climbed to the top of the tower, high up where
only Brother Angelus, the bell master, went. And there, lying
under the chapel's bell, was an iron bar.

"I have never seen it before," said Brother Angelus with
awe. "It is a miracle."

The abbot merely nodded and sighed again, this time in
thanks. Such miracles, he knew, often occurred when one was
as old and as forgetful as the bell master. Still, when the four
had descended the stairs, the abbot blessed the bar and gave it
to Kenan.

"Go you must," he said, "so go with God."

The three monks left the monastery and took the road
going north. Only to the north was the land empty of towns.

Brother Kenan was in the lead, carrying the iron bar like a
banner before them.

Brother David was next, his pack filled with bread and

cheese and string with which to practice knots, for his fingers always had to be busy with something.

Brother John was last, his basket filled with herbs and simples in case of any accidents or ills.

The three monks traveled for nearly three weeks. Their food ran out, and John found berries and mushrooms and roots. Their wine gave out, and David found a fresh, flowing spring. Their spirits ran low, and Kenan cheered them on with a psalm. And always the silent iron bar went before.

One day, though, Brother David grew weary. He thought to himself, "Perhaps it was not a holy dream after all. I swear that that bell will never ring on its own. I must make the miracle happen." So that night his clever fingers fashioned a sling of the strings. And in the morning, as they marched along, he walked behind and aimed several small stones at the iron bar. But the stones went left or the stones went right. Each shot missed, and Brother Kenan marched on with the bell as silent as ever.

The next day Brother John grew weary. He thought to himself, "All dreams do not come from God. That bell will never ring by itself. Sometimes one must help a miracle along." So he waited until he found a bush with hard, inedible berries growing along the path. He grabbed up a handful and threw the lot of them at Kenan's back. But the berries went left or the berries went right. Not one of them struck the bar, and Brother Kenan marched on with the bell as silent as ever.

The next day the monks came upon a broad meadow that stretched down to the banks of a tumbling stream.

"This would be a lovely place to build a house of God," thought Kenan with a sigh, for he, too, was weary. But putting such a thought behind him as unworthy of his dream, he shouldered the iron bar and walked on.

Just then, a small brown bird flew across the meadow, fleeing from a hawk. The little bird ducked and dived to escape its pursuer, and in its flight it flew straight toward the three monks. At the last minute, noticing them, it turned sharply and rammed into the iron bar. It broke its wing and fell.

As the hawk veered off into the woods, the iron bar sang out from the collision with a single clear and brilliant tone.

"The bell!" cried David and John as one.

"The bird!" cried Brother Kenan. He jammed the iron bar into the soft sod of the meadow and took up the wounded bird. And when he picked the bird up, the iron bar standing straight and true in the meadow grass rang out again and again and again. Each note was like a peal of hosannas to the Lord.

So the monks built their house of God in the meadow by the river. Brother David's wonderful hands and Brother John's wonderful simples cured the wounded bird. And with patient care, Brother Kenan melted down the iron bar and cast a perfect bell.

Ever after, the little brown bird sang outside Brother Kenan's window to call the many monks who worked in the abbey to their prayers. And its voice was as clear and as loud and as pure as the monks' own iron bell.

Sans Soleil

THERE WAS ONCE A PRINCE called Sans Soleil, which is to say, Sunless. It had been prophesied at his birth that he would grow so handsome his beauty would outshine the sun. That he might not be killed by the jealous star, he had to be kept in the dark, for it was said that he would die if ever a shaft of sunlight fell upon his brow.

So the very night he was born, his father, the king, had him carried away to a castle that was carved out of rock. And in that candlelit cave-castle, the young prince grew and flourished without ever seeing the sun.

Now, by the time Sans Soleil was twenty years old, the story of his strange beauty and of the evil prediction had been told at every hearth and hall in the kingdom. And every maiden of marrying age had heard his tragic tale.

But one in particular, Viga, the daughter of a duke, did not believe what she heard.

"Surely," she said, tossing her raven-black hair from her

face, "surely the king has hidden his son from the light because he is too monstrous to behold."

Her father shook his head. "Nay," he replied. "I have been to this cave-castle and have seen this prince. He is handsomer than the sun."

But still Viga did not believe what her father told her. "The sun cannot harm anyone," she said. "There is no sense in what you say." And she took herself to the king dressed in her finest gown of silver and gold.

"Sire," she said, "at court you have been taken in by lies. The sun is not harmful. It nourishes. It causes all things to grow. It will not kill the prince."

The king was touched by the girl's sincerity. He was moved by her beauty. He was awed by her strength of purpose, for it is no little thing to contradict a king. Still, he shook his head and said, "It was prophesied at his birth that he would die if ever a shaft of sunlight struck his brow."

"Old wives and young babes believe such tales. They should not frighten you, sire. They do not frighten me," Viga replied.

"They do not frighten you because you are not the one who would die," said the king, and at these words all the courtiers smiled and nodded their heads and murmured to one another. "Still, I will give the matter more thought."

Viga gave a low curtsey. And as she rose, she said quietly, so that only the king could hear it, "It does seem strange that *sun* and *son* do sound the same." Then she smiled brightly and departed.

The king was true to his word and gave the matter more thought. And what he concluded was this: that his son and Viga should be wed. For he liked her courage and admired her beauty, and thought she would make his son a most suitable wife. So the king and the duke set the wedding date for a week from the following night.

When the night was deep and no spot of sun still lit the kingdom, a carriage with drawn curtains arrived at Viga's door. Out stepped the handsomest man she had ever seen. He was dressed all in red and gold, like the sun.

They were wed by candlelight, and their golden rings were carved with images of the sun. There was feasting and dancing till three. Then the two talked and kissed far into the night, as befits a couple who are but newly wed.

But at the crowing of the village cocks announcing that the sun would soon rise, Sans Soleil stood up. "I must go. I cannot allow the sun to shine upon me."

"Do not leave me," Viga said. "Now that we are wed, I cannot bear to have you away from my sight. Do not be afraid of the sun. It will not harm you. Stay here with me."

"No, I am safe only in my cave. You are my wife; come and live in my cave-castle with me."

"Live in a cave?" said Viga. "Never."

So the prince tore himself from her grasp and ran out into the waiting golden carriage. With a crack of the whip, the horses were away before the sun could gain the sky.

However, Viga was a woman of strong will. So determined was she to prove to Sans Soleil that she was right and he would not be killed by the sun, she devised a plan. That very day she sent her maidservants to buy up all the cockerels in the kingdom. Then she had her footmen bind the birds and throw them down into the duke's deepest dungeons, where it would always be dark as night.

But there was one rooster the servants could not buy, the pet of the potter's boy. The child cried so much at the thought of losing his bird, his father would not part with it.

"What is one cockerel out of so many?" the servants asked themselves. And so they neglected to tell their mistress of the last bird.

That evening again Sans Soleil's carriage came to Viga's door. As before, the prince was dressed all in red and gold like the sun, and the feathers on his cap stood out like golden rays. In his hand he carried a sunburst, a ruby brooch with beams like a star.

"This is my only sun," he said to Viga. "Now it is yours."

And they forgave one another for the harsh words of the morn. They touched and kissed as married couples do, far into the night.

At the coming of the dawn, far off in the village, the cockerel belonging to the potter's child began to crow.

"Is that a cockerel I hear?" asked Sans Soleil, sitting up.

"There is no cockerel," replied Viga sleepily, for she thought indeed there was none.

But again the rooster crowed out, and, hearing no answering call from his brothers, he sang out louder than before.

"I am sure I hear the warning of the sun's approach," said Sans Soleil.

"It is nothing but a servant's snore," Viga replied. "Stay quiet. Stay asleep. Stay with me."

But on the third crow, Sans Soleil leaped up. "I must go," he said. "I cannot allow the sun to shine upon me."

"Do not put your faith in such old wives' tales," cried Viga. "The sun cannot hurt you. Put your faith in me."

But it was too late. The prince was gone, running down into his golden carriage and away to his cave–castle before the sun could start up in the sky.

However, Viga was a woman of strong will and passion. She was determined not to lose her lover for a single day because of such a foolish tale. She was convinced that if the prince but forgot the sun, he would learn that it could do him no harm. So she decided to have the last rooster put in her father's dungeon.

But she did not trust her servants anymore. With her cloak wrapped about her and covering her face with a sleeve, Viga slipped out into the streets. By the potter's hut she saw the bird strutting and preening its feathers in the sun. Quickly, she looked around, but there was no one in sight. She reached down, snatched up the cockerel, and hid it under her cloak. In the night of her garment the bird made no sound.

She was back in her own home before the potter's child could set up his wail. The cockerel she put with its brothers in the dark. Then she waited impatiently for the sun to set that she might see her lover again.

That evening, so great was his haste, Sans Soleil himself drove the golden carriage to the door. He leaped to the ground and in a graceful bound ran to the waiting girl.

They ate and touched and sang and danced and talked until the night was through. But there were no cockerels to crow and warn them of the dawn.

Suddenly the prince glanced out of the window. "It is becoming light," he cried. "I must leave. You know that I cannot allow the sun to shine on me."

"Love me. Trust me. Stay with me," said Viga, smoothing his hair with her strong hands.

But Sans Soleil glanced out of the window again. "Is that the sun? Tell me, for I have never seen it shine."

Viga smoothed his neck with her fingers. "Forget your foolish fears. The sun nourishes. It does not kill. Stay with me here and greet the dawn."

The prince was moved by her plea and by his love for her. But just as he was about to stay, fear, like an old habit, conquered him. He jumped up and blinked at the light. "I must go to my cave. Only there will I be safe," he cried. And before she could stop him, he tore from her grasp and sped out into the dawn.

Viga ran after him. "Do not be afraid," she called. Her long black hair streamed out behind her like the rays of a black star. "It is but a tale. A tale for children. *You* are the sun."

But the prince did not hear her. As he ran out into the courtyard, the sun rose in full brilliance over the wall. Sans Soleil had never seen anything so glorious before. He stood and stared at the burning star. The sunlight struck him full in the face. And with a single cry of pain or anger or regret, he fell down dead.

Viga saw him fall. She cried out, "Oh, Sans Soleil, it was true. Who would have believed it? Now it is I who am sunless, for you were my sun."

She threw herself upon his still form, her breast against his, her cool white brow on the ashes of his, and wept.

The next year, in the courtyard where Sans Soleil had fallen, a single sunflower grew. But unlike others of its kind, it bloomed all year around and always turned its face away from the sun.

Viga had a belvedere built around it. There she spent her days, tending the flower, watering it, and turning its soil.

When visitors arrived at her father's house, she would tell them the story of her love for Sans Soleil. And the story always ended with this caution: "Sometimes," Viga would say, "what we believe is stronger than what is true."

The Seventh Mandarin

ONCE IN THE EAST, where the wind blows gently on the bells of the temple, there lived a king of the highest degree.

He was a good king. And he knew the laws of his land. But of his people he knew nothing at all, for he had never been beyond the high stone walls that surrounded his palace.

All day long the king read about his kingdom in the books and scrolls that were kept in the palace. And all day long he was guarded and guided by the seven mandarins who had lived all their lives, as the king had, within the palace walls.

These mandarins were honorable men. They dressed in silken robes and wore embroidered slippers. They ate from porcelain dishes and drank the most delicate teas.

Now, while it was important that the mandarins guarded and guided their king throughout his days, they had a higher duty still. At night they were the guardians of the king's soul.

It was written in the books and scrolls of the kingdom that each night the king's soul left his body and flew into the sky on the wings of a giant kite. And the king and the seven mandarins believed that what was written in the books and scrolls was true. And so, each mandarin took turns flying the king's kite through the long, dark hours, keeping it high above the terrors of the night.

This kite was a giant dragon. Its tail was of silk with colored tassels. Its body was etched with gold. And when the sun quit that kingdom in the East, the giant kite rose like a serpent in the wind, flown by one of the seven mandarins.

And for uncounted years it was so.

Now, of all the mandarins, the seventh was the youngest. He was also the most simple. While the other mandarins enjoyed feasting and dancing and many rich pleasures, the seventh mandarin loved only three things in all the world. He loved the king, the books and scrolls of the law, and the king's giant kite.

That he loved his king there was no doubt, for the seventh mandarin would not rest until the king rested.

That he loved the books and scrolls there was also no doubt. Not only did the seventh mandarin believe that what was written therein was true. He also believed that what was *not* written was *not* true.

But more than his king and more than the books and scrolls of the law, the seventh mandarin loved the king's kite, the carrier of the king's soul. He could make it dip and soar and crest the currents of air like a falcon trained to his hand.

One night, when it was the turn of the seventh mandarin to fly the king's kite, the sky was black with clouds. A wild wind like no wind before it entered the kingdom.

The seventh mandarin was almost afraid to fly the kite, for he had never seen such a wind. But he knew that he had to send it into the sky. The king's kite *must* fly, or the king's soul would be in danger. And so the seventh mandarin sent the kite aloft.

The minute the giant kite swam into the sky, it began to rage and strain at the string. It twisted and turned and dived and pulled. The wind gnawed and fretted and goaded the kite, ripping at its tender belly and snatching at its silken tail. At last, with a final snap, the precious kite string parted.

Before the seventh mandarin's eyes, the king's kite sailed wildly over the palace spires, over the roofs of the mandarins' mansions, over the high walls that surrounded the courtyards, and out of sight.

"Come back, come back, O Magnificent Wind Bird," cried the seventh mandarin. "Come back with the king's soul, and I will tip your tail with gold and melt silver onto your wings."

But the kite did not come back.

The seventh mandarin ran down the steps. He put his cape about his face so that no one would know him. He ran through the echoing corridors. He ran past the mandarins' mansions and through the gates of the high palace walls. Then he ran where he had never been before—past the neat houses of the merchants, past the tiny homes of the workers, past the canals that held the peddlers' boats, past the ramshackle, falling-down huts and hovels of the poor.

At last, in the distance, hovering about the hills that marked the edge of the kingdom, the seventh mandarin saw something flutter like a wounded bird in the sky. And though the wind pushed and pulled at his cape and at last tore it from his back, the seventh mandarin did not stop. He ran and ran until he came to the foot of the mountain.

There he found the king's kite. But what a terrible sight met his eyes. The wings of the dragon were dirty and torn. Its tail was shredded and bare. The links of its body were broken apart.

It would never fly again.

The seventh mandarin did not know what to do. He was afraid to return to the palace. It was not that he feared for his own life. He feared for the life of his king. For if the king's soul had flown on the wings of the kite, the king was surely dead.

Yet, much as he was afraid to return, the seventh mandarin was more afraid not to. And so he gathered the king's kite in his arms and began the long, slow journey back.

He carried the king's kite past the canals and the ram-shackle, falling-down huts and hovels of the poor. And as he passed with the broken kite in his arms, it came to him that he had never read of such things in the books and scrolls of the kingdom. Yet the cries and groans he heard were not made by the wind.

At last, as the first light of the new day touched the gates of the high palace walls, the seventh mandarin entered the courtyard. He climbed the stairs to his chamber and placed the battered, broken kite on his couch.

Then he sat down and waited to hear of the death of the king.

Scarcely an hour went by before all seven of the mandarins were summoned to the king's chamber. The king lay on his golden bed. His face was pale and still. His hands lay like two withered leaves by his side.

Surely, thought the seventh mandarin, I have killed my king. And he began to weep.

But slowly the king opened his eyes.

"I dreamed a dream last night," he said, his voice low and filled with pain. "I dreamed that in my kingdom there are ramshackle hovels and huts that are falling down."

"It is not so," said the six mandarins, for they had never been beyond the high palace walls and so had never seen such things.

Only the seventh mandarin was silent.

"I dreamed that in my kingdom," continued the king, "there are people who sigh and moan—people who cry and groan when the night is dark and deep."

"It is not so," said the six mandarins, for they had never read of such things in the books and scrolls.

The seventh mandarin was silent.

"If it is not so," said the king, slowly raising his hand to his head, "then how have I dreamed it? For is it not written that the dream is the eye of the soul? And if my soul was flying on the wings of my kite and these things are not so, then how did my dream see all this?"

The six mandarins were silent.

Then the seventh mandarin spoke. He was afraid, but he spoke. And he said, "O King, I saw these same things last night, and I did not dream!"

The six mandarins looked at the seventh mandarin in astonishment.

But the seventh mandarin continued. "The wind was a wild, mad beast. It ripped your kite from my hands. And the kite flew like an angel in the night to these same huts and hovels of which you dreamed. And there are many who moan and sigh, who groan and cry beyond the high palace walls. There are many—although it is not written in any of the books or scrolls of the kingdom."

Then the seventh mandarin bowed his head and waited for his doom. For it was death to fail the king. And it was death to damage his kite. And it was death to say that what was *not* written in the books and scrolls was so.

Then the king spoke, his voice low and crackling like the pages of an ancient book. "For three reasons that you already know, you deserve to die."

The other mandarins looked at one another and nodded.

"But," said the king, sitting up in his golden bed, "for discovering the truth and not fearing to reveal it, you deserve to live." And he signaled the seventh mandarin to stand at his right hand.

That very night, the king and his seven mandarins made their way to the mountain at the edge of the kingdom. There they buried the king's kite with honors.

And the next morning, when the kingdom awoke, the people found that the high walls surrounding the palace had been leveled to the ground.

As for the king, he never again relied solely upon the laws of the land, but instead rode daily with his mandarins through the kingdom. He met with his people and heard their pleas. He listened and looked as well as read.

The mandarins never again had to fly the king's kite as a duty. Instead, once a year, at a great feast, they sent a giant dragon kite into the sky to remind themselves and their king of the folly of believing only what is written.

And the king, with the seventh mandarin always by his side, ruled a land of good and plenty until he came to the end of his days.

The Soul Fisher

IN A TIME WHEN THE RIVERS RAN crystal clear all the way down to the sea, there lived a man in a cave. The cave was in the center of the world and was fed by many streams. It was mostly dark in the cave, and the spring waters made it slippery and cold. Yet the man lived there alone all the year around.

He bathed in the cold, clear streams. He caught the blind fish that swam in the dark, whose shapes were ugly but whose meat was sweet. And he fished out stoppered bottles that washed into a central pool.

In each bottle was a message from the world outside the cave.

And when the man had taken the bottle from the pool and unstoppered it, he would read the message by the light of his single torch. Then, with a pen made from the rib of a fish and silver ink made from fish scales, he would try to scribe an answer. The answer he placed back in the bottle, which he set upright in a whittled boat with a miniature torch at the bow.

Sailing out, the flickering bowlight would cast its answer onto the sides of the cave.

The man was called the Fisher of Souls.

Now there was, at that time, a great and terrible war in the world outside the cave, and even little children took to carrying swords. Where once the land had been green with spring, it was now sere and torn with a thousand wounds. During one gasp in the respiration of battle, someone had an idea.

"Why don't we ask the Fisher of Souls to come out of the cave. Instead of sending us messages one by one by one, he could tell all of us what to do at the same time, and in this way end the war."

At first it was just one man and one thought, and the war overwhelmed the one. But a woman took up his cry, so then there were two of them wandering the land.

"Call up the Fisher of Souls from his cave," they cried. "Instead of helping one by one, he can help us all at the same time."

They wandered from village to town, from city to farm, and the one who had become two became ten and then twenty and then forty and then hundreds.

But the Soul Fisher could not hear them, living as he did far down under the land in his cold, dark home.

"Why don't we send him a message?" asked a child. "Each message could read the same."

So the hundreds of men and women and children laid down their swords and wrote the same message on scraps of paper. They placed these messages in stoppered bottles and tossed them into the streams. And soon all the bottles swam their slow, blind passage to the Soul Fisher's pool.

"Come up to the light. Help us stop the war," read the notes.

The Soul Fisher read note after note, and each was the same. The message moved him deeply. He thought that he would like to tell the people all at once what to do. But then he shook his head wearily and brushed his long, gray hair out of his eyes with a thin hand. He took up his pen and wrote "If there is real need, I will come."

Within days, the men and women and children replied: "There is need. We all need."

The Soul Fisher read note after note, and each was the same. So he wrote a simple answer—"I am coming"—and sent it into the stream. Then, with his torch in one hand, the other touching the dark, dank walls of the cave, he followed the answer through the twisting tunnel up and up toward the light of the world.

It took him many days to reach the mouth of the cave. The sudden wind guttered his torch. The late-afternoon sun hurt his eyes. The sound of the animals in the fields broke like great waves upon his ears.

Emerging from the cave, the Soul Fisher saw hundreds of people standing in silence on the plain before him. Then they waved their arms wildly, and the vision cut like a thousand swords.

They cried out, "Fisher of Souls, Fisher of Souls!" and the noise of it would have turned him around if the messages they had sent had not carried him forward.

The Fisher of Souls stepped into the crowd, and it parted as if struck by an invisible blow. The ground felt strangely familiar beneath his feet. He walked without willing it to the gates of a palace. Then he moved through the gates to the palace itself, through room after room till he came to a golden throne. He mounted the steps and sat on the throne.

And all the while the hundreds of people followed crying out his name: "Fisher of Souls! Fisher of Souls!"

With a great effort, he raised his hands for silence. And there fell upon the palace a silence as deep as any he had ever heard in a cave.

"I am here *in* answer to your one great need," he said. "I have come *to* answer your one great need." His hands felt along the throne's ornate sides, remembering on their own. Then, speaking to himself, the Soul Fisher said, "Once long ago—so long ago there are hardly any of you here who might remember it—this was my throne and I was your king. I tried to rule wisely. But whenever I made a judgment, not everyone was pleased. One ruling led to another, and again there were those who were not pleased. So I ran away from my throne and fled to the cave." He sighed, his voice cracking. "It is a hard life, the cave," he said, "but far easier than here. To answer one wish at a time, to solve one small problem at a time, to please each seeker without hurting another, is easier than trying to answer many."

But no one was listening to the Soul Fisher. For no sooner had he begun to speak than the people broke the silence, too.

"I need," shouted one woman.

She was jostled aside by another. "We need . . ." began a man.

Two women shoved him aside. "Listen to us, O Fisher of Souls," they cried.

A small child ran up to the throne and pulled at his hand. "I need—" and was slapped away by a crone.

"One at a time," the Soul Fisher begged.

But no one heard. The people jostled and shouted and pushed and shoved to get to him. They argued and wrangled and finally a sword was lifted.

No one noticed the Soul Fisher slipping away.

He walked slowly down the marble halls and out into the rent land. He walked past the broken houses and torn fields, past burned-out farmyards and gutted barns, until he came at last to the mouth of his cave. Sadly he looked around at the hills and valleys of his kingdom. Then he made a small fire and relit his torch.

Holding his torch in one hand, he descended the winding, slippery tunnel back to the center of the cave.

There in the sputtering light of the torch, he sat down on the cold rocks. He watched the blind fish swim back and forth. And he waited for the first stoppered bottle to arrive with a question.

He knew he would not have long to wait.

One Old Man, with Seals

THE DAY WAS CLEAR AND SHARP AND FRESH when I first heard the seals. They were crying, a symphony of calls. The bulls coughed a low bass. The pups had a mewing whimper, not unlike the cry of a human child. I heard them as I ran around the lighthouse, the slippery sands making my ritual laps more exercise than I needed, more than the doctor said a seventy-five-year-old woman should indulge in. Of course he didn't say it quite like that. Doctors never do. He said: "A woman of your age . . ." and left it for me to fill in the blanks. It was a physician's pathetically inept attempt at tact. Any lie told then would be mine, not his.

However, as much as doctors know about blood and bones, they never do probe the secret recesses of the heart. And my heart told me that I was still twenty-five. Well, forty-five, anyway. And I had my own methods of gray liberation.

I had bought a lighthouse, abandoned as unsafe and no longer viable by the Coast Guard. (Much as I had been by the county library system. One abandoned and no-longer-viable children's librarian, greatly weathered and worth one gold watch, no more.) I spent a good part of my savings renovating, building bookcases, and having a phone line brought in. And making sure the electricity would run my refrigerator, freezer, hi-fi, and TV set. I am a solitary, not a primitive, and my passion is the news. With in-town cable, I could have watched twenty-four hours a day. But in my lighthouse, news magazines and books of history took up the slack.

Used to a life of discipline and organization, I kept to a rigid schedule even though there was no one to impress with my dedication. But I always sang as I worked. As some obscure poet has written, "No faith can last that never sings." Up at daylight, a light breakfast while watching the morning newscasters, commercials a perfect time to scan *Newsweek* or *Time*. Then off for my morning run. Three laps seemed just right to get lungs and heart working. Then back inside to read until my nephew called. He is a classics scholar at the university, and my favorite relative. I've marked him down in my will for all my books and subscriptions—and the lighthouse. The others will split the little bit of money I have left. Since I have been a collector of fine and rare history books for over fifty years, my nephew will be well off, though he doesn't know it yet.

The phone rings between ten and eleven every morning, and it is always Mike. He wants to be sure I'm still alive and kicking. The one time I had flu and was too sick to answer the phone, he was over like a shot in that funny lobster boat of his. I could hear him pounding up the stairs and shouting my name. He even had his friend, Dr. Lil Meyer, with him. A *real* doctor, he calls her, not his kind, "all letters and no learning."

They gave me plenty of juice and spent several nights, though it meant sleeping on the floor for both of them. But they didn't seem to mind. And when I was well again, they took off in the lobster boat, waving madly and leaving a wake as broad as a city sidewalk.

For a doctor, Lil Meyer wasn't too bad. She seemed to know about the heart. She said to me—whispered so Mike wouldn't hear her—just before she left, "You're sounder than any seventy-five-year-old I've ever met, Aunt Lyssa. I don't know if it's the singing or the running or the news. But whatever it is, just keep doing it. And Mike and I will keep tabs on you."

The day I heard the seals singing, I left off my laps and went investigating. It never does to leave a mystery unsolved at my age. Curiosity alone would keep me awake, and I need my sleep. Besides, I knew that the only singing done on these shores recently was my own. Seals never came here, hadn't for at least as long as I had owned the lighthouse. And according to the records, which the Coast Guard had neglected to collect when they condemned the place, leaving me with a week-long feast of old news, there hadn't been any seals for the last hundred years. Oh, there had been plenty else—wrecks and flotsam. Wrackweed wound around the detritus of civilization: Dixie cups, beer cans, pop bottles, and newsprint. And a small school of whales had beached themselves at the north tip of the beach in 1957 and had to be hauled off by an old whaling vessel, circa 1923, pressed into service. But no seals.

The lighthouse sits way out on a tip of land, some sixteen miles from town, and at high tide it is an island. There have been some minor skirmishes over calling it a wildlife preserve, but the closest the state has come to that has been to post some yellow signs that have weathered to the color of old mustard and are just as readable. The southeast shore is the milder shore, sheltered from the winds and battering tides. The little bay that runs between Lighthouse Point and the town of Tarryton-across-the-Bay, as the early maps have it, is always filled with pleasure boats. By half-May, the bigger yachts of the summer folk start to arrive, great white swans gliding serenely in while the smaller, colorful boats of the year-rounders squawk and gabble and gawk at them, darting about like so many squabbling mallards or grebes.

The singing of the seals came from the rougher northwest shore. So I headed that way, no longer jogging because it was a rocky run. If I slipped and fell, I might lie with a broken hip or arm for hours or days before Mike finally came out to find me. *If* he found me at all. So I picked my way carefully around the granite outcroppings.

I had only tried that northern route once or twice before. Even feeling twenty-five or forty-five, I found myself defeated by the amount of rock-climbing necessary to go the entire way. But I kept it up this time, because after five minutes the seal song had become louder, more melodic, compelling. And, too, an incredible smell had found its way into my nose.

I say *found,* because one of the sadder erosions of age has been a gradual loss of my sense of smell. Oh, really sharp odors eventually reach me, and I am still sensitive to the intense prickles of burned wood. But the subtle tracings of a good liqueur or the shadings of a wine's bouquet are beyond me. And recently, to my chagrin, I burned up my favorite teakettle because the whistle had failed and I didn't smell the metal melting until it was too late.

However, this must have been a powerful scent to have reached me out near the ocean, with the salt air blowing at ten miles an hour. Not a really strong wind, as coastal winds go, but strong enough.

And so I followed my ear—and my nose.

They led me around one last big rock, about the size of a small Minke whale. And it was then I saw the seals. They were bunched together and singing their snuffling hymns. Lying in their midst was an incredibly dirty bum, asleep and snoring.

I almost turned back then, but the old man let out a groan. Only then did it occur to me what a bizarre picture it was. Here was a bearded patriarch of the seals—for they were quite unafraid of him—obviously sleeping off a monumental drunk. In fact I had no idea where he had gotten and consumed his liquor, or how he had ever made it to that place, sixteen miles from the nearest town by land, and a long swim by sea. There was no boat to be seen. He lay as if dropped from above, one arm flung over a large bull seal which acted like a pup, snuggling close to him and pushing at his armpit with its nose.

At that I laughed out loud, and the seals, startled by the noise, fled down the shingle toward the sea, humping their way across the rocks and pebbly beach to safety in the waves. But the old man did not move.

It was then that I wondered if he were not drunk but rather injured, flung out of the sea by the tide, another bit of flotsam on my beach. So I walked closer.

The smell was stronger, and I realized it was not the seals I had been smelling. It was the old man. After years of dealing with children in libraries—from babies to young adults—I had learned to identify a variety of smells, from feces to vomit to pot. And though my sense of smell was almost defunct, my memory was not. But that old man smelled of none of the things I could easily recognize, or of anything the land had to offer. He smelled of seals and salt and water, like a wreck that had long lain on the bottom of the ocean suddenly uncovered by a freak storm. He smelled of age, incredible age. I could literally smell the centuries on him. If I was seventy-five, he had to be four— no, forty—times that. That was fanciful of me. Ridiculous. But it was my immediate and overwhelming thought.

I bent over him to see if I could spot an injury, something I might deal with reasonably. His gray-white, matted hair was thin and lay over his scalp like the scribbles of a mad artist. His beard was braided with seaweed, and shells lay entangled in the briary locks. His fingernails were encrusted with dirt. Even the line of his face were deeply etched with a greenish grime. But I saw no wounds.

His clothes were an archeological dig. Around his neck were the collars of at least twenty shirts. Obviously he put on one shirt and wore it until there was nothing left but the ring, then simply donned another. His trousers were a similar rag-bag of colors and weaves, and only the weakness of waistbands had kept him from having accumulated a lifetime supply. He was barefoot. The nails on his toes were as yellow as jingle shells, and so long they curled over each toe like a sheath.

He moaned again, and I touched him on the shoulder, hoping to shake him awake. But when I touched him, his shoulder burst into flames. Truly. Little fingers of fire spiked my palm. Spontaneous combustion was something I had only read about: a heap of oily rags in a hot closet leading to fire. But his rags were not oily, and the weather was a brisk sixty-eight degrees, with a good wind blowing.

I leaped back and screamed, and he opened one eye.

The flames subsided, went out. He began to snore again.

The bull seals came out of the water and began a large, irregular circle around us. So I stood up and turned to face them.

"Shoo!" I said, taking off my watch cap. I wear it to keep my ears warm when I run. "Shoo!" Flapping the cap at them and stepping briskly forward, I challenged the bulls.

They broke circle and scattered, moving about a hundred feet away in that awkward shuffling gait they have on land. Then they turned and stared at me. The younger seals and the females remained in the water, a watchful bobbing.

I went back to the old man. "Come on," I said. "I know you're awake now. Be sensible. Tell me if anything hurts or aches. I'll help you if you need help. And if not—I'll just go away."

He opened the one eye again and cleared his throat. It sounded just like a bull seal's cough. But he said nothing.

I took a step closer and he opened his other eye. They were as blue as the ocean over white sand. Clear and clean, the only clean part of him.

I bent over to touch his shoulder again, and this time the material of his shirt began to smolder under my hand.

"That's a trick," I said. "Or hypnotism. Enough of that."

He smiled. And the smoldering ceased. Instead, his shoulder seemed to tumble under my hand, like waves, like torrents, like a full high tide. My hand and sleeve were suddenly wet; sloppily, thoroughly wet.

I clenched my teeth. Mike always said that New England spinsters are so full of righteous fortitude they might be mistaken for mules. And my forebears go back seven generations in Maine. Maybe I didn't understand what was happening, but that was no excuse for lack of discipline and not holding on. I held on.

The old man sighed.

Under my hand, the shoulder changed again, the material and then the flesh wriggling and humping. A tail came from somewhere under his armpit and wrapped quickly around my wrist.

Now, as a librarian in a children's department I have had my share of snake programs, and reptiles as such do not frighten me. Spiders I am not so sanguine about. But snakes are not a phobia of mine. Except for a quick intake of breath, brought on by surprise, not fear, I did not loose my grip.

The old man gave a *humph,* a grudging sound of approval, closed his eyes, and roared like a lion. I have seen movies. I have watched documentaries. I know the difference. All of Africa was in that sound.

I laughed. "All right, whoever you are, enough games," I said. "What's going on?"

He sat up slowly, opened those clean blue eyes, and said, "Wrong question, my dear." He had a slight accent I could not identify. "You are supposed to ask, 'What *will* go on?' "

Angrily, I let go of his shoulder. "Obviously you need no help. I'm leaving."

"Yes," he said. "I know." Then, incredibly, he turned over on his side. A partial stuttering snore began at once. Then a whiff of that voice came at me again. "But of course you *will* be back."

"Of course I *will* not!" I said huffily. As an exit line it lacked both dignity and punch, but it was all I could manage as I walked off. Before I had reached the big rock, the seals had settled down around him again. I know because they were singing their lullabies over the roar of his snore—and I peeked. The smell followed me most of the way back home.

Once back in the lighthouse, a peculiar lethargy claimed me. I seemed to know something I did not want to know. A story suddenly recalled. I deliberately tried to think of everything but the old man. I stared out the great windows, a sight that always delighted me. Sky greeted me, a pallid slate of sky written on by guillemots and punctuated by gulls. A phalanx of herring gulls sailed by, followed by a pale ghostly shadow that I guessed might be an Iceland gull. Then nothing but sky. I don't believe I even blinked.

The phone shrilled.

I picked it up and could not even manage a hello until Mike's voice recalled me to time and place.

"Aunt Lyssa. Are you there? Are you all right? I tried to call before and there was no answer."

I snapped myself into focus. "Yes, Mike. I'm fine. Tell me a story."

There was a moment of crackling silence at the other end. Then a throat-clearing. "A story? Say, are you sure you're all right?"

"I'm sure."

"Well, what do you mean—a story?"

I held on to the phone with both hands, as if to coax his answer. As if I had foresight, I knew his answer already. "About an old man, with seals," I said.

Silence.

"You're the classics scholar, Mike. Tell me about Proteus."

"Try Bulfinch." He said it for a laugh. He had long ago taught me that Bulfinch was not to be trusted, for he had allowed no one to edit him, had made mistakes. "Why do you need to know?"

"A poem," I said. "A reference." No answer, but answer enough.

The phone waited a heartbeat, then spoke in Mike's voice. "One old man, with seals, coming up. One smelly old god, with seals, Aunt Lyssa. He was a shape-changer with the ability to foretell the future, only you had to hold on to him through all his changes to make him talk. Ulysses was able . . ."

"I remember," I said. "I know."

I hung up. The old man had been right. Of course I would be back. In the morning.

In the morning I gathered up pad, pencils, a sweater, and the flask of Earl Grey tea I had prepared. I stuffed them all into my old backpack. Then I started out as soon as light had bleached a line across the rocks.

Overhead a pair of laughing gulls wrote along the wind's pages with their white-bordered wings. I could almost read their messages, so clear and forceful was the scripting. Even the rocks signed to me, the water murmured advice. It was as if the world were a storyteller, a singer of old songs. The seas along the coast, usually green-black, seemed wine-dark and full of a churning energy. I did not need to hurry. I knew he would be there. Sometimes foresight has as much to do with reason as with magic.

The whale rock signaled me, and the smell lured me on. When I saw the one, and the other found my nose, I smiled. I made the last turning, and there he was—asleep and snoring.

I climbed down carefully and watched the seals scatter before me. Then I knelt by his side.

I shook my head. Here was the world's oldest, dirtiest, smelliest man. A bum vomited up by the ocean. The centuries layered on his skin. And here was I thinking he was a god.

The I shrugged and reached out to grab his shoulder. Fire. Water. Snake. Lion. I would outwait them all.

Of course I knew the question I would *not* ask. No one my age needs to know the exact time of dying. But the other questions—the ones that deal with the days and months and years after I would surely be gone—I would ask them all. And he, being a god who cannot lie about the future, must tell me everything, everything that is going to happen in the world.

After all, I am a stubborn old woman. And a curious one. And I have always had a passion for the news.

Names

Her Mother's Number had been D248960. It was still imprinted on her arm, burned into the flesh, a permanent journal entry. Rachel had heard the stories, recited over and over in the deadly monotone her mother took on to tell of the camp. Usually her mother had a beautiful voice, low, musical. Men admired it. Yet not a month went by that something was not said or read or heard that reminded her, and she began reciting the names, last names, in order, in a sepulchral accent:

ABRAHMS
BERLINER
BRODSKY
DANNENBERG
FISCHER
FRANK
GLASSHEIM
GOLDBLATT

253

It was her one party trick, that recitation. But Rachel always knew that when the roll call was done, her mother would start the death-camp stories. Whether the audience wanted to hear them or not, she would surround them with their own guilt and besiege them with the tales:

HEGELMAN

ISAACS

KAPLAN

KOHN

Her mother had been a child in the camp; had gone through puberty there; had left with her life. Had been lucky. The roll call was of the dead ones, the unlucky ones. The children in the camp had each been imprinted with a portion of the names, a living *yahrzeit*, little speaking candles; their eyes burning, their flesh burning, wax in the hands of the adults who had told them: "You must remember. If you do not remember, we never lived. If you do not remember, we never died." And so they remembered.

Rachel wondered if, all over the world, there were survivors, men and women who, like her mother, could recite those names:

LEVITZ

MAMOROWITZ

MORGENSTERN

NORENBERG

ORENSTEIN

REESE

Some nights she dreamed of them: hundreds of old children, wizened toddlers, marching toward her, their arms over their heads to show the glowing numbers, reciting names.

ROSENBLUM

ROSENWASSER

SOLOMON
STEIN

It was an epic poem, those names, a ballad in alphabetics. Rachel could have recited them along with her mother, but her mouth never moved. It was an incantation. Hear, O Israel, Germany, America. The names had an awful power over her, and even in her dreams she could not speak them aloud. The stories of the camps, of the choosing of victims—left line to the ovens, right to another day of deadening life—did not frighten her. She could move away from the group that listened to her mother's tales. There was no magic in the words that told of mutilations, of children's brains against the Nazi walls. She could choose to listen or not listen; such recitations did not paralyze her. But the names:

TANNENBAUM

TEITLEMAN

VANNENBERG

WASSERMAN

WECHTENSTEIN

ZEISS

Rachel knew that the names had been spoken at the moment of her birth: that her mother, legs spread, the waves of Rachel's passage rolling down her stomach, had breathed the names between spasms long before Rachel's own name had been pronounced. Rachel Rebecca Zuckerman. That final *Zeiss* had burst from her mother's lips as Rachel had slipped out, greasy with birth blood. Rachel knew she had heard the names in the womb. They had opened the uterine neck, they had lured her out and beached her as easily as a fish. How often had her mother commented that Rachel had never cried as a child. Not once. Not even at birth when the doctor had slapped her. She knew, even if her mother did not, that she had been silenced by the incantation, the *Zeiss* a stopper in her mouth.

When Rachel was a child, she had learned the names as another child would a nursery rhyme. The rhythm of the passing syllables was as water in her mouth, no more than nonsense words. But at five, beginning to understand the power of the names, she could say them no more. For the saying was not enough. It did not satisfy her mother's needs. Rachel knew that there was something more she needed to do to make her mother smile.

At thirteen, on her birthday, she began menstruating, and her mother watched her get dressed. "So plump. So *zaftik*." It was an observation, less personal than a weather report. But she knew it meant that her mother had finally seen her as more than an extension, more than a child still red and white from its passage into the light.

It seemed that, all at once, she knew what to do. Her mother's duty had been the Word. Rachel's was to be the Word Made Flesh.

She stopped eating.

The first month, fifteen pounds poured off her. Melted. Ran as easily as candle wax. She thought only of food. Bouillon. Lettuce. Carrots. Eggs. Her own private poem. What she missed most was chewing. In the camp they chewed on gristle and wood. It was one of her mother's best tales.

The second month her cheekbones emerged, sharp reminders of the skull. She watched the mirror and prayed. *Barukh atah adonai elohenu melekh ha-olam.* She would not say the words for bread or wine. Too many calories. Too many pounds. She cut a star out of yellow posterboard and held it to her breast. The face in the mirror smiled back. She rushed to the bathroom and vomited away another few pounds. When she flushed the toilet, the sound was a hiss, as if gas were escaping into the room.

The third month she discovered laxatives, and the names on the containers became an addition to her litany: Metamucil, Agoral, Senokot. She could feel the chair impress itself on her bones. Bone on wood. If it hurt to sit, she would lie down.

She opened her eyes and saw the ceiling, spread above her like a sanitized sky. A voice pronounced her name. "Rachel, Rachel Zuckerman. Answer me."

But no words came out. She raised her right hand, a signal; she was weaker than she thought. Her mother's face, smiling, appeared. The room was full of cries. There was a chill in the air, damp, crowded. The smell of decay was sweet and beckoning. She closed her eyes and the familiar chant began, and Rachel added her voice to the rest. It grew stronger near the end:

ABRAHMS

BERLINER

BRODSKY

DANNENBERG

FISCHER

FRANK

GLASSHEIM

GOLDBLATT

HEGELMAN

ISAACS

KAPLAN

KOHN

LEVITZ

MAMOROWITZ

MORGENSTERN

NORENBERG

ORENSTEIN

REESE

ROSENBLUM

ROSENWASSER

SOLOMON

STEIN

TANNENBAUM

TEITLEMAN

VANNENBERG

WASSERMAN

WECHTENSTEIN
ZEISS
ZUCKERMAN

They said the final name together and then, with a little sput-
ter, like a *yahrzeit* candle at the end, she went out.

Sister Light, Sister Dark

The Myth:

THEN GREAT ALTA plaited the left side of her hair, the golden side, and let it fall into the sinkhole of night. And there she drew up the queen of shadows and set her upon the earth. Next she plaited the right side of her hair, the dark side, and with it she caught the queen of light. And she set her next to the black queen.

"And you two shall be sisters," quoth great Alta. "You shall be as images in a glass, the one reflecting the other. As I have bound you with my hair, it shall be so."

Then she twined her living braids around and about them, and they were as one.

The Legend

It was in Altenland, in a village called Alta's Crossing, that this story was found. It was told to Jonna Bardling by an old cooking woman known only as Mother Comfort.

"My great-aunt—that would be my mother's mother's sister—fought in the army as blanket companion to the last of the great mountain warrior women, the one that was called

259

Sister Light. She was almost six foot tall, my great-aunt said, with long white braids she wore tied up on top her head. Her crown, like. She kept an extra dirk there. And she could fight like a dust demon, all grit and whirling. 'Twas known that no one could best her in battle, for she carried a great pack on her back and in it was Sister Dark, a shadow who looked just like her but twice as big. Whenever Sister Light was losing— and that weren't often, mind—she would reach into her pack and set this shadow fighter free. It was faster than eyes could see and quiet as grass growing. But Sister Light used that shadow thing only when she was desperate. Because it ate away at her insides as it fought. Fed on her, you might say. My great-aunt never saw it, mind you. No one did. But every-one knew of it.

"Well, she died at last, in a big fight, a month long it was, with the sun refusing to shine. And the shadow could only work with the sun overhead. When after a month the sun came out, Sister Dark crept out of the pack and looked around. The land was blasted, and she looked in vain behind every shriveled tree. But she couldn't find Sister Light. She was long buried.

"They say Sister Dark can still be seen, sometimes, at night under the full, high moon. Looking for her mate. Or perhaps for someone else to carry her, someone else she can eat away at. You have to be careful out there on the high moors. Especially when the moon is full. That's where the saying 'Never mate a shadow' comes from. They'll eat away at you, if they can."

The Story:

Under the eye of the leprous moon, two shadows pulled them-selves along a castle wall. The ascent had been laborious: a single step, a single rock gained.

One of the figures was tall, muscular, and sturdy, yet seemed exhausted by the effort. The other, nearly a twin of the first in dress, was thin and wraithlike, almost insubstantial, yet was not winded at all. They clung, dispatched a foot, then a leg, seemed to wait for gathered strength, then stepped together. They worked synchronically across the rock face. The soft leather of their boots was scraped. Their leggings each had a hole in the right knee. Still they climbed.

The moon's sores were suddenly hidden by a shred of cloud, and the thin figure disappeared—one moment clinging to the wall, the next gone.

The sturdy twin, so intent on the rock underhand, never noticed.

A minute later, and three more slow foot-and-hand holds farther on, the moon came out again. With it, the thin twin appeared on the rock, clinging with effortless ease.

"You breathe hard, sister," said the thin woman with a laugh. The laugh was soft, like a south wind, suddenly hot and then gone.

"If I could appear and disappear under the light as you do, Skada," groused her companion, "I wouldn't need to breathe at all."

"I breathe," Skada answered dispassionately.

"In my ear," came the reply. "You do it to annoy. And I wish to Alta you would stop."

"Sister, as you know, your wish is my . . ." but the moon disappeared behind another rip of cloud and cut off Skada's retort. And when the moon pushed through again, the two were silent with one another, a silence born of long companionship. They had been reflectors, image sisters, and blanket companions since Jenna's thirteenth year. It took many knots on a string to count their time together.

The wall, shadow-scarred and crumbling, fooled the eye and hand. What seeemed a chink was often solid. What appeared solid, a handful of dust. The mistakes cost them precious minutes, took them equally by surprise. Their goal was a small, lighted tower window. They knew they would have to be into it before dawn.

The sturdy climber stopped a moment, cursed, put her left

palm to her mouth. She licked a small, bloody shred there. Her wraithlike companion did the same, seeming to mock her. Neither of them smiled.

They climbed on.

Inches were gained. The wall did not fight them, but it did resist. Their own bodies became their worst enemies, for there is only so much stretch in the ligaments, so much give in the muscles, so much strength in arm and thigh.

At last the sturdier woman felt the top of the wall under her fingers.

"We're here, Skada," she whispered down to her companion. But the moon was again behind a cloud and there was no longer anyone there to whisper to.

"Alta's hairs!" she muttered, and pulled herself up and over the top. Even with the heavy brocade panels as protection, she felt the scrapes on her breasts. She rolled to her knees and found herself staring at a large pair of boots.

"Look up slowly," came the voice. "I would like to see the surprise on your face before I strike you down. Look up, dead man."

From her knees, Jenna looked up slowly and never stopped praying for a sliver of light. When she finally stared at the guard, his face was suddenly lit by a full and shining moon.

Jenna smiled.

"By the god Alto, you are no man," said the soldier, relaxing for a fraction of a second and starting to smile back.

Jenna looked down coyly, a maneuver she had learned in a minor court. She held out her hand.

The soldier automatically reached out to her.

"Now!" Jenna shouted.

Startled by her cry, the guard stepped back. But he was even more startled when, from behind him and below his knees, he was struck by another kneeling form. He tumbled over and was dead before the blade came sliding easily out of his heart.

Jenna hoisted the guard's body on her shoulder and heaved it over the wall. She did not wait to hear it land.

"You took your time, Skada. I hate to flutter at a man. But I knew no other way to stall."

"You know it is not my time to take or to give, Jenna."

"Don't preach at me." Jenna wiped her blade on her leggings, then shoved it back in the loop of braids on top of her head. "It is about time we got up that tower wall. In case there are other guards. Once daylight comes, you are of no practical use anyway."

Skada smiled.

"And protect my back! If *I* die . . ."

Skada nodded. "You do not have to remind me. Every Shadow Sister knows the rules of living and of light. I am called from your substance at the whim of the moon. I live as you live, die as you die, and so forth. Live long, Jenna, and prosper. Only get up that wall. I can't start without you, you know."

Jenna moved to the wall and stared up. The bricks were newer than along the Great Wall, but the ravages of the northern winds had pulped part of the facade. Bits of every brick crumbled underhand.

As the two began their ascent, whispered curses volleyed between them, though none so loud that they would awaken any guards. The curses were only variations on old standbys, as meaningless as love taps, but the antiphonal play between the two voices made the swearing sound fierce and full of raw anger.

Jenna reached the tower window first, but only fractionally. Below one of her torn fingernails blood seeped like a devil's spot. She paid it no mind. All of her effort was concentrated on the sill. Under her dark tunic, muscles bunched as, with a final pull, she hoisted herself up to the sill and over. She landed heavily on her stomach, her legs tangling with her companion's head.

"Out of the way, Skada," she huffed.

"It is your legs that are at fault. My head is only movable in a limited direction," Skada said breathily, pushing herself up. They slipped off the sill together and fell ungracefully onto the floor of the room. It was much farther down than they expected. As they landed, the lights suddenly flickered and went out.

"My lord," Jenna began hopefully, "it is Jo-an-enna, your white goddess. I have come to rescue you and . . ."

"Have you indeed?" came a mocking voice from one of the dark corners. "Well, I fear you have come to the wrong room, my friend."

Jenna felt her arms seized. She was pushed to her knees and the sword belt slashed from her waist.

The torches were lit again, slowly.

There was a sudden scrambling from the corner, and the mocking voice cried out, "There's a second one, fools! Bring the torches. Over there!"

Two men—one with a torch and one with a drawn blade—ran to the corner, but the strong light dispelled all shadows. Only along the far wall, dark patterns, unfocused but tempting, danced. A shadow leg, a quick arm.

"There is no one here, Lord Kalas."

"It was just a trick of the light," said Jenna quickly. No one but the mountain women knew how to call up the shadow side. It was a secret they kept well hidden. She shrugged extravagantly. "I came alone. I *always* come alone. It is, if you will, my one conceit." She looked up at Lord Kalas. She had heard many things about him, and none of them good. But could this faded coxcomb, with his dyed red hair and dyed red beard that emphasized the pouching under his eyes, be the infamous Lord K? "Do not tell me that Lord Kalas of the Northern Holdings is afraid of shadows?"

"Ah, I know you now. You are Longbow's white goddess. I recognize you by your mouth. He said it opened as quickly as your legs."

"Carum would never . . ."

"A man on the rack says many things, my dear."

"Few of them true," Jenna added.

Lord Kalas walked over to her. He put his hand lightly on her head as if to stroke her. Then, without warning, he grabbed a handful of her thick white hair. The hidden dirk clattered to the floor.

"Women playing at warriors bore me," Kalas said, pulling a smile over his discolored teeth. It was *piji* nut, not age, that had yellowed them. *Piji* addiction was a slow rotting. "And you, pretty girl, do it badly. We moved your Carum Longbow to the dungeon ten days and nine would-be rescuers ago. So all your climbing has been for naught save to strengthen your long, pretty legs." He tapped her right knee with the flat of his blade.

"By Alta's hairs . . ." she began.

"Alta's hairs are gray and too short to keep her warm," said the smooth, mocking voice. "And that is what we have you by—Alta's short hairs." He laughed at his own crudity. "But if you insist on playing a man's game, we will treat you like a man. Instead of warming my bed, you will freeze with the others in my dungeon."

Jenna bit her lip.

"I see you have heard of it. What is it they call it?" He yanked her head back once again and brought his face close to hers, as if for a kiss. Jenna could smell the sickly sweet odor of *piji*.

"They call it Lord Kalas' hole," she said.

"Enjoy it," Kalas said and pushed her to her knees. He turned from her quickly, and his lizard-skin cape sang like a whip around his ankles. Then he was gone.

The guards pushed Jenna down the stairs. They descended it quickly—much more quickly, Jenna mused, than her laborious climb up. Her hands were so tightly bound behind her, she had lost the feeling in her fingers by the second level. Her one consolation was that the man with the torch went ahead, and so the shadows of their moving bodies were ranged behind them. If he had been at the end of the line, there would have been a second bound woman on the stairs, with braids down her back and a brocade tunic and leggings with a hole in the knee. *And* a head that still ached.

Jenna promised herself that she would do nothing to make any of the guards look back, for she knew that Skada was following. Whether in dark or in light, Skada was never far away. They were pledged by ties deeper than blood, bound by magic older than either of them could guess. From the first blood of womanhood to the last blood flowing in Jenna's veins, Skada would be with her. But only where shadows could be counted.

They came suddenly to the stairs' end where a heavy wooden door barred the way. It took three keys to unbolt the door, and when it was finally opened, Jenna was thrown in without ceremony.

The dungeon deserved its name. Lord Kalas' hole was dark, dank, wet, and smelled like the hind end of a diarrhetic ox. Jenna had marched behind sick cattle in the Retreat of Long Acre and she knew that smell well. She kept herself from gagging by flinging a curse at the departing guards.

"May you be hanged in Alta's hairs," she began when the wooden door slammed shut. So she finished the swear at a splinter of light that poked through the barred window. "And may She thread your guts through Her braids, and use your skull . . ."

"It's not that I mind women cursing," came a low, cracked voice made almost unfamiliar with fatigue. "But you should try . . ."

". . . to be more original," Jenna finished for him. "*Carum!* You're here." She spun around and tried to find him in the dark. As she peered into the blackness, she began to distinguish some shadows, though she could not tell which one was Longbow and which the nine other half-starved men who had preceded her. Of Skada there was no sign at all, but with only the patch of window light, Jenna had hardly expected to see her dark sister.

She felt fingers working slowly at her bonds and heard a muttering.

"Besides, haven't I told you before, you have the legend

wrong. It's *by Alta's heirs*—the sons and daughters She bore—not the long braids you copy."

Jenna rolled her eyes up and sighed. Even in the dark, Longbow lectured. He loved to talk and plot, lecture and argue, while she was always the doer of the two. His "bloody right hand," he called her.

"What good," Longbow continued, "is my bloody right hand if she's tied?"

"What good am I at all," said Jenna angrily, "if I'm caught? By Alta's . . . no, by my sword, which I have unfortunately lost, and my dirk, which is also gone, and my temper, which is fast going, *I can't think in the dark.*"

"You can't think with your hands tied. You do very well in the dark," Longbow said.

There was a slight murmur from the floor, as of cold water over stones. Jenna realized that the other men in the dungeon were laughing. It might have been their first laugh in days, and it stumbled a bit in their mouths. She knew from long experience that men in dangerous situations needed laughter to combat defeatism. So she added a line to Longbow's. "You do fairly well in the dark yourself." But then she spoke rapidly, as if to herself. "But why *so* dark? Why is there *no* light here?"

One of the men stood up. First Jenna heard the movement, then made it out.

"Lord Kalas' jest, lady. He says one's enemies are best kept in the dark."

Jenna was trying out variations on the bad joke in her head, but none had reached her lips when Longbow announced, "There, you are free."

Jenna rubbed first one wrist, then the other. "And when do they feed us?"

"Once a day," Longbow said. "In the morning, I think. Though, as you can imagine, day and night have little meaning here."

As casually as she could manage, Jenna asked, "And do they bring a light then?"

Carum was not fooled by her tone. He already knew something of her shadow sister. Anyone who spent time with a mountain warrior woman had had a chance to see blanket companions at work, and Carum had spent a great deal of time with Jenna over the past five years of almost continuous warfare. But he did not understand their relationship, not entirely. He thought Skada merely a lowlander who fought furiously at Jenna's side. He had never seen her by day, only at night. There was some strangeness there.

"Is *she* here?" he whispered. "Your dark sister? Did she slip in somehow? Or is she outside with a legion?"

"She's around," Jenna answered. "By herself. You know she dislikes company. Now, about that light?"

"They bring a single torch. And they set it on the wall—there." He pointed near the door. "And all the good it does is to show us how degraded we have become in ten short days." He laughed, a short, angry bark. "Is it not ironic what a little bit of dirt and damp and dark and a delicate diet can do to beggar a man?"

"Carum, this does not sound like you."

"This does not look like me, either," he answered. "And I am glad of the dark this moment, for I would not have you, my white goddess, see me thus."

"I have seen you many ways," Jenna answered, "and not all of them handsome. Do you remember the Long Acre march? And the fording of Crookback's Ravine?"

The one other standing man put his hand on Jenna's arm. "They put something in the food, lady. It takes a man's will away. It eats at his soul. And Longbow has eaten the food longer than the rest of us. Do not tax him with his answers. We are all like that now—high one minute, low the next. I am the latest to arrive, save yourself. And I feel the corrosion of will already."

Jenna turned toward the shadow man and put her hand on his cheek. "Carum Longbow, it will be better by and by. I promise."

Longbow laughed again, that hoarse, unfamiliar chuckle.

"Women's promises . . ." he began before his voice bled away, like an old wound reopened.

"*You* know I keep my promises," Jenna said under her breath to him. "All I need is that light."

Longbow's voice grew strong again. "It will do you no good. It does none of us any good. They hold the light up to the hole in the door and then make us lie down on the floor, one atop another. Then they count us aloud before they open the door. After each lock is opened, they count us again."

"Better and better," said Jenna mysteriously.

"If you have a plan, tell it to me," demanded Longbow.

"Tell it to all of us," came a voice from the floor. The others chimed in with gritty, tough, angry voices.

Jenna smiled into the dark, but none could see it. "Just be sure," she said slowly, "that I lie on top of the pile."

The men gave their muttering laughs, and Carum laughed loudest. "Of course. It would not do to have the white goddess underneath."

Jenna laughed with them. "Though there have been times . . ." she said.

"Now *that*," said Longbow, his voice again on the upswing note, "you do well."

Jenna ignored him and walked over to the door. She held her hand up into the little sliver of light. Skada's hand appeared faintly against the far wall. Jenna waved, and was delighted to see Skada return it.

"Will you be ready?" she called to the wall.

The shadowy figures ranged along the floor grunted their assent. Carum called out, "I will." But Jenna had eyes only for the hand on the wall. It made a circle between thumb and finger, the goddess's own sign. For the first time Jenna felt reason to hope.

Jenna forced herself to sleep, to give her body time to recover from the long climb she had had to endure. Curled up next to Longbow, she forced herself to breathe slowly, willing each limb to relax in turn. She knew she could put herself to sleep within minutes even on the cold, damp, sandy floor. If it was an uncomfortable bed, she had been in worse. She stopped herself from remembering the night she had spent in the belly of the dragon beast of Kordoom. Or the time she had passed the dark hours astraddle the horns of the wild Demetian bull-man.

When she slept at last, her dreams were full of wells, caves, and other dark, wet holes.

The clanging of a sword against the iron bars of the window woke them all.

"Light count," came the call through the slit. "Roll up and over."

The prisoners dragged themselves to the wall and attempted a rough pyramid, not daring to complain. Jenna was the last to sit up, and she watched as the sturdiest four, including Carum, lay down on the floor. The next heaviest climbed on top of them. Then two almost skeletal forms scaled wearily onto the pile, distributing their weight as carefully as possible. At last the slightest, almost a boy, scrambled up to perch a bit unsteadily on top. All this Jenna could see with the help of the additional light shining through the door slit.

The sound of the guard's voice counting began. "One, two, three . . ."

"Wait, you misbegotten miscalculators," came the smooth mockery of Lord Kalas' voice. "Don't deny me the best. You have all forgotten our lady friend, our latest guest. There seems no room at the top for her. Had you planned laying her somewhere else?" He laughed at his own words and his men echoed his laughter a beat behind.

The exhausted prisoners rolled off their pyramid and ranged around Longbow. He started, slowly, to explain what must be done.

"Start with five on the bottom this time," suggested Lord

Kalas. His voice threaded out with a bored drawl. "Sooner or later another will come along to be added to your pyramid of lost hopes. Though why anyone would want to rescue Carum Longbow is beyond me. However, heroes being heroes, I expect another one soon. And then I shall have a full pyramid again. I do like pyramids. They are an altogether pleasing figure."

The prisoners began again.

"Why do you do this?" Jenna whispered to Longbow.

"We tried denying them their pleasure," Carum said, "and they simply refused to feed us until we stacked ourselves at their command." He lay down on the floor, in the middle of four men. Four crawled on top of them. Then the boy nestled on them, and Jenna climbed carefully on top of the pile, leaving a space between the boy and herself. She settled gingerly, trying to distribute her weight.

"Will they bring the light now?" Jenna whispered to the man under her.

"Yes," he whispered back. "Look, here it comes."

Two men—one with a torch—entered the room. They had their swords drawn. Lord Kalas, disdaining to draw his own weapon, entered after them.

The light-bearer stood at the head of the pile of bodies, counting them aloud once again. The second went to a corner, sheathed his sword, and took a bag off his shoulders. He emptied its contents onto the floor. Jenna made out a pile of moldy breads. She wrinkled her nose. Then she looked up at the wall nearest the door, where shadows thrown by the flickering torch moved about.

"Now!" she shouted, flinging herself from the pile.

She calculated her roll to take her into the shoulder of the guard at the pyramid's peak. His torch flew into the air, illuminating another hurtling body that seemed to spring right out of the far wall. It was Skada. She rammed into the unsuspecting Lord Kalas, knocking him forward just as he had unsheathed his sword.

Jenna reached for the guard's weapon as Skada grabbed for Lord Kalas'. They completed identical forward rolls in a single fluid motion, then stood up, their newly captured weapons at the ready.

Longbow and the other lordlings had at the moment of impact collapsed their pyramid and leaped to their feet. They surrounded the guard with the bread, and stripped him of his sword and a knife in his boot. Carum now held the torch aloft.

"There were eleven of you," Lord Kalas said. "I counted you myself. Where did this twelfth come from?"

Skada laughed. "From a darker hole than you will ever know, Lord Kalas."

Jenna hissed through her teeth, and Skada said no more. For the mountain women had been sworn never to reveal the secret of the shadow sisters, nor tell of the years of training where they met and mastered the dark side of their own spirits.

Lord Kalas smiled. "Could it be . . . but no . . . the mages tell of a practice in the highlands of raising black demons, mirror images. I thought it was a tale. Mages do not lie, but they do not always tell all the truth."

Skada made a mocking bow. "Truth has many ears. You must believe what you yourself see."

"I see sisters who may have had the same mother, but different fathers," Kalas said, his mouth twisted in a scornful smile. "It is well known that mountain women take pleasure in many men."

"Do not speak of my mother," Jenna said threateningly. "Do not soil her with your *piji* mouth."

Kalas laughed and in the same moment dashed the torch from Longbow's hand. It fell to the floor, guttered, and almost went out. At the same moment, his sword fell from the darkness at his feet. He bent down and picked it up.

"*Piji*," Kalas said, "stains the teeth. But it gives one wonderful night sight." His sword clanged against Jenna's.

"Dark or light," cried Jenna, "I will fight you. Stand back, Carum. Keep the others away."

Lord Kalas was well versed in the traditional thrusts and parries, but he counted too much on his night sight. What he did not know was that Jenna had learned her swordplay first in a darkened room before progressing to the light. And though she could not see as well as he in the blackness, she had been taught to trust her ears even before her eyes. She could distinguish the movement of a thrust that was signaled by the change in the air and the hesitation of a breath. She could smell Lord Kalas, the slight scent of fear overlayered with the constant *piji* odor. In less than a minute it was over.

"Light," Jenna called.

Carum picked up the torch and held it overhead. Out of the damp sand, it fluttered to life again smokily.

Lord Kalas stood without his sword, and Jenna held her blade point in his belly. Behind him stood Skada, her blade in his back. If he moved, he would be spitted like a sheep over a roasting pit.

"Sisters indeed," said Skada. "But, as you have noted, not quite alike. I do not have your blood on my sword—yet."

Jenna turned to Longbow. "Keep the torch high and stand at the head of the line. Skada and I will be at the back. Look forward, my lord. Always forward. Skada and I will follow."

They went out of the dungeon in a line. Outside it was daylight, and Skada, in an instant, was gone. The sun was at its height. But Longbow, as Jenna had asked, never once looked back.

The History:

In the sixth century AEFM (after the establishment of the First Matriarchy), in the second decade of the so-called Gender Wars, there rose a woman warrior of phenomenal battle skill but little formal education. Her name has been variously given as Jenna, Janna, J'hanna, and Jo-an-enna. She came from a mountain clan known for its great beauty, height, and fair coloring who worshiped the white goddess Alta of the World

Tree, hence the name Jo (lover)—an (white)—enna (tree). Swearing blood sisterhood with a woman of the smaller, dark-skinned valley clans, Skada or Skader or Shader (the low-tongue word for *dark* or *shadow*), Jo-an-enna and Shader offered their swords to Queen Falta IV. But the blood sisters did not take well to military discipline and were, according to contemporary legion records, dismissed from the regular forces. They were given their swords, a sack of flour, and muster-out pay of forty *pesta,* as was common. There was a dishonorable mark inked in and then partially erased after their names. Whether the fault lay with one or both is impossible to say at this date. Blanket companions were traditionally treated as one entity in the rigid military system of the day.

The two hired out as bodyguards and occasionally fell in with short-lived mercenary bands that roamed freely over the countryside, and their adventures gave rise to many local legends. The song "Jenna at the Ford" (Carne Ballad 17) is one, as is "Bold Skada and the Merchant's Lament" (Carne Ballad 46) and the bawdy "Lord Kalas' Hole" (Carne Ballad 69). The recently revived passion play "Sister Light and Sister Dark" contains many folk motifs that have only tangential connection with the history of Jo-an-enna.

By accident or design (Burke-Senda's account suggests graphically that serendipity was at work, while Calla-ap-Jones writes convincingly of a Great Matriarchal Plan), the two women rescued the soldier of fortune Carum Longbow from prison. Longbow, later known in the low tongue as Broadbreaker, became the first King of the Low Countries and was famous for bringing down the First Matriarchy and expunging the armies of all female fighters. Whether this was from economic need (Burke-Senda cites the failing birthrates due to the practice of salting soldiers' food with *pedra,* a common anti-ovulent) or passion (Calla-ap-Jones offers striking evidence that Longbow won Jo-an-enna from Skader in a ritual trial by arms, and in revenge Shader killed Sister Light, throwing Longbow into a bloody genocidal frenzy which was levied against every fighting woman in the forces) is not clear. It is ironic, however, that the famous Dark and Light Sisters of the songs, stories, and myths should have been the ones to bring down, all unwittingly, the generous, enlightened, art-centered rule of the first great queens of Alta.